Mandy Magro lives in Cairns, Far North Queensland, with her daughter, Chloe Rose. With pristine aqua-blue coastline in one direction and sweeping rural landscapes in the other, she describes her home as heaven on earth. A passionate woman and a romantic at heart, she loves writing about soul-deep love, the Australian rural way of life and all the wonderful characters who live there.

www.facebook.com/mandymagroauthor

www.mandymagro.com

Also by Mandy Magro

MANDY MAGRO

Moment of Truth

mira

First Published 2017
Second Australian Paperback Edition 2022
ISBN 9781867249047

MOMENT OF TRUTH
© 2017 by Mandy Magro
Australian Copyright 2017
New Zealand Copyright 2017

Published by
Mira
An imprint of Harlequin Enterprises (Australia) Pty Limited (ABN 47 001 180 918), a subsidiary of HarperCollins Publishers Australia Pty Limited (ABN 36 009 913 517)
Level 13, 201 Elizabeth St
SYDNEY NSW 2000
AUSTRALIA

* and TM (apart from those relating to FSC*) are trademarks of Harlequin Enterprises Limited or its corporate affiliates. Trademarks indicated with * are registered in Australia, New Zealand and in other countries.

Cataloguing-in-Publication details are available from the National Library of Australia www.librariesaustralia.nla.gov.au

Printed and bound in Australia by McPherson's Printing Group

MIX
Paper from
responsible sources
FSC® C001695

For my mum, love you a million xo

CHAPTER

1

**Diamond Acres Horse Sanctuary, Blue Ridge,
North Queensland**

A resounding boom echoed throughout the cottage, sending a black
wave of fruit bats soaring from the surrounding mango trees in
search of safer perches. Kicking off the bed sheets, thirteen-year-old
Alexis Brown stirred from a dream where she was travelling through
a magical world. For a split-second she fought not to return to
reality, the wonderful feeling of her horse, Wild Thing, galloping
beneath her as they rode across a luminous rainbow arch was
enticing her to stay in dreamland a little longer. If only she could
get to the end of it and finally see what treasures lay at the foot of
the band of colours that arched across the bright blue sky – her
mum was always telling her about the pot of gold and she wanted
to know if it was true. But to her disappointment she tumbled back
into the real world, her nightie stuck to her sweaty skin and her
heart still racing from the invigorating ride. Resting her hands on

her chest she took a few deep breaths, slow and steady, the rhythm returning to normal as she opened her eyes.

A deafening crash of thunder made her start and then a bright flash of lightning briefly lit up the room as if someone had just switched a light on. The wet season was finally upon them. The much-needed rain was here, the thirsty ground desperate for it. She almost clapped her hands in delight, but refrained so she didn't wake her younger sister. Her mother's many wind chimes jingled from the front verandah, the clangs melodious. The sheer white curtains flapped in the breeze, allowing the full moon to cast its silver–grey light through the window, illuminating the entire bedroom like the colours in an otherworldly dream. The big old fig tree she liked to climb so she could read her books in peace scraped its branches along the side of the house as the wind blew noisily through its leaves. The scent of the balmy summer night, of the jasmine blossoms and the freshly mowed grass, mixed with the scent of imminent rain floated in through the open window, all of it tantalising her senses – she truly felt alive when she was outside and she felt drawn there now. Her mother was always trying to get her to hang out in the kitchen, wanting her to learn boring things like baking; but she much preferred to be with her dad (if she wasn't reading) – not because she didn't love her mum, she loved her to bits – it's just that her father worked outdoors and did much more exciting stuff, like fixing tractors and fences, and her most favourite job of all, helping Mister King take care of the wild horses that he and her dad brought here when they rescued them. Her father was the best horse trainer around, or that's what the people at the local agriculture shop always said to her, and she liked to believe it was so.

Heavy raindrops suddenly hit the tin roof in a roar, making it almost impossible to hear anything else. Unperturbed by the noise,

Alexis breathed in deeply – she loved the smell of rain. It was so new and pure, and made her feel super alive. She thought about how her Grandpa Bob had once told her that the rain was God watering his garden. But if it were the case, God had been a bit slack in that department, because they hadn't had a drop for almost a month now.

Turning away from the window she gazed at the stars and moon that appeared to be dancing across the ceiling, projected by the revolving bedside lamp – her favourite gift from her favourite Nanny Fay. She couldn't wait to see her again, and Grandpa Bob, in a few months time; it was going to be so much fun spending the Easter school holidays at their place in Townsville. She just hoped her mum came along because she didn't seem too keen on the idea.

Wide awake now and with her mind wandering, she thought about going for a ride on Wild Thing at first light, if the rain stopped, when loud voices caught her attention. Trying hard to hear over the storm Alexis caught words from a heated conversation. It was coming from the kitchen at the other end of the cottage. She could hear her father's distinctive deep voice, but as much it made her feel happy to know he'd arrived home a day early from visiting her grandparents, his angry tone worried her. He rarely got mad. And her mum sounded like she was crying as she said things Alexis couldn't quite comprehend. Instantly blaming herself for the argument, because her dad had gone to her great grandad's funeral on his own, Alexis choked back a sob. She chewed on her bottom lip to try to stop it quivering. Although they sometimes grumbled at each other, she'd never heard her parents argue like this. Thinking back to the tension that had hung over the dinner table when her mother had said they wouldn't be able to come along to the funeral because Alexis had to go to school made her feel as though this was all her fault. Luckily she'd had what looked like a billion peas on her dinner plate at the time, because she could focus on moving them around with her fork rather than thinking about the glare her father had given her mother.

Rolling on to her side so her back was now to the window she looked at the strip of light under the closed bedroom door, the pale moonlight shining on her Polaroid camera, which hung on the doorknob. Her heart jumped up to her throat as she tugged the doona in closer. She and her younger sister Katie never slept with their door closed. Her parents both knew how much it scared them. So who had closed it? The voices grew louder. Fear stabbed at her belly as she squeezed her eyes shut. Something wasn't right. Part of her wanted to fix whatever it was, but another big part of her wanted to stay right here, where she felt safe. Katie was asleep beside her. She had crawled in with Alexis after having yet another bad dream, and being the big sister Alexis felt it was her job to make sure her sister was safe too.

Staying right here was the best thing to do.

But then the rain eased and her father's voice got even louder, and all the more angry.

Clutching her favourite blue teddy bear, scruffy as it was after thirteen years of cuddles, Alexis shot up to sitting when she heard him. She was so unsure of what she should do – go out and stop her parents arguing, or protect her sister? Rubbing the bear's fluffy ears in the same place she always did when she was sad or worried, she looked down at Katie; her sister's petite features were even more adorable as she slept but also made her seem even more vulnerable. And that made Alexis feel even more protective. She huffed. Renewed determination filled her. Her parents should quieten down, and maybe she'd better go out there and tell them so. Perhaps, with all the noise from the storm, they didn't realise just how loudly they were talking.

Her father's voice became harsher, his bad language not something Alexis was used to. Her stomach tightened and hot tears stung her eyes. Her mum was saying sorry over and over again while begging him to understand. Understand what? Alexis felt like her heart was going to bang its way out of her chest, it was beating so fast now. She wanted to go and comfort her mother, and tell her dad to stop being so nasty, but then something smashed, maybe a glass hitting the floor. Twirling a strand of her long blonde hair tightly around her finger she held her breath, terrified of what might happen next as her eyes darted back and forth from the open window to the closed door.

Warily slipping from the bed she tiptoed towards the sliver of light and pressed her ear up against the plywood door.

'I can't take any more of this, Peggy,' her father's voice boomed.

'Please, stop yelling, Jason, the girls are asleep.' Her mum's sobs got louder.

'And so they should be at three in the morning, just like you should be, too. I can't believe you've done this to me, to us. We're a family. I thought we were happy. I thought we were going to live out our days together, side by side.'

'I'm so sorry, Jason. I don't know what to say.'

'Then don't say anything, Peggy, because there's really nothing more to say. I've seen it for myself, you can't talk your way out of it now.'

Hearing the rustle of sheets Alexis turned around as Katie stirred and her eyes flickered open. Alexis's sisterly instincts kicked into full force – she didn't want Katie to hear any of this. She dashed over to her as quietly as she could, placing her hand on her arm. 'Hi there, Pebbles, did the rain wake you?'

'I don't know.' Katie looked past her to the door and her eyes grew misty. She hugged her knees to her chest. Her lips quivered as she sucked in a shaky breath, then the welling tears rolled down her cheeks. 'Sissy, why's the door shut?'

Before Alexis could answer a strong draught of wind blew through the open window, lifting the curtains, and gave her the perfect answer. 'I think the wind might have shut it, Pebbles. I was just going to open it when you woke up.'

'Okay, can you open it now?'

Alexis wished she could but was too terrified to do so. 'In a sec, I want a cuddle first.' Climbing back onto the bed she cradled Katie, making sure to subtly cover her little sister's ears as Katie wrapped her arms around her neck.

Just as things seemed to quieten, her parents' voices no longer loud and the rain now more of a soft pitter patter on the roof, Jack, their bits-of-everything-dog (well that's what her father had called him when they saved him from the pound a few months ago) began to bark from where he was locked away in his kennel out the back. Her dad roared for Jack to *Shut the hell up*. Instead, the barking became more insistent. Alexis silently prayed for her newest best furry buddy to do as he was told, while she pressed her hands in harder against Katie's ears.

Heavy footfalls stomped down the hallway, past the bedroom, and moments later whoever it was pounded back past again. A gunshot followed, so close to the cottage it seemed to echo through the walls. Katie jumped, her eyes filled with fear and a wail escaped her. Rocking Katie, Alexis swallowed down hard as she squeezed back tears. She needed to be strong for Katie, no matter how terrified she felt. As her dad always said, it was a big sister's job to be the strong one, to lead by giving a good example.

'It's all right, Pebbles, I think Dad might have been shooting at one of those pesky dingoes again.' It seemed to calm Katie but

Alexis knew better – her dad must be real mad, shooting his gun like that to warn Jack. It had worked, though; Jack was silent now.

But then the voices got louder, more urgent, and Alexis was sure she heard a third voice, but she couldn't be certain with Katie's wailing filling her ears. Her already racing heart beat faster. The hair stood up at the back of her neck. Maybe it was time to think about hiding under the bed? Or in the cupboard, like ET had with all those toys? But that would scare Katie even more – she hated the dark. With her mind in a spin Alexis tried to think quickly. Their favourite place, that's where she should take Katie until her parents stopped fighting, and they could get to it by climbing out of their bedroom window. They often climbed out through the window to avoid walking all the way down the hall and out the back door, much to her mother's annoyance.

'Come on, Katie, let's go and have a tea party in the cubby house.'

Katie smiled through her tears. 'Now?'

Alexis tried to fake calmness by shrugging. 'Why not?

Katie looked to the open window. 'Because it's dark outside and the boogieman might get us.'

'Don't be silly, Katie, like I always tell you, there's no such thing as the boogieman. We still have Daddy's big torch in there, remember, so it won't be dark once we turn that on.'

'But aren't we going to get wet?'

'When have you ever been afraid of the rain, Pebbles?'

'Okay then, Sissy.' Katie didn't sound so sure as she climbed from the bed, her comforter blanket clutched tightly in her small hands. 'Why are Mummy and Daddy yelling?'

'I don't know, Pebbles.' Springing from the bed, she gathered Katie into her arms. 'Sometimes people just get mad at each other, like you and I do, I suppose.'

'Yeah,' Katie said with a giggle. 'You get mad at me a lot.'

'I do not.'

'Yes you do, all the time.'

'Okay, I do, but only because you're a little ratbag and you drive me nuts.'

'Am not.'

'Are too.'

Katie giggled.

Alexis tried to keep the mood light as she walked over to the window. She helped Katie to climb out first and then it was her turn, her feet hitting the sodden ground before she had even let go of the windowsill. Hand in hand, the two girls then dashed the few metres to the cubby house, both of them drenched through to the skin when they got there. The small backyard of the worker's cottage didn't allow for much, but her dad had built the finest cubby house Alexis had ever seen. If she had her way, she would turn it into her bedroom.

Just as she switched on the torch, igniting the cubby in so much light that she and Katie both squinted, another gunshot rang out, its boom piercing the quiet countryside and ricocheting off the surrounding mountains. Heart-wrenching screams from her mother were immediately followed by her father's cries. Katie burst into uncontrollable tears, her sobs only quietened when she needed to draw a breath. Although wanting to comfort her sister Alexis stood frozen to the spot, her breathing ragged as she felt a part of her snap in two. She'd never been so terrified in all her life. What was she meant to do? Go inside and make sure her parents were all right, or do everything she could to protect her sister and herself? Was that selfish, to want to protect herself?

She grabbed Katie's hand. Hurrying out of the cubby house she tugged her towards the scrub at the side of the cottage. Like she always did, Katie followed in her footsteps without complaint, and within seconds they were standing at the edge of the paddock that led down to Mister and Missus King's house – their neighbours and also their father's bosses. She had no idea what was going on but she instinctively knew she had to get down there, fast, to get Katie to safety and to ask for help for her parents.

The wind blew wet tresses of her long hair across her face as more gunshots rang out, her mother's blood-curdling screams driving Alexis into a wild run. No longer hand-in-hand with Katie, she could hear her sobbing so she knew Katie was beside her, even though it seemed as if her sister were a million miles away, all of Alexis's senses feeling as if they'd short-circuited. With her chest burning from the exertion and her breath hard to catch, she reached the driveway that led to the big homestead. If only Wild Thing wasn't all the way up the other end she would have run to him for comfort. Mud splashed up her leg as Katie tripped and fell into a puddle, her little body heaving with angst-ridden sobs, and she rolled into a ball, her knees cuddled to her chest.

Crouching down Alexis tried to help Katie back up, but her sister refused to move.

'Come on, Pebbles, please, we have to go and get help.' Taking her wrist she gave it a tug.

Katie yanked her arm free and slowly sat up, her bottom lip trembling. 'I want to go home to Mummy.'

'I know, Katie, me too,' Alexis said softly as she placed her hand on her sister's shoulders. 'We will soon.' Using the corner of Katie's blanket, she wiped her sister's face and nose before tucking the loose dark curls behind her ears. 'Don't worry, as long as you and I stick together everything's going to be all right, okay?'

'You promise?' Katie mumbled, her fingers in her mouth.

'I promise, Pebbles.' Alexis's throat was so tight with emotion she was finding it hard to speak.

'I don't want to go to the big house. I don't like Missus King. She's grumpy and she scares me.'

Alexis gently wiped the hair back from Katie's forehead. 'I know, she scares me too, but hopefully Mister King will answer the door. He's never grumpy, is he?'

'No, he's really nice.'

'Yes, he is, and he always gives us those yummy butterscotch lollies when Mrs King isn't looking, doesn't he?'

A hint of a smile shone through Katie's tear-stained face. 'He does, naughty Mister King.'

'Will we go and see if he has any left?'

Nodding, Katie got up. Her powder-pink singlet was now mud spattered, as too was her beloved cuddle blanket. Moving into more of a jog, Alexis breathed a sigh of relief when Katie did the same. She couldn't go shouting at Katie to hurry up, she was upset enough. Not long and they would be able to knock on the front door and ask for help. She wondered if Ethan was staying at his grandparents' place this weekend – he was always so calm, even when she'd fallen off Wild Thing and broken her arm, he knew what to do. Being three years older than her, he was smarter about certain things. How she wished he were with her right now, so she didn't have to be the adult.

The rambling homestead finally came into view and with her galloping heart feeling as though it was about to explode she slowed, as did Katie. Stealing a second glance back up at the only home she'd ever known, Alexis gritted her teeth to stop from crying. Something very bad had happened and she didn't dare think what it was right now for fear of crumbling into a million tiny pieces. She had to believe her mum and dad were okay and, most importantly, alive.

Hurrying through a white picket fence they took a short cut and headed across the front lawn instead of following the winding garden path. The wet grass was cold on Alexis's bare feet. Casper, the Kings' pet Border Collie, still only a pup, barked incessantly from his kennel at the side of the house. As they climbed the five front steps a floodlight fired to life. Alexis held her free hand up to shield her eyes, the other still holding tightly to Katie's. The front door swung open and Mister King appeared. When he heard Casper barking, he must have raced down to the door to get there so fast. Pulling his robe in tighter he stepped towards them, concern twisting his already wrinkly features.

'Oh my goodness, Alexis, Katie ... ' He looked from one to the other. 'What are you two girls doing up and about at this time of the night, and in this horrible weather? Is everything okay?'

Katie burst into inconsolable tears. Momentarily unable to speak for the growing lump in her throat Alexis shook her head as she peered down at her mud-covered toes. 'Mum and Dad were fighting ... ' she choked out. 'And then there were gunshots, and now I don't know if they're okay.' She brought her eyes back up to meet Mister King's. 'Please, we have to go and help them.'

'Oh my goodness, you poor darling girls.' Mister King knelt down and took them into his arms. Alexis crumpled into him; the comfort he gave with such a simple gesture was overwhelming.

The flyscreen door creaked open. Alexis peered over Mister King's shoulder to see Missus King standing at the doorway, her hair in rollers and her arms folded across her fluffy pink robe. The frown creasing her thick black brows was even bigger than it usually was. 'For goodness sake, what's happened at the Browns' place now, Charlie? Can't they give us a rest from their incessant dramas?'

Dramas? Alexis felt confused.

Mister King turned, his arms still enfolding the two sisters. 'Go and call an ambulance, Mavis.' His tone was firmer than Alexis had heard it before, especially when speaking to Missus King. Usually it was the other way around.

Missus King rolled her eyes and clucked her tongue. 'Surely we don't need an ambulance, Charles, whatever it is it can't be that bad, hmmm?'

'Oh, for goodness sake, woman, can't you just do as you're asked one time without damn well questioning me?' Mister King dropped his arms and stood, his well-built, six-foot-tall frame seeming to tower over them. 'There have been shots fired at the cottage and the girls have no idea what's happened or if their parents are all right.'

Shock stole Missus King's frown as she raced back inside without another word.

Mister King placed a hand on each of the girls' shoulders. 'Now, you two, come on inside and wait with Missus King while I go up to the cottage to find out what's going on, all right?'

'Okay,' they said in unison. Mister King ushered them inside, ran upstairs to get dressed and then quickly strode over to his ute, parked beneath a paperbark tree near the house.

Now standing on the other side of the flyscreen door, her hands and face pressed up against it, Alexis watched Mister King speed off down the driveway. The back of his ute was sliding this way and that. She couldn't help but wonder what he would find when he got there, and she prayed with everything she had that this was just some misunderstanding and soon she and Katie could give their mum and dad a great big cuddle.

With the taillights finally disappearing she turned to find Katie nowhere in sight and neither was Missus King. She called out to them, but there was no answer. Strange. Katie never left her side when they had visited the Kings' place before. She called out again as she wandered around, going from room to room. Walking towards the staircase, she looked up. She didn't want to go up there. It was so very dark and, besides, she and Katie were never allowed upstairs. Missus King had made that very clear over the years. She heard a muffled cry and knew it was Katie's. Why was she upstairs, and where was Missus King? Sighing, she did what she knew she shouldn't and climbed the steps. Missus King would be very angry if she found Katie wandering around up there, so she needed to find her little sister and bring her back down before they both got into trouble.

A bright light shining into Alexis's eyes made her reflexes fire to life. The sounds and smells were unfamiliar to her, as too was whatever she was laying on. Panic filled her and her breath snagged in her chest. She felt herself wrestling a desperate feeling of grogginess as she fought for consciousness. As though summersaulting through mid-air, she struggled to come to a standstill, at the same time afraid of where she might land. Her head pounded like it had never had before. Her stomach twisted and plummeted as if she were tumbling off a cliff. Suddenly she had the urge to vomit as she slammed into reality hard and fast.

Quickly climbing to the surface in her mind, a deep sorrow filled her, making her want to burst into tears. Something was upsetting her but she didn't know exactly what it was. Was she having a bad dream? Questions bombarded her as she wrestled the haziness, the lack of answers making her mind spin even faster. Where was she? Where was Katie? Where was her mum? Her dad? Why weren't her parents here, comforting her like they usually did when she had a nightmare? Her panic fuelled her building anxiety and she tried to push away whoever was shining the torch into her eyes. A firm but gentle hand came down on hers as a reassuring voice told her she was okay, that she was in Blue Ridge hospital. But those words did nothing to curb her anxiety; if anything they made everything ten times worse. She slipped into a blurry world, her gaze finally focussing on the face of the kindly woman who stood at her bedside, a torch in her hand.

Wincing from the shooting pain at the side of her head, Alexis peeled her tongue from the roof of her mouth. 'Why am I in hospital?' Her voice was croaky, and she suddenly felt extremely thirsty as if she hadn't had a drop of water for weeks. She stared at the lady's bright shock of fiery red hair and recognised her light blue uniform as one a nurse would wear.

The lady removed her glasses and left them dangling from a cord around her neck, and then gently patted Alexis's arm. 'You've had a bit of a mishap, my dear. But don't worry, you'll be fine.' She reached for a glass of water that sat on the bedside table. 'You'll feel a bit groggy from the anaesthetic so just make sure you take it easy ... we don't want you falling and hurting yourself again.'

'Falling *again*?'

The nurse looked perplexed. 'Yes, don't you remember anything that happened earlier tonight?'

Alexis shook her head, her lips trembling.

'I'll make sure to mention this to your doctor.'

Another rush of fear shot through her. 'Is it serious, if I can't remember anything? Does it mean my brain is broken?'

'Don't get yourself all worked up.' With a gentle smile the nurse gave Alexis's arm a reassuring pat. 'You had quite a big tumble, and memory loss can be a short-term side effect. I'm surprised you didn't break anything – it's a miracle if I've ever seen one.'

'Really?'

'Yes, really. You arrived concussed, and needed twenty stitches at the side of your head to fix you up. Once you've had time to rest it should all come back to you.'

'Okay then.' Alexis sounded as unsure as she felt. Unclenching one of her hands from the bed sheet she gently touched the side of her head, lightly running her fingertips over the bandage. 'Where are my mum and Katie?'

The nurse bent the straw in the glass and then held it to Alexis's lips. 'Don't you worry, sweetheart, Katie's okay. She's out in the waiting room with Mister and Missus King, waiting for your grandparents to arrive from Townsville.'

Confused, Alexis slowly shook her head. 'But it's a five-hour drive ... they'll be waiting for ages. Is my dad driving back with them? And why isn't my mum with Katie?'

'So many questions.' The nurse plucked a folder from the end of the bed. 'Actually, you've been asleep for quite a few hours now, Alexis, so your grandparents are probably almost here, I'd say.' She pulled a pen from her pocket and scribbled something down.

Alexis was about to ask more questions when the sound of footsteps drew her attention to the doorway. She expected to see her mum but was met with another familiar face, which helped to ease some of her anxiety, but only a little.

'Oh, sweetheart, you're finally awake.' Mister King rushed towards her. 'Thank goodness. We've been so worried about you.' He placed a hand on her arm and it felt cold against her skin. 'What happened at the homestead was just a terrible accident.'

Fear almost overwhelmed Alexis. None of this made any sense. 'Why are you at the hospital with me, Mister King, and why are

Nanny and Grandpa driving all the way here? Is Dad coming home with them?' She tried to sit up, but feeling woozy she stopped halfway. 'And where is Mum?' Her skull began to pound like there was a jackhammer inside it. Reaching her hand to her forehead, she felt a lump the size of an egg.

'Please be gentle with yourself, Alexis.' The nurse touched her shoulder. 'You've hit your head very hard, and you've had some strong medicine to help with the pain, so it would be best for you to stay lying down for now. Just until the doctor has had a chance to check you over again.'

Alexis's heart was racing. 'Can you please tell me what happened, Mister King?' Desperation laced her every word.

'You don't remember anything?' He gave the nurse a tense sideways glance.

'No, I don't.' Alexis was growing increasingly annoyed that no one was answering her questions.

Charlie King sighed as though the weight of the world was upon him. 'We're not sure, sweetheart. Missus King said she heard a loud crash and then found you at the bottom of the stairs. You must have tripped and fell.'

'The front steps?'

'No, you fell down the steps inside,' Mister King said, shaking his head. 'You gave Mavis, and me, quite a fright.'

The nurse nodded. 'Yes, poor Missus King was beside herself when they brought you in. Fifteen steps is quite a way to tumble.'

Alexis slowly shook her head. She couldn't remember any of what they were saying, and it was scaring her. 'Why was I upstairs, Mister King?'

'I don't know, sweetheart.'

'That's really weird.'

The creases in Mister King's forehead deepened. 'Why's that?'

'Missus King has told Katie and me not to go up there, so I don't think I would have just gone up by myself. I'd be too scared I'd get into trouble.'

Mister King shrugged. 'Maybe you went to use the bathroom.'

'But there's a bathroom downstairs.'

'Maybe it was being used?'

'Maybe.' Alexis wished she could put the pieces of the puzzle together. 'I'm sorry, but I don't remember any of this, or why I was at your house in the first place.' Pulling the sheet up to her neck she clutched it beneath her quivering chin. It was all she could do to stop from crying. Two sets of concerned eyes looked back at her. 'I want my mum. Where is she?' The tears welled and rolled down her cheeks before she could blink them away.

Sadness flashed across Mister King's big brown eyes. He tried to hide it by rubbing his face but it was too late. Alexis almost covered her ears, she really wasn't sure she wanted the answer now. She held her breath as she waited for him to say something, anything that would help to alleviate the fear coursing throughout her.

Mister King went to answer, but then, shoving his hands in his pockets, he paused. He closed his eyes for a few brief moments before blowing out a heavy breath. His shoulders slumped even more so as he looked at her again. 'You honestly don't remember anything?'

She shook her head. The terror of the unknown was crushing her. She wanted her mother. Now. So she could fall into her arms and feel safe as she listened to her heartbeat, like she always did when her mum cuddled her to her chest.

Silence hung heavy.

Mister King turned to the nurse as if asking a tongue-tied question. The nurse nodded and mumbled something about amnesia. Alexis had no idea what that meant. Was it some terrible disease she was going to die from? Or was it something her mum had? What if her mother died from it? She stopped a scream escaping just in time.

With another hefty sigh, Mister King pulled up a seat and slumped down as though his legs would no longer hold him. Folding his hands together, he rested his elbows on his knees and leant forwards. Alexis watched the apple in his throat bob, like he was about to cry, and it made her want to cry even harder. Sniffing, he wiped his left eye quickly. This wasn't good. Mister King never cried; even when his dog died last month he hadn't shed a tear.

'Please say something, Mister King.'

He nodded and then cleared his throat, three times. 'Well, you arrived at my place with Katie at about three o'clock this morning, very disorientated and very upset.' He stopped and cleared his throat again.

'Did I really? Why would I come over to your place in the middle of the night, especially with Katie? And why was I so upset?' She tried to smile. 'Maybe I was sleepwalking and Katie was taking care of me.'

He shook his head and looked down at the floor. 'I'm afraid you weren't sleepwalking, Alexis.' He went to say something and then stopped himself. Instead, he rubbed the grey stubble on his chin and stretched back in the seat, the world seeming to be weighing down on his shoulders.

Alexis crumpled her face up as she tried to recall something, anything ... but there was nothing. 'So where's Mum now? Is she in hospital too? Is that why she's not here with me? Because she's hurt?'

Mister King looked to the nurse as if for guidance. The nurse subtly shook her head. 'I think we should wait until her grandparents get here, Charlie.'

'But I ... ' He seemed to stumble over his words.

The nurse gave his shoulder a pat. 'It's for the best that we leave it to them.'

What was the big secret? Panicked even more, Alexis squeezed her eyes closed. Maybe this *was* just a bad dream – one where everything seemed real. When she opened her eyes again she would be at home in her bedroom, and her mum and dad and Katie would be there, and everything would be back to normal. Silently counting to ten, she found the courage to open them again, her heart sinking even further when she saw that nothing had changed.

The nurse tucked the sheet in tightly around Alexis. 'Your grandparents will be here very soon, and then they can explain everything to you, okay, sweetheart?'

'But why can't you?' Alexis choked out.

The nurse sucked in a breath. 'Because it's not my place to, and neither is it Mister King's.' Blinking fast, she placed her hand over Alexis's and gave it a squeeze. 'I promise it won't be long, and then you'll be able to talk to them.'

'Please just tell me my mother is okay?' Terrified of the answer, it came out as a whisper.

The nurse busied herself scribbling on the chart again. 'Okay, my job's done here, so how about I go and check if your grandparents have arrived?' She turned to Mister King. 'Can you stay here with her please, Charlie?'

He nodded very fast. 'Yes, yes, of course.'

With fear swirling inside her, Alexis watched the nurse disappear out the doorway, her shoes squeaking on the shiny floors with each step. It was as if she couldn't get away fast enough.

Alexis looked to Mister King and he gave her a tight-lipped smile before staring past her and out the window to the sun-drenched garden. She could tell he didn't want to talk anymore. So she tried to remember anything that would give a clue as to what was going on. But there was nothing but a big, blank space. Her mind felt hazy, her thoughts scattered. She recalled leaving her best friend's birthday party in the afternoon, filled to the brim with chips, cordial, lollies and cake. Her mother had been so happy to see her when she had picked her up – so much so she had hugged her tight. Then Alexis and her mother had sung along to the songs on the radio as they'd driven home, with Katie giggling in the back seat. As a treat for being such good girls while their father was away her mum had made them their favourite dinner of apricot chicken and a yummy apple pie and custard for dessert. After watching *Family Feud*, a ritual in their house, Katie had gone to bed and their mother had read her a story until she'd drifted off to sleep. Alexis went to bed a bit later and read her own book for a while. She vaguely recalled Katie crawling into bed with her because she'd had a bad dream, and that was it. As hard as she tried she couldn't remember anything more until right here, right now.

A shuffle at the door caught her attention. She turned to see the towering figure of her grandpa coming into the room, a sleeping Katie cradled in his strong arms. Nanny remained in the doorway, her voice hushed as she talked with the nurse. Alexis noticed that her nan was dabbing her eyes with a tissue. She looked beyond them, waiting to see her father's face appear, and was saddened when it didn't. Maybe he was still in Townsville. But that didn't make any sense. None of this did.

'Hi, Bubbles,' Grandpa said, his lips not smiling but instead set in a grim line. The scent of tobacco followed him in, which was a surprise. He'd told her he'd given up smoking after she'd said how much it worried her that he might die from cancer. He leant in and placed a kiss on her cheek, his stubble scratching her skin as he pulled away.

'Hey, Grandpa.' Although delighted to see him, Alexis felt her heart sink lower. He was usually so happy to see her. 'Where's Dad? Did he drive back with you and Nanny?' She watched as he gently placed Katie down on the end of the bed and then covered her with the spare blanket. He blew out a big breath, as though he'd been holding onto it forever, and folded his arms across his chest.

'How are you feeling, Bubbles?' Worry wrinkled his brow.

Hadn't he heard her ask about her dad? Or was he ignoring her questions too? He looked so much older than when she'd seen him a few months ago. The weight in his eyes upset her even more. 'I'm really confused and my head hurts a lot, but I'm okay, I suppose. Have you seen Mum yet? And where's Dad?'

He stepped back as though he'd been struck. Covering his mouth he coughed, and then the tight-lipped smile returned. 'Well, that's good you're doing okay, Bubbles.' He sounded weird, like he was straining to appear happy. He looked to the lump on her head, his bushy eyebrows rising. 'You did hit your head a beauty by the looks of it.' He peered to where the bandage was covering her stiches. 'It must be very sore.'

'Uh-huh, apparently I fell down fifteen steps ... ' She said it as though it were a feat to be proud of. 'But I don't remember anything.' She noted how red his eyes were, as though he'd been crying, but then he'd had a long drive so that was probably why. He was just really tired, she told herself.

Grandpa acknowledged Mister King with a curt nod. 'Thanks for bringing her in, Charlie, and taking care of Katie. Fay and I really appreciate it.'

Mister King fidgeted in his chair and looked uncomfortable. 'Don't mention it, Bob. It's the very least we could do.' He stood up, groaning as he did. Holding his lower back, he reached out his free hand.

Grandpa did the same. Alexis looked from one to the other. The two men shared a quick handshake, both of them looking as though they were about to break down at any moment.

Mum? That one word swirled in her head, worrying her sick. Why wouldn't anyone tell her how or where she was?

'I'm so sorry, Bob. Please let me know if there is anything Mavis or I can do to help.'

'Will do, Charlie. Thanks.' Grandpa looked away as he cleared his throat yet again.

Mister King turned to Alexis. 'I best be going. You get better now, sweetheart.' He gave her a wobbly smile before making his way to the door, where her nanny gave him a quick hug. Alexis couldn't be sure, because her nanny had her back to her, but with the way her shoulders were trembling it seemed that she was crying very, *very* hard.

Grandpa returned to her bedside and took her hand in his. His felt so big compared to hers. And that's when she noticed the tears welling in his eyes.

'Hey there, my darling baby girl.' Nanny scooted in beside him, her eyes red and puffy with smudgy black marks beneath them. She cupped Alexis's cheeks and placed a firm kiss on her lips. 'I'm so glad you're doing okay, my darling girl.' She looked to Grandpa as heavy tears began to fall down her cheeks. 'Do you want me to tell her, Bob?'

'No, Fay, I'll do ... ' Grandpa's voice cracked. In three big strides he was standing at the window with his back to them, his head in his hands.

Alexis felt her bottom lip tremble just before a sob escaped her, and then another. This was very bad. 'Are Mum and Dad okay?' She looked to her nanny for a reply, her breath held as she waited.

'Oh, Alexis, sweetheart.' Breaking into a sob, her Nanny reached out and wrapped her arms around her.

Grandpa came back to join them and placed his hand on Nanny's back. Alexis looked up at him for answers. His lips were quivering and there was so much sadness in his eyes it tore her already breaking heart to shreds. 'Grandpa?' She choked out.

He shook his head. 'Sweetheart, I'm so sorry, but your mum and dad, they're … '

Alexis didn't hear anything more, her heart-wrenching screams echoing around the room.

CHAPTER

3

Townsville – seventeen years later

'Have you thought any more about what I suggested last time, about going back there? It might help you remember.' It was said so gently, but the force of the question hit hard.

Alexis Brown felt the all too familiar rise of emotions as she stared point blank at her psychologist. Stepping back into the cottage was the last thing on her mind. Even thinking about it terrified her. There had to be another way to get over her parents' deaths, surely. But after all this time, wouldn't she have found that way by now? She'd need something very big to drag her back there, a sign from the gods perhaps. 'I really don't think that's a good idea.'

'On the contrary, I do, Alexis.'

Alexis shrugged. What else was there to say when she'd given every excuse under the sun not to go back to Blue Ridge?

Doctor Anita Jacobs didn't reply but wrote something down on her notepad. Although Alexis hated that notepad, she longed to see what was secretly scribbled in it each session. The short pause in their conversation was a welcomed reprieve. A smile tugged at her lips as she admired the oriental lilies filling the room with their intoxicating scent, her photographer's eye imagining them captured within the lens. For Alexis, like anything born from the womb of the earth, fresh flowers always had a way of lighting up even her darkest days. She made it her weekly indulgence to go to her local florist on a Saturday morning and buy whatever colourful bunch she liked – sometimes it was lilies, other times it was roses or tulips. It was such a simple but gratifying pleasure. The way the flowers would boldly open over time was breathtaking, and just when she thought they couldn't open any further, they would go and open some more. If only she could do the same, open her heart and soul up with such effortless faith so as to allow another love into her life. Her longing to start a family was perhaps more hormonal than a choice – being thirty she was at prime child-bearing age, but her inner light had been dulled after enduring her fair share of relationships that had gone bad.

'Are you still here with me, Alexis, or are you floating off somewhere?'

'Oh, sorry, I was just admiring your flowers.'

Anita put her pen down and turned to glance at the vase on her desk. 'Oh, yes, aren't they just gorgeous? David had them delivered to me yesterday, for our thirtieth wedding anniversary.'

'Naw, how sweet, if I live to share a love like you two do I'll be one very happy woman.' Her heart aching for that one true love she was yet to meet, she looked down at her hands that were now folded in her lap.

'If you truly believe you'll find the love of your life you will, Alexis, just give it time.'

'I don't know about that, Anita. I haven't yet, and I've probably been on about five dates so far this year, thanks to everyone trying to set me up on them.'

'That's because none of the men you've gone out with has been the right one, but don't give up ... he'll be out there waiting for you.' Anita smiled kindly.

'Yeah, we'll see,' Alexis said a little cynically. 'And besides, from my experience, most of the people I've ever truly loved have died, Mum and Dad, Grandpa and Nan ... makes me scared to love again, if I'm to be completely honest.' She shrugged. 'Maybe that's why I go out with the men I do, because unconsciously I'm choosing the ones who will never fully commit to me. That way I won't fall too far head over heels and risk being completely crushed.'

'We've all loved and lost, in many different ways, and yes, you've lost too many in your short life, but don't let that turn you cold, Alexis. Life is for living, and loving.'

'I'll try and take that on board.'

'Good.' Anita stared at her a little longer than comfortable and then her finger popped up in the air as if she'd just remembered something. 'I meant to say earlier, your photo on the front cover of Saturday's newspaper was beautiful.'

'Cheers.'

'I didn't think you were working for the newspaper anymore?'

'I'm not, but when I heard about the local woman trying to raise money to help pay for her child's multiple sclerosis medication, I just had to take some photos of them together to get her story in the paper.'

'That's so typically selfless of you.' Anita shook her head as though amazed. 'The way you captured the love that mother has for her sick child as she held her moved me to tears.'

Not one to accept compliments easily, Alexis felt heat rise to her cheeks. 'Thank you. I just hope it encourages people to help her out, financially or otherwise.'

'You truly have a gift when it comes to capturing life and emotion through a lens, Alexis, and you're putting it to good use. I'm so glad you found the courage to give up your desk job at that awful mechanic's shop and follow your calling.'

'That was all thanks to you pushing me to make the change.'

'Give credit where credit is due ... it was you who took the brave steps forwards, not me.'

'I've got to admit it's been a tough year, the photo industry is lethal, but all the blood, sweat and tears were worth it now I'm freelancing for a couple of different magazines.'

'Glad to hear it, I'm so very proud of you.' Anita resumed her professional position in her chair, her posture straightening and her pen now poised and ready. 'That was a nice distraction, but we better get back to it.' She drew in a slow breath. 'So how do you feel when someone disagrees with your belief about what happened that night?'

To help expel some of the nervous energy Alexis tapped the air with her foot. It was always the same when she talked about that horrible night – the anguish of it had never eased, she'd just come to accept it was always going to be that way and had learnt to somehow manage her life around it. Keeping busy was the key. 'I know I've told you this a hundred times, and I know you've told me I need to come to grips with it, but I refuse to believe my father would do such a thing. He was a good man, a wonderful father and he loved my mum to bits, so when someone agrees with what the police had to say about it all, I feel annoyed and very angry that they cannot bring themselves to believe *me*, the one person other than my mum who was the closest to my father.'

'Even when I disagree?'

'Yes, Anita, even when you do.'

'I've never disregarded your thoughts, Alexis, I've just tried to explain that the police investigation was very thorough, and they are adamant it was a murder–suicide, so who am I to assume otherwise?' Although a brash statement, Doctor Jacob's voice was as it always was – soft, soothing, compassionate.

'Fair enough, but that doesn't mean the police are correct, there's hundreds of cases where they've been wrong.' Alexis's eyebrows rose in question. 'Right?'

'Yes, and that might well be the case in your parents' deaths, but how will you ever truly know? And you're going to drive yourself around the bend trying to piece something together when you have no memory of it in the first place.'

She had a very good point. Annoyingly so. At a loss for words, Alexis silently studied the sixty-nine year-old woman she'd watched age gracefully over the past sixteen years, appreciative of the fact that someone as committed and compassionate as Anita Jacobs had been her psychologist from when she first needed her. Knowing Anita was about to retire was hard, and scary. It felt as though she were losing her pillar of strength. But she needed to be courageous enough to stand on her own two feet now – it was high time she learnt to. 'I know I should let it go, just like a few other things in my life, and try and move on, but it's so damn frustrating. I just want to remember something, anything. It's like having a jigsaw puzzle where none of the pieces fit. And I can't talk to anyone about it anymore either, other than you.'

'Oh, why's that?' There was something in Anita's question that insinuated she already knew the answer. And so she should, also being Katie's psychologist.

Regardless, Alexis chose to respond as calmly as she could. 'With losing both Nan and Grandpa so close together last year, Katie is already heartbroken enough without reminding her of Mum and Dad's death time and time again, so I won't talk to her about it.'

'Yes, it's probably best to allow her time to heal from the shock of it all. Your grandfather's cancer was hard enough for you both to cope with, let alone your nan's heart attack two weeks later.'

With a wave of emotions making it almost impossible to breathe, Alexis stared down at the floor and blinked back tears. 'Yes, it was devastating. At least with Grandpa we had plenty of warning, but Nan left before we could say goodbye.' She brought her eyes back to Anita's. 'I know she died of a broken heart. She loved Grandpa so much, she just couldn't live without him.'

'Now that's true love if I've ever heard it.' Anita smiled softly as she pushed her reading glasses up her nose. 'What about talking to your friends?'

'My close friends try and be understanding but they don't know what to say anymore because nothing they say or do makes the heartache go away.'

Anita quickly jotted something down on her notepad and then looked up. 'Have you come to accept that Katie has a different opinion from yours about your parents' death?'

'It still makes me feel angry and hurt, but I can't blame her, I suppose. She was too young to remember anything about that night, which is a good thing in the scheme of things, and she can't really remember Mum and Dad, either. So in a way she's found it a hundred times easier to move on in her life. I mean, how can you miss something you never really remember having?'

Anita drew in a slow, steady breath, her kind eyes never leaving Alexis's. 'Does the fact that she can move on and live a fulfilled life make you envious of her?'

Alexis's heart squeezed. 'Sometimes, although I feel terrible when I think like that.'

'Why do you feel terrible?'

'Well, because I should be happy for her ... which I am. I want nothing more than for Katie to be content in life. Although I do have to admit, I don't like where she's working, there's so many shady people in the nightclub business.'

'There are, but you know you can't protect her all her life; you have to let her make her own mistakes sometimes. And who knows, this may not be a mistake, but a stepping stone in the direction of her dream to being able to travel the world as a well-known DJ.'

'I know, but it's easier said than done when it's such a big dream.'

'You have to dream big to make it in this world, Alexis. Look at your path, from working at the local mechanic's, to a journalistic photographer for a small newspaper, to a freelancer who travels the world for the perfect shot ... even as far as Antarctica last year.'

'That's true, so who am I to doubt her ability to do the same?' Alexis smiled. 'She does love her job, so the shady people come with the territory ... I suppose it's not something she can do at the local library, is it?'

'No, it certainly is not. Don't be too hard on yourself for your feelings, though, Alexis. You're an empathetic person, so it's natural for you to be hypersensitive to everything around you, including what goes on inside you.'

'Yes, I know, I can't even watch the news without starting to cry over something. And if there is anything about a child or animal being hurt ... ' She held her hands up. 'Don't even get me started or I'll start bawling like a baby.'

'I'm one of those kinds of people myself,' Anita said, 'so I understand what you're saying. That's all part of being an empath, Alexis. It may feel like a burden at times, but believe me, it makes you the kind and thoughtful person you are. It's okay to be envious as long as you don't project that envy onto Katie and make her feel guilty for being happy and living the life she chooses.'

'No, I never do that ... not that I know of anyway.' She grimaced. 'Do I?'

Anita smiled. 'I'm fairly certain Katie would let you know if you were. She's not afraid to speak up.'

Alexis laughed along with her. 'No, she's not backwards in coming forwards, is she?' She twirled a stray tendril of jet-black hair around her finger. 'I just wish I could get past my parents' deaths because I know that's what's blocking me from living a happy, satisfying life. But as hard as I try I just can't seem to free myself of the guilt of not going into the kitchen that night.'

'It was not your job to save your parents. You have to try to believe in the fact you did the right thing.'

'And just how do I do that?'

'It's as simple as you deciding to allow yourself to let it all go, Alexis.'

'Maybe, but I feel I owe it to Dad and Mum to remember something, to uncover the truth, because no matter how much I try to push the doubt away, I believe the police have it all wrong.'

'Do you think that might be your own inner desires speaking? It's your way of dealing with your unwarranted guilt of not saving your parents and not wanting to see your father in such a light?'

'Quite possibly.' Alexis sighed, her heart heavy. 'I always keep hoping that something will jog my memory, that maybe I might wake up one day and remember, even if that does mean I recall something that points directly at my father – at least then I will have some sort of closure. I just can't comprehend how a person can lose a whole section of their life and never remember it.' She wiped a tear from her cheek. She could get through three hundred and sixty four days a year without crying over her parents' death, but the anniversary of that fateful night always brought up the same unwanted feelings, the same unanswered questions. That is why she made sure one of her two visits with Anita each year fell on or at least close to that date.

The doctor shifted in her seat. 'You know my favourite saying, Alexis, and as much as I'm sure you're tired of hearing it I will say it again ... Never say never.'

'Yes, I know, but honestly, if my memory hasn't returned by now, why would it ever come back?'

'You can never pinpoint when it will, if ever, as frustrating as that is, but your memory could come back at any given moment, at a time when you least expect it.' Anita put down her notebook and pen on the table and delicately folded her hands in her lap. 'As I've explained many times before, Alexis, it's your subconscious way of handling the unsettling reality of what happened the night your parents died. It's not an easy thing to accept that your father took your mother's life before taking his own, and then when you factor in the amnesia from the fall, well ... just don't be too hard on yourself, okay?' She offered a compassionate smile before glancing up at the clock on the wall. 'I'm sorry, but we really need to wrap the session up for today.'

'Sorry we've gone over time again.'

'Not your fault at all, but I better not let my next patient wait much longer.' Anita Jacobs stood and walked over to her door; her long grey hair that was usually free and loose was tucked up into a neat bun today, making her seem more business-like then her usual bohemian aura exuded. 'If you feel you'd benefit from coming in for one last appointment before I head off overseas, I will fit you in, even if I have to stay back late one evening to do so.'

'Oh, thank you, but I should be fine.' Alexis picked up her bag from beside her, popped her favourite comfy heels back on and then hugged the psychologist who'd become more like a friend over the years.

Anita hugged her back, her embrace warm and genuine. 'What was that for?' she said as the two women stepped apart.

'For always making me feel so much better than when I walked in,' Alexis said. 'I honestly don't know how I would have got through it all without you.' Her throat tightened with emotion and she fought back the tears. 'So thank you, from the bottom of my heart, for everything.'

'Thank you for the kind words, Alexis, but ... ' Anita reached out with both hands and gave her arms a squeeze. 'You have yourself to thank for that. You're a very strong woman, a lot stronger than you give yourself credit for, and with so much love to give in that big generous heart of yours. Just promise me you will never give up on finding that special man who will love you for who you truly are ... you *are* allowed to move on with your life.'

'I promise I will try and keep an open mind, and heart.' Alexis was amazed at the absurdity of what she'd just said. As if she were able to find a way to do that.

'Good, a positive mindset ... that's what I like to hear.' Anita looked at her thoughtfully. 'I know you're tired of hearing it, but I meant what I've said about you going back to Blue Ridge, when and if you're ready, of course. I think it will really help you with your healing process and it may even help wake up that part of your memory that's closed itself off.'

'I've taken what you've said on board. I've thought about going back there, I truly have, many times, and I've almost talked myself into it, many times too, but the thought of *actually* doing it terrifies me.'

'That's understandable. There'll be a lot of memories you may not want to resurface, but I think I'm safe in saying there may be quite a few you're fond of too. You'll know when you are ready, if ever, to face that challenge. Just don't put too much pressure on yourself in the meantime, okay?'

'Yes, okay. Thank you, Anita. You make sure you have yourself a wonderful time travelling the world. You deserve the time of your life after all the amazing work you've done over the years with people like me,' she said warmly. 'Katie raves about what a miracle worker you are, and I have to agree with her.'

'Thank you, Alexis, I do my best.' She opened the door from her cosy office. 'You take care of yourself, and please pass on my regards to Katie.'

'Will do.' Alexis waved as she headed into the waiting area, only to be given the evil eye by the next patient, who had waited an extra twenty-five minutes for his appointment.

'Sorry,' she whispered as she passed him.

He rolled his eyes and grunted in response.

Alexis bit her tongue and instead flashed him a smile. Kindness cost nothing, and she couldn't blame him for being a bit pissed off.

CHAPTER

4

Stepping out of the office block and into the hustle and bustle of everyday life, Alexis begrudgingly slid back into the real world, leaving behind the cocoon that was Doctor Jacob's consulting room. It had offered her a nice, safe escape, if only for an hour or so, for many years. She tried not to think about the fact that this was her last session.

Alexis glanced at her watch and swore beneath her breath. She had to catch a bus to the mechanic's to pick up her car and she was going to be cutting it fine to make it home in time to get changed and be ready to walk out the door again by six. Being the school holidays the footpaths were busier than normal, and with roadworks in full swing on the highway the traffic was going to be a nightmare. Some days were just so much harder than others. Sighing, she pounded the pavement towards the bus stop. She hadn't caught a bus in years so this was going to be an experience.

All she wanted to do was to go home to the beachfront apartment she shared with Katie, have a relaxing bubble bath with a glass of red, order some Thai food to be delivered and then curl up on the couch with a good book. But it wasn't to be. Her date for the night was apparently going to collect her in less than two hours, and in that time she needed to get her car and then wrestle with the bumper-to-bumper traffic until she could take her turn-off to Bushland Beach, a drive that would usually take twenty-five minutes but being a Friday afternoon would most probably take much longer. Then she needed to shower, tame her mop of long crazy curls into something appropriate for a dinner date, probably get changed five times until she decided on the outfit she'd put on first, and then skull a glass of wine to calm her nerves – blind dates just weren't her thing. Actually, men in general just weren't her thing – they were too much like hard work. She really wished people would stop setting her up on dates, and she wished she would learn to say no to them.

At the very thought of her night ahead she groaned and her shoulders slumped. After being hounded for two entire days to say yes, she had caved in and promised Katie she'd join her and her boyfriend. Katie and Zane meant well, wanting to see her happy and in love. She just hoped the guy wasn't a douche-bag because she wasn't in the mood to put up with someone who spent more time in front of a mirror than she did, or thought the only conversation worth having was one about himself. It would be like scraping her fingernails down a blackboard for two hours until she could respectfully excuse herself and go home.

If only she could meet the man she'd always imagined in her daydreams – a down-to-earth kind of bloke with a love for country music, one who enjoyed lots of cuddles and good conversation beneath a blanket of stars after a night out at a club, who also loved the beach, who had a bottomless depth to his heart and soul, knew how to cook, clean, worked hard, who would love her and protect her fiercely, and one who still believed in old-fashioned chivalry. Was that too much to ask? Was she, as Katie and her friends often told her, setting the bar too high? She always defended herself when they said that, but if she was being honest with herself, yes, she was setting the bar super high and that was the plan, because that shielded her from the pain of love. She shook her head to clear it of these thoughts. It was a waste of her time, daydreaming about her Mister One-in-a-million, because if he were out there, some lucky woman would have snapped him up or in a twist of fate he was quite possibly gay and completely unattainable.

Preoccupied with her thoughts she jumped as a man bumped into her in passing. It wasn't much of a surprise that he didn't even pause to apologise, his head bent down, looking at his phone as he hurried along the street. What was with life these days, everyone so busy that they couldn't even take the time to stop and look you in the eyes? It saddened her that technology had stolen most people away from common courtesies and face-to-face conversation. Katie would quite often text her from the kitchen to say dinner was ready, rather than walk a few steps to let her know – it drove Alexis insane.

As she strode towards the bus station thinking evil thoughts about mobile phones, her own chimed and she dug it out from her handbag, groaning when she spotted the caller ID. Her experience of late told her this wasn't going to be a short call. She loved her best mate, but really, now of all times? Pushing the pedestrian button so she could cross the busy street, she squeezed her phone to her ear with her shoulder, unable to even get a *Hello* out before the shrill voice at the other end began.

'Lexi, where have you been? I've been trying to get hold of you for over two hours.'

Usually a calm, cool, collected woman, Melanie, her cousin's bride-to-be and one of her dearest friends, was turning into a bridezilla. Alexis gritted her teeth and smiled through it. 'I've been at my psychologist appointment. What's up?'

'Oh, bugger, I'm so sorry. I'd forgotten all about that. I'm being such a bad friend at the moment, aren't I?'

'No, you're not,' Alexis lied. What good was it going to do to speak the truth? With the wedding just over a week away, Melanie had a lot on her plate, and Alexis knew that once it was over, she'd have her loving, thoughtful friend back.

'Stop being so nice, Lexi. I'm a she-devil from hell who needs a good slap over the head with a fry pan to put me and everyone else out of their misery.'

Alexis couldn't help but laugh.

'So you agree?'

'Um.'

'Be honest.'

'Kinda sort of.'

'Ha-ha, don't blame you.' The chink of ice against what Alexis knew would be a glass of white wine echoed down the phone line. 'Did it go okay?'

'Did what go okay?'

'Your appointment.'

'Oh, yeah, pretty good.'

'Great. Anything new to report?'

'Not really, same as every other time ... ' Alexis didn't want to rehash everything she'd told Melanie countless times. 'Anyways, what's up?'

'I went to the bridal shop to pick my dress up this morning, only to discover they've misplaced it.'

'What do you mean, they've *misplaced* it?'

'That's exactly what I said, amongst a few other things. I think I actually said the F word three times, and you know me, I only swear around those I love.'

'Naw, that makes me feel super spesh because you swear around me constantly.'

'Of course you're super spesh, you're my maid of honour.' She laughed. 'But in all seriousness, how in the hell can you lose a wedding dress of all things!'

'Oh no, Mel ... what are they doing about it?'

'Apparently, a few dresses were picked up by a courier yesterday afternoon that were going to be dropped off at the casino, so they're madly trying to find out if mine accidentally went with them.'

'Oh shit, well, let's not panic just yet. At least there's hope.'

'Don't panic! Are you fucking serious, Lexi? What am I going to wear if I don't have my wedding dress?' There was a sharp intake of breath. 'Oh my god, I think I'm going to have a panic attack just thinking about it.'

'Deep breaths, it'll all be fine. You'll see.'

'I wish I could believe you, Lexi, but holy crap, this is bad. What happens if I've lost too much weight, or heaven forbid, somehow put weight on, and I don't have time for an alteration? And oh my goodness, what if ... '

Crossing the street and then dashing down the steps that led to the bus station, Alexis patiently waited for the drop-dead gorgeous Melanie Jones to finish all the *what ifs* she could conjure up in her overanxious state. Clearing the bottom two steps and out of breath, she just caught the bus before it pulled out from the curb and into the traffic. It was only then that Melanie finally stopped to draw a breath.

After what felt like an eternity Alexis eventually got a word in. 'You know what, you need to calm your farm because no matter what happens we will deal with it together, okay? There's nothing you and I can't conquer, and stressing isn't going to achieve anything.' Realising that she needed to heed her own advice sometimes, Alexis was mindful to keep her voice low, not wanting to annoy the other passengers.

'Lexi ... ' There was a pause as Melanie sucked in a noisy breath. 'Okay, all right, yes, you are right, I need to calm the fuck down.'

'I didn't really say it like that, but yes, you do.'

'I know, but that's my take on it.'

'You've got a way with words, my friend.'

'That I do, I need to go and wash my mouth out with soap,' Melanie replied playfully.

Alexis took the last available seat halfway down bus, beside a man who smelt as if he hadn't bathed in a week. It was too late to abandon ship now. With Melanie muttering something about a piercing Alexis fought her gag reflex when the smell hit, but at the same time refusing to budge just in case she insulted the man. He looked as if he could use more than a shower, the despondency written all over his face tugging at her heart strings. The people who were still standing gave her a look as if to say 'That's why we didn't sit there', and she felt like telling them all to stop being so mean. She subtly turned in her seat to try to capture some fresh air.

'Alexis, are you still there?'

'Oh, sorry, yup. What were you saying about a piercing?'

'Well, wanting to stick with the theme of having the most glitter-infused, diamanté encrusted, extravagant wedding my guests have ever seen, I went out on a whim and had my thingy pierced this morning.'

'You mean your nether thingy?'

'Yes, I do.'

Screwing her face up, Alexis crossed her legs tightly with the thought of it. 'No way, are you serious?'

'Deadly. And fuck me, it hurt like a bitch.' There was silence for a brief second. 'I'm looking at it right now and it's as swollen as a ... '

'I'm okay for a visual, thanks, Mel.' Alexis tried her best not to picture it, but she couldn't hold back the laughter when her creative mind won out. She stifled her giggles as much as she could. 'I can't believe you'd do something so crazy. Actually, erase that, yes I do.' She had a habit of snorting when she laughed, and although she tried to stop it a small snort escaped her. The unkempt man sat beside her grinned, and she was pleased that she could make him break a smile.

'I'm glad you can see the funny side of it, Lexi ... ' Melanie giggled. 'I probably will too, once the pain goes away. Hopefully it will be worth the look on Henry's face when he sees it, which is not going to be until the wedding night now.'

'I'm sure he will love it, Mel. So are you playing the virgin until then?' Alexis whispered.

'I'm doing my very best to ... seeing I'm wearing white I should make some kind of effort to be one, even though its late for that now.'

'Go you.' The phone beeped. 'Sorry, Mel, but I have to run. Another call is coming in.'

'Okay, Hun, chat later.'

'Yes, will do, make sure you let me know as soon as you hear anything about your dress. Bye, Mel.' She ended the call and the next one came in. 'Hey, Katie.'

'Hey, Sis, where are you?'

'I'm on my way. I'll be home in about an hour, fingers crossed.'

'Shit, that long?'

'Yeah, sorry, I've had one of those days that have got away from me, and I still have to pick my car up, so please tell me you're calling to say the date is off.'

'No, but I kind of wish I was.' Katie's voice trembled.

Alexis sat up straighter. 'You don't sound good. Is everything okay?'

'Not really.'

'Why, what's happened?' The guy beside her gave her a sympathetic sideways glance, and Alexis showed her gratitude for that with a smile of her own.

'Well, I just collected our mail from the post-office box and there was a letter addressed to both of us, so of course I opened it, and ... ' her voice broke and she calmed it by clearing her throat. 'Inside there was a really weird note, typed, not hand written.'

Alexis waited for the rest with bated breath, but it didn't come. 'So, don't leave me hanging, what did the note say?'

'I'm so sorry, Sis, but I only rang to see how long you will be. I'll fill you in when you get here.'

'Oh, Katie, come on, that's not fair at all. Just tell me now so I don't have to worry myself sick on the way home.'

'No, sorry, Lexi, this will have to wait until you get here.' It was said with absolute conviction.

Katie was as stubborn as a mule when she had her mind set on something so Alexis knew there was no talking her round. 'Oh bloody hell, Katie. Really?'

'Yes, really ... just hurry the hell up, okay, before I burn holes in the carpet from pacing.'

'It's that bad, huh?'

'Yup.'

'I really wish you would just tell me.'

'Can't. Won't. So don't even bother trying to beg me.'

'Okay, okay. I'm going as fast as I can. I will see you soon.'

'Yup, see you then.'

'Katie?'

'Yes.'

'Please just tell me it has nothing to do with anyone being hurt, or dying.'

'I can't really promise you that, Sis.'

Shock hit Alexis like a slap in the face and the confinement of the overcrowded bus suddenly made her feel as though she couldn't catch her breath. For the second time that day, Alexis bit her tongue. She knew she could be overbearing when it came to telling Katie what to do and what not to do, but she just couldn't help herself, she was the big sister, the mother Katie hadn't had since she was little, so she was only looking out for her and wanted to do her damndest to keep her safe. 'Yes, yes, okay.'

'Good.' Katie's voice trembled.

'Great.' The lilt of sarcasm was something she couldn't control.

'I love you, Lexi.'

'Love you too, Pebbles.'

And then the phone went dead, leaving Alexis's mind swirling as if a cyclone was tearing through it. Was it some sick love note by an obsessed admirer of Katie's? That was possible seeing as they'd had one of them before. Or perhaps a threatening note because they sometimes played their music too loud, or a note about some debt she wasn't aware of? For goodness sake, had Katie got herself into some sort of trouble at work? There were so many possibilities and not one that curbed her growing anxiety. Deep breaths, everything was going to be okay.

Why, oh why, on the eve of the anniversary of her parents' death did something like this have to go and happen? Now the blind date didn't seem so bad after all. She swore under her breath at the universe. Hadn't she gone through enough already? And it was then that the bus came to a grinding halt, everybody on board grabbing the nearest thing to stop from slipping. For Alexis it was the scruffy bloke sitting beside her. 'Oops, so sorry,' she said with a smile.

The man smiled back at her. 'No worries.'

She fought to refrain from finding the bottle of hand antiseptic in her bag and pouring it all over herself as she quickly wriggled back to her side of the bench seat.

'Sorry about that, ladies and gentleman,' the bus driver turned and addressed everyone. 'Just a hiccup of a few rogue cattle on the road, they must have snuck out of the feedlot up the road. We should be back on our merry way as soon as we can moooooove them off.' He said it as if it was hilarious, but only a few passengers joined in his mirth. Usually Alexis would have too, but today she wasn't in the mood. He cleared his throat. 'Anyhow, please remain where you are and we'll be on our way again soon.'

Alexis slumped in her seat and, pulling her mobile from her bag, she sent Katie a text.

Cows on road. Go figure! Might be home later than expected. Maybe think about cancelling dates. And just for the record, this not knowing is killing me. Xx

As if she'd had her finger at the ready, a bubble popped up on Alexis's phone to let her know Katie was texting straight back. She hoped her sister had had a change of heart and would tell her what the damn note said. She held her breath as the bubble vanished and she waited for the message to pop up.

Cows? From the feedlot? I've already cancelled tonight with Zane. See you when you get here. Xoxo

Sighing, Alexis tossed her phone back in her bag. Whatever the note had to say she had a feeling it was going to pack a punch.

CHAPTER

5

The elevator in the seaside apartment block felt as if it were moving in slow motion as Alexis waited for it to reach her floor. Her lip bled lightly on the inside from where she'd been chewing on it in nervous anticipation. Before the lift doors had fully opened she dashed out, excusing herself as she bumped into people, and then ran down the hall towards her front door. Keys at the ready she slipped them into the lock, pushed the door open, accidentally slammed it shut behind her, and then tossed her bag onto the entrance table. 'Katie, I'm home.' Usually a stickler about taking her shoes off at the door, she didn't even think to do so now.

'Oh thank god for that,' Katie called out. The two sisters met in the middle of the hallway in a tight embrace.

'So?' Alexis said as she pulled back, her heart hammering against her chest.

Katie's usually tanned face looked very pale. 'I think you better come and sit down first.'

'It looks as if you need to sit down too, Pebbles.' Alexis followed her sister into the lounge room and took her usual seat on the couch.

Katie slumped down beside her, staring at the note in her hands. 'I seriously don't know what to make of it, or if I even believe it.'

Alexis held out her hand. 'Well come on, give it to me so I can make up my own mind.'

With anguish written all over her face Katie passed it to Alexis. 'Please, whatever you do, don't say I told you so.'

'Why in the heck would I do that?' With her heart in her throat Alexis quickly unfolded the A4 piece of paper that looked as if it had been folded and unfolded a million times already. She wondered if it were Katie, or the sender, that had done so. As she began to read, the words slipped past her quivering lips in a breathless whisper.

Dear Alexis and Katie,

I hope this finds you both well. I'm so very sorry it's taken me all these years to get in touch, but circumstances prevented me from doing so before. I want you to know that your father didn't kill your mother, or take his own life. They were both murdered. I need to die knowing I have told you this, and may the good Lord forgive me for keeping it from you. I don't want to go to hell ...

As if someone had just punched her in the back, Alexis exhaled a sharp breath. She looked at the bottom of the page, but there was nothing to indicate who the writer was. No name, no initials, no clue as to who would be so nasty as to withhold this life-changing information all these years. Could it be true? Had her intuition been right all along? Or was someone playing a really nasty prank?

Her palms felt clammy. The room seemed to be spinning. Nausea swirled in her stomach. She tried to take a deep breath but her chest was too tight to draw air. Katie was saying something but she sounded a million miles away. A hand came down lightly upon her back and rubbed it tenderly. Hot tears blurred her eyes and she tried to wipe them away before turning her attention back to the note. Her hands shook so badly she was finding it almost impossible to read the rest, but she just had to. Tears dripped from her cheeks and onto the paper, blurring some of the inked letters as the words slipped from her lips in more of a sob now.

> *... I feel so ashamed of myself for keeping this secret all this time, but I hope you can find it in your heart to understand I had to protect my family. I only hope this at least gives you some kind of closure, some kind of peace. I can't begin to understand the heartache you both must have suffered with not only losing your parents but also thinking your father would do such a horrible thing. I can vouch for the fact that he was a good man, and a loving father and husband. You two girls, and your mother, were his world. He does not deserve the disgrace that is attached to his name. I wish I could do more, but it's with a heavy heart that I feel it's out of my hands, and at God's will. If you are meant to discover more, he will show you, and I, the way. May God forgive me and may he bless you both.*

Whoever it was, they were clearly religious. How dare they fob it off and leave it in God's hands. Anger and resentment coursed throughout Alexis. 'Who would do such a terrible thing?'

'I have no idea, Sis.' Katie twirled her thumbs around each other, and her left leg bobbed nervously. 'Do you believe it's for real?'

Alexis placed her hand on Katie's leg in a bid to stop it bouncing. 'I really want to, but part of me is scared to just in case it's a hoax.'

Much to Alexis's surprise, Katie nodded. 'Yeah, me too.'

Alexis focussed on the note again and Katie on her wine. Silence hung between them.

'I'm so sorry, Sis.'

Alexis tilted her head to the side. 'What for, Pebbles?'

'For sitting on the fence and not backing you up about Dad. I always thought the police would've known what they were doing and ... ' She broke into a sob.

Alexis gently rubbed Katie's back. 'Oh, Katie, please don't apologise. We don't even know if this note is genuine.'

'Yeah, I know, but still, I haven't really been the supportive sister, have I?' She took a big glug from her wine, leaving the glass empty.

Alexis couldn't disagree.

Katie sighed wearily as she peered down at her black-painted toes. 'I suppose, for me, believing Dad did it gave me a good reason not to miss him.'

Stunned with Katie's frankness and also with the tears welling in her eyes when Katie was rarely emotional, Alexis went to say something but faltered. She bit back the sob rising in her throat as she placed the note down beside her and then reached out and took hold of Katie's hands, her heart aching. She remained silent, giving Katie time.

'It allowed me to hate him, Lexi, to conjure up an image of a monster in my mind, so then I only had to cope with the heartache of losing Mum.' Katie sniffled, her tears running down her cheeks. 'And now I feel horrible thinking like that. Poor Dad, not being alive to clear his name, that is of course, if this note turns out to be the truth.'

'I'm so sorry, Pebbles. I never knew that was how you were dealing with it all.'

'Yeah, well, I'm not really one for talking about deep stuff, so how could you?'

'True ... but don't beat yourself up over it, it's just your way of coping.' Alexis pulled her into a hug, realising now that Katie's ability to move on in her life made perfect sense. 'We all deal with grief in our own way. And trust me, I'll get to the bottom of this. If it is true, I'll make sure I clear our father's name, come hell or high water.'

Katie nodded, her sobs squeezing Alexis's heart even tighter. After a few quiet moments Katie sat up straight and wiped her tears, leaving black mascara smudged on her cheeks. 'How do you think they got our address?'

'Whoever it was only had to look my name up on Google to find my photography website, which has our post-office box listed in the contact details.'

'Oh, I didn't think of that. Do you have any thoughts on who might have sent it?'

'I honestly have no clue. Mum and Dad had quite a lot of friends that knew you and I well ... too many candidates and not enough information to narrow it down at the moment. I need some time to get my head around it. Have you got any ideas?'

'I've tried hard to come up with something while I was waiting for you to get home, but I don't remember anyone from Blue Ridge, other than a vague memory of Mister and Missus King, and my guess is they'd both be well and truly through the pearly gates by now.'

'Yeah, possibly. They were in their late sixties when we lived there, so who knows?' Alexis turned and looked at her sister. 'How much do you remember about them?'

'Not much, but I can remember how much of a grump Missus King was,' Katie said. 'I remember hiding behind you whenever she was around.'

Alexis was struck with an overwhelming sense of sadness. 'You remember that but you can't recall anything about Mum or Dad?'

'Yeah, weird, huh? I have this really hazy memory of Missus King grabbing me by both arms and yelling at me, and I was terrified, but I can't remember what it was about or what I'd done wrong.'

'Really? It must have been something pretty bad. I never remember her ever touching either of us. She did do a heck of lot of yelling, and not only at us, but at Ethan too.' Alexis couldn't help but smile as she thought about her childhood crush.

'You used to always call him the dashing Ethan King,' Katie said softly. 'It's been a while since you mentioned him. I wonder what he looks like now.'

'He's probably old, and ugly and balding – nothing like what I imagine him to look like.'

'Oh come on, Sis, he'd only be in his early thirties, wouldn't he? He'd be in his prime.' Smiling, Katie picked up her empty glass of wine from the coffee table and held it up. 'Want one?'

Not wanting to imagine Ethan in his prime, Alexis gestured to the half-empty bottle of red beside another empty glass. 'More like, *need* one, fill her up, buttercup.' She looked back at the note, the shock beginning to wane, allowing her hope to climb up a few notches. 'I so want to believe this is authentic. But I wonder why someone would wait this long to let us know the truth, if in fact it is. Would someone really be so nasty to lie about such a thing?'

Katie shrugged as she poured them both a full-to-the-brim glass. 'Who knows why they'd wait so long, and it's very possible it's a hoax. It was plastered all over the news when it happened, and there are a lot of sick people out there who apparently get their kicks out of doing stuff like this.'

Taking her glass from Katie, Alexis stood. She needed to move, pace, do anything but sit still. 'Yes, very true, but if this is real it means the person who murdered our parents is walking free, and has had the privilege of living the past seventeen years when they took that right from Mum and Dad.'

'That's spot-on, and also very fucking wrong.' The tone in Katie's voice was fierce and her dark brown eyes were stormy. 'Do you think we should take it down to the police station and let them handle it?'

'Yeah, right, if this note is true look how they handled it last time.' Alexis's tone was filled with cynicism and anger.

'Hmmm, good point, but then again forensics have come a long way compared to seventeen years ago, Lexi.' She pointed at the note. 'There might be fingerprints all over that thing.'

'I know, but we need to give it to someone who actually gives two hoots, otherwise it won't get the attention it deserves. I'm not going to risk giving this to some random desk cop only to have it getting lost in police red tape. And I'm sure as hell not going to risk the one chance for our parents to finally get the justice they damn well deserve.'

'Should we give Henry a call, see what he reckons?'

Already on her way to pick up her mobile to call her cousin, Alexis shot Katie a sideways glance. 'Great minds think alike, Pebbles.'

It only took three rings for Henry to answer. 'Hey, how's your day been?'

'Yeah, you know, not stop.' Alexis sat back down beside Katie, who reached out and gave her sister's hand a squeeze.

'Tell me about it ... between work and planning this wedding I don't have time to scratch my butt.' Henry sighed. 'Melanie told me she called you a little while ago, sorry if she's becoming a bit, how should I put it, frenzied.'

A bit? At the moment, Melanie was the epitome of the word. 'No, not at all.' She wasn't about to tell him the truth.

'Oh, that's good. So what do I owe this call?'

'I've got a favour to ask.'

'Of course, shoot.'

'Katie and I got a really weird note in the mail today ... '

'What kind of note?'

She went on to explain everything, Henry remaining quiet the entire time. Any normal person would gasp, but not Henry; seven years as a forensic photographer had taught him to be extremely level-headed, and completely pokerfaced – she could just imagine his deadpan expression.

'My God, Lexi, what a shock. This is something that could confirm what you've felt all along.' His voice was even, steady.

'It was, is, but I don't want to go getting myself too hopeful, just in case it's a hoax. Do you think you can look into it for us, without making it official just yet? You know, ask one of your mates in forensics to do you a favour without any questions asked.'

'Of course I can. I start my shift in an hour, so how about I call in on my way to work. If you don't mind, I'll take it in and get a friend of a friend to check it for fingerprints and see if I can get any leads. As long as you understand, if I do uncover something, I'll have to make it official police business or I could lose my job.'

'Of course, Henry, I don't want to get you in any trouble.'

'Did you have a look at the envelope, to make sure it came from Blue Ridge?'

'Oh no, I didn't even think to look at it.' She turned to Katie and shook the note. 'Where's the envelope this came in?'

'Not sure, maybe still on the kitchen bench.' Katie jumped up and ran to the kitchen. 'Yup, got it,' she called out. She was back in seconds.

Seizing it from Katie's hand, Alexis scanned it. 'It's definitely from Blue Ridge – the post office stamp says so.'

'Well, that's a good start ... unless someone is hell bent on messing with you it gives some indication that this is quite possibly genuine. I gather there's no return address on the back?'

'Doubt it.' She flipped it over, not surprised to see it was blank. 'Nope, nothing.'

'Okay, well, I'll see you two soon.'

'Thanks, Henry, what would I do without you?'

'You'd probably go to Blue Ridge and try to work it all out for yourself.'

'Yeah, I probably would,' Alexis said, the seed he'd just planted blooming within seconds. Maybe this was the sign she'd been looking for to go back there.

CHAPTER
6

**Diamond Acres Horse Sanctuary, Blue Ridge,
North Queensland**

The shrill ringing of his mobile phone sent Ethan King leaping from
the bed and onto a pile of dirty clothes on the floor. On autopilot,
his mind tried to catch up with what his body was already doing.
Had his mum been rushed to hospital again? Had the cancer finally
won? He almost fell to his knees with the thought. His heart in
his throat, he prayed it wasn't the news they'd all been expecting,
because at this time of the night he was only too well aware that
it wouldn't be a friendly call. Rummaging through his jeans in the
dark he yanked his phone out just in time to spot the caller ID was
private before answering it.

'Hello,' he said with a tremble in his voice that was rarely there.

'Hey, Ethan. Sorry. Did I wake you, buddy?'

Hearing his best mate's voice, Ethan's heartbeat slowed to normal.
'No, I'm always awake at midnight ... of course you woke me.'

'Ha-ha, good point.'

'Everything okay there in Brownsville?' That was the far northerners' name for Townsville – rain always seemed to swing away from the place as though it were allergic to it.

'Yeah, kind of ... you got a minute?'

Heading back to the comfort of his tousled bed Ethan flopped down, chuckling. 'Yeah, Todd, it's not like I'm doing anything right now ... and why the hell are you whispering anyway?'

'Because I'm at work, and I don't want this bloke who has just come in to hear me. Look, hold on a minute, I'm going into the office.'

As he waited, Ethan tucked his free arm behind his head and stared out at the acreage that owned his heart, the softly rolling land glowing beneath the light of a full moon, and he looked at the silhouettes of his horses grazing in the paddock opposite the homestead. He felt like the luckiest man alive, calling this place home, and being able to make a living from what he loved most in this world – saving and training wild horses.

'Are you there, mate?'

'Yeah. What's up?'

'A truckload of brumbies just got brought in.'

Ethan shot up straight, his heart beating erratically again. An abattoir wasn't a place for brumbies. Never. Ever. No matter what. The thought of the horses, alive or dead, being used for pet food made his stomach heave. 'Alive?' He held his breath.

'The majority of them.'

'How many?'

'Dead or alive?

'Jesus.' Ethan's jaw tightened, as did his grip on his phone. 'Both.'

'Five dead, six alive.'

Ethan was up now, pacing the floor of his bedroom, kicking things out of his way as he did. 'Fuck me, how can a third of them be dead?'

'That I can't tell you right now, because they've only just turned up, but my guess is broken necks from being tied to trees, dehydration or shot.'

'Bastards.'

'Yup, and speaking of, the bloke reckons they caught them up north, at the Cape, and he wants to sell them, now, tonight ... said he couldn't wait until the boss gets here in the morning. He's a shady bastard, if you ask me. I reckon he's caught them in a state forest in New South Wales, and then crossed the border to avoid the law.'

The red haze of anger Ethan had grown accustomed to over the years of working beside his grandfather and bearing witness to the cold-blooded murder of such majestic creatures threatened to take over, but he fought it back. He'd learnt all too well that it did nothing to help his cause, and this was a time when he had to be rational. 'How much does he want?'

'Two hundred bucks a head ... even for the dead ones, and we only usually pay eighty bucks for them if they're alive.'

'Son of a bitch.' Ethan's blood boiled. 'Tell him a hundred bucks a head, and only for the ones that are still alive. Can you cover the six hundred bucks and I'll bring it with me to give to you?'

'Sure can buddy. I'll just take it out of the till for now, and put it back in when you get here – nobody will know any different. Hang five and I'll pass the message on.'

Heavy footfalls landed and the sound of muffled voices followed. The red rage continued to course through Ethan as he waited.

'You still there, buddy?'

'Yup.'

'Done deal.'

'Good, I'll be there in just under five hours. Give or take depending on the traffic. What time does the boss get in?'

'Around nine.'

Ethan quickly did the math. They were going to be cutting it fine. 'You there by yourself until then?'

'The day-shift blokes start at eight-thirty. I'm on my own for a while now.'

'I'll make sure I'm there and gone well before then. I don't want you getting sacked for helping me and the horses out.'

'Yeah, as much as I think it's a good thing to give the horses a second chance, the boss doesn't. He'd have my hide if he found out the night watchman had done a deal behind his back.'

Putting his phone on loudspeaker, Ethan tugged on a shirt and jeans and then grabbed a pair of socks from his drawer. 'He won't, buddy, we'll make sure of it.'

'Righto, just let me know if there's any hold ups on the road.'

'Will do, Todd, and thanks, mate, really appreciate the call.' He checked his wallet, now glad that the bank had been shut when he'd gone there the day before to deposit the two thousand bucks he'd made on the sale of one of his brumbies.

'No worries, Ethan, talk to you a bit later on.'

'You will.'

'Take care with all the roos about, buddy,' Todd said.

'Will do, catch ya as soon as I can.' The call ended and with the truck keys in hand, Ethan raced down the hallway, flicked on the verandah light and headed out into the night. He'd kill for a coffee for the road but didn't have a minute to spare to make one. He tugged on his RM Williams and cleared the steps two at a time. The gravel of the drive crunched beneath his boots as he dashed to the shed. Time was of the essence, and he had himself some horses to save.

*

Both hands on the steering wheel, Ethan looked at the gold wedding band on his finger. It had fit him perfectly eight years ago, but was on the verge of being overly snug now. It was going to be a struggle to try to get the thing off – but then why would he ever want to? It wasn't like he was going to meet anyone else worthy of taking Jasmine's place. It felt wrong even thinking such a thing. He shook his head, fighting to change his train of thought. He didn't want to do this. Not here. Not now. But after four and a half hours on the road and with nothing but the blur of the centre white lines and the hum of the radio to keep him company, his mind was taking on a life of its own. And just like that, it wandered back to the day he decided to leave high school and do as his step-grandfather did. Ethan smiled – although he was technically his step-granddad, Ethan thought of him completely as his own grandfather. This was a good distraction from his earlier thoughts.

Like it was only yesterday, he remembered the haunting images of the carcasses. Sixteen years young and climbing from his grandfather's four-wheel drive, he was hit with the stench of death. And then he'd seen it. A slain palomino horse lay rotting with her neck twisted grotesquely. It was exactly how she had fallen when a sniper had shot her in cold blood. Further down the road was a chestnut foal, its belly deflated into crinkled leather. Flies buzzed where its eyeballs should've been. Another eight horses sprawled dead in a trail, their insides seeping from where feral pigs had feasted.

Ever since that day he'd devoted his life to saving and training wild horses so they could go to loving homes or become stars in the saddle bronc arenas, much to his stepfather's disappointment. Not that he cared what Peter King thought – the man was not one to judge, with his shitty track record. A police officer for all of his life, his stepfather had wanted Ethan to do the same. But there was no way in hell, especially after catching him having an affair, and when he saw who the woman was Ethan would never have believed it if he hadn't seen them with his own eyes. That was the day every ounce of respect he'd held for his stepfather disappeared. Putting up with the man for his mother's sake was a gross understatement. Ethan wished he'd had the guts to speak up at the time, but with so many people's happiness at risk and his grandfather swearing him to silence, he'd kept the dirty secret hidden. He still battled with the fact that he believed his mother deserved to know the truth, as did a few others, but what good would it do to bring it all to light now?

It was nearing quarter past five when he pulled into the abattoir. The drive had been a breeze, thank goodness for small mercies. He found his best mate waiting for him at the gate. A plume of cigarette smoke lingered above Todd's shock of copper hair. Pulling to a stop, Ethan wound down his window. 'Hey, mate, those things will kill ya.'

Putting the butt out beneath his boot Todd grinned. 'Yeah, that's what Cheryl keeps telling me,' he said. 'Something's got to, though, so why not enjoy it?'

'Whatever blows your hair back, I suppose.' Rolling his eyes at his mate, Ethan looked at the T-intersection ahead. 'We better get a move on. Which way are they?'

Todd climbed the side steps of the truck and joined Ethan at his height, one hand gripping the safety bar. He pointed to the left track that bumped off into some scrub. 'Head thataway. I put them in a holding pen down the back, just in case any of the blokes turn up early. There's a run we can send them down to get them onto the truck quickly and there's a track that gets you onto the highway so you don't have to come back out this way. It'll be nearly daylight by the time you leave.'

'Good thinking.'

Todd grinned. 'I'm always full of good ideas.'

'More like full of shit.' Ethan cracked up, as did Todd.

Reaching the holding pen in a matter of minutes, Todd jumped down and waited at the gate while Ethan reversed the truck. Parked up flush, he kicked his door open and jumped down. His thumbs hooked into the belt loops of his jeans, Ethan rested one boot up on the bottom railing of the rustic timber fence as he eyed his next lot of equine mates. In the floodlight he could see that five looked in pretty good nick, albeit a few scratches and treatable wounds, but the foal looked worse for wear. 'Bastards, doing this to them.'

Todd nodded as he opened the gate and stepped into the holding pen. 'Yup. They need to be taught a bloody lesson.'

Ethan followed him in. Assessing the scar on his hand from a time in a Cape York pub when he'd knocked a bloke out who'd been skiting about shooting horses, he couldn't help but smirk. 'I tried that, not sure if it did much good though.'

Todd looked at the scar too, and grinned. 'Yeah, I remember that night. I can't believe the arrogant son of a bitch got off with a broken nose and two cracked teeth. A light sentence, I reckon.'

'Yeah, he was lucky Grandad stepped in and broke the fight up. The judge seen otherwise, though.'

The two men got to work, gently pushing the horses in the direction of the run, which led to the back of the truck. Ethan was cautious not to spook them, not wanting any, especially the foal, to be hurt any more than they already were. He wished he could check them over, take his time, but that would have to wait until he got back to Diamond Acres. Todd's job was at risk.

'Giving you two months in the slammer was a bit harsh,' Todd said with a shake of his head.

'The look on the idiot's face when I'd socked him was worth every second I spent in the hell hole but.'

'Yeah, true that.'

The horses followed each other and filed onto the truck with ease. Ethan breathed a sigh of relief as he quickly shut the backdoors. Todd switched off the floodlight and closed the gate to the holding pen. Job done, they gave each other a man hug – a brisk hold and a slap on the back.

Ethan shoved his hands in his pockets. 'Make sure you say g'day to Cheryl and the kids for me.'

'Will do.' Todd's face turned solemn. 'I'm so sorry about your mum, Ethan. Wish there was something I could do to help.'

'Thanks, Todd, but nobody can really do much about it.'

'How's your grandad doing?'

'He has his good and bad days.'

Todd gestured towards the gold band on Ethan's wedding finger with a flick of his eyes. 'And how's all of that going? Getting any easier?'

Todd had never been good at deep and meaningfuls. Ethan instinctively touched the gold ring with his fingertips, not wanting to say too much about it. 'Nah, not really. I think I'm just learning to live with it. They say time heals, but I don't know about that. In my opinion, time just makes you stronger, more resilient.'

'After three years I'd have hoped things would be getting easier for you. I'm so sorry, mate.' Todd reached out and gave Ethan's arm a slap. 'I'm here anytime you need, hey.'

'I know, buddy, as you have been all along.'

Todd's lips quivered and it looked as if he was about to cry. 'Life can really suck sometimes.'

Ethan nodded. 'Yeah, it can. I've just got to try and focus on all the good in my life though, otherwise it'll break me … and that's not an option. I want to bring Diamond Acres back to its glory days, and I need a good head to do it.'

'I'll come up for a weekend, when I can get some time off. We can catch up over a few beers. But only if you build a ripper fire to sit around.' Todd finally broke a smile as he jabbed Ethan in the ribs. 'Think you can handle that?'

Ethan laughed, his hand coming to rub where Todd had just got him a beauty. 'Sounds like a master plan to me.'

'Good. It's a date. Who's helping you unload at the other end?'

'I rang Big Al, and asked him to call over.'

'Oh, say g'day to him for me. It's been years since I seen him.'

'He still looks the same, just a little greyer.' Ethan glanced at his watch. 'I better head before you get busted.'

Todd pointed to a track leading off behind the holding pen. 'Just follow that, it'll take you straight to the highway.'

Ethan pulled out his wallet, and handed six hundred dollar bills over. 'Thanks again, mate.'

'No wuckers. Catch you on the flip side.'

'Yeah, catch you round like a rissole.'

Both men laughed. It was the farewell they'd said to each other since they were teenagers. Ethan found it hard, walking away from his one true lifelong mate. He knew it might be months, maybe even a year, before they saw each other again, but Todd's life was here now, with his wife and kids, as his was at Diamond Acres with his brumbies.

CHAPTER

7

The sound of the truck groaning as it headed up the rise brought a smile to Ethan's freshly chap-sticked lips. Even after almost twenty years of witnessing brumbies arriving in their new home, the rush was always the same, the only difference this time was that his beloved grandfather wasn't standing shoulder to shoulder with him, enjoying the moment. The thought tore at his heart, but he shook it off. This wasn't the time to grieve for those he was losing. There'd be plenty of time for that down the line. For now, he needed to remain a pillar of strength for his mum and grandad, and do everything in his power to keep Diamond Acres alive for generations to come.

Feeling sweat rolling down his back, Ethan leant onto the steering wheel and rolled his neck from side to side. The midday sun was scorching its way through the windscreen, his sunglasses not doing much to ward off the glare. Wiping the beading sweat from his brow he tugged the rim of his wide-brimmed hat down further, his five o'clock shadow darkened by the shade now spread over his chiselled jaw. Not long now and he could release the breath he felt as if he'd been holding onto for the last twelve hours. The newest additions to his herd of brumbies were home, safe and sound. It comforted him to know they were out of harm's way. How the government thought it was okay to cull them was beyond his comprehension. If only he could get his hands on the bastards who sat in the choppers, taking aim and pulling the trigger on such magnificent creatures, creatures that were the epitome of freedom as they ran wild among the rugged bushlands. What right did they have to take away the wild horses right to live?

A towering figure leant on the timber fence up ahead. Big Al was already there, as promised. Ethan pulled the truck to a stop, parking the back flush against the roundyard. Swatting a fly from his face, he smiled as the burly, pot-bellied man wandered towards him, his swagger one of confidence and his six and a half foot frame casting a shadow along the ground worthy of his nickname. A scruffy looking Kelpie-cross-Blue Heeler scampered behind him, the old dog a familiar sight alongside his master. Ethan jumped down from the truck and strode towards the two, his hand outstretched. The dog came to a skid beside Big Al, panting, his tail tapping the ground rhythmically. With his weathered face wrinkling even more with his broad smile, Alan Johnston chose to ignore the handshake and instead pulled Ethan into a hug.

The man was like an uncle to Ethan, who returned the gesture wholeheartedly. 'Cheers for dropping everything to help out, Al. I bloody well owe you one, mate.' He leant in and gave Bluey a ruffle behind the ear and the dog's tail tapped the ground even faster.

'Don't even mention it, buddy. It's about time we caught up anyway. I haven't seen you for yonks.' Now held at arm's length Alan gave Ethan's shoulders a tight squeeze. 'Your grandfather would be bloody proud of you, following in his footsteps the way you have. He couldn't want for anything more from the heir to his throne.'

'I don't know about that, Al ... ' Ethan shrugged, embarrassed with the compliment. 'I'm only doing what's been bred into me, so it's no biggy.'

'You're doing what a lot of people wish they could do, and as much as you don't want to acknowledge it, you've made a solid name for yourself. You're not just going along in the shadow of Charlie's reputation. Mate, you should give yourself a pat on the back.'

'I've tried but I can't reach that far,' Ethan said with a throaty chuckle. 'Trust me, trying to wash my back in the shower sucks.'

Alan folded his brawny tattooed arms across his chest, his bushy brows furrowing. 'I'm being deadly serious.'

'Yeah, sorry, but I'm just a man doing his best to try and keep the family business alive, Al, and save as many of the wild horses as I can along the way.'

'And you're doing a damn fine job of it.'

Ethan peered down at his boots and drew an arc in the dirt with one well-worn toe. 'Thanks, Al, appreciate it, mate.'

Silence hung for longer than was comfortable before Alan broke it. 'So how's everything else?'

Ethan knew exactly what Al meant from where he was looking – at his wedding ring. The same as Todd, even though he hadn't so much said it in words, people thought it was time he took the ring off and moved on. And he couldn't blame them. He was still young, and without the joys of a family, of children. Even though he appreciated everyone's concern, he really didn't want to talk about it anymore. He'd done that for two years after his wife's death, with a psychologist, and had gone as far as he could with talking. He looked back up and the concern written all over his friend's sixty-seven-year-old face meant one hell of a lot to him. 'Yeah, good … getting there.'

'It's been a long haul for you, hasn't it?'

'Sure has, Al, but what can I do, other than try and get on with things? It's not like she's ever coming back?'

'Harsh but true, buddy.' Al sighed. 'I suppose just keep the faith that whatever powers that be have a grand plan for you, and one day you might meet another woman you can love as much as you loved Jasmine.'

'I hope you're right, Al, but only time will tell.'

Alan reached out and gave his shoulder a squeeze. 'I reckon I am.' He chuckled. 'I'm usually always right, just ask the missus.'

Ethan returned his laughter and shook his head.

'I heard you sold your Landcruiser,' Al said, changing the subject. 'How much did you get for it?'

'Much less than I paid for it, but it had to go. I needed money for feed and the horses come first. I'm driving Granddad's old one now.'

Alan's brows furrowed. 'Are you getting ahead at all, Ethan, or still slipping behind?'

'Oh, I'm slowly getting ahead. It's been a hard slog but at least I'm not going backwards.'

'Good to hear.' Alan shook his head. 'Sorry you had to sell the Landcruiser. I know it was your pride and joy.'

'Shit happens, Al.' They were quiet for a second or two, then Ethan stepped past the tower of a man. 'Ah well, we better get these brumbies off, hey?' he said. He lifted his sunglasses and tried to peer through the rungs of the livestock crate in the back of the truck. Hooves shuffled and stomped, and the neighs were high pitched and fear-filled.

Alan joined him, hands on hips as he looked through the railings. 'They all look in pretty good shape, except for the foal,' Al said. Taking off his sunglasses he sniffled and then wiped at his eyes. 'I ain't one to tear up, but fuck me, seeing this just breaks my heart.'

Ethan's heart squeezed tight, just like his fisted hands. 'It's so bloody wrong, hey?'

'My oath it is, Ethan.'

Stopping at a roadhouse on the way home, Ethan had stolen the chance to quickly check the young horse over. 'The foal's hind legs are pretty cut up, and he's got some deep gashes on his muzzle. Looks to me like he gave quite a fight trying to get away from the bastards that caught him. And the fear in his eyes ... ' he shook his head. 'It's just plain horrible to see.'

'The bloody bastards.' Alan cleared his throat. 'At the very least I s'pose we have to be thankful he's alive.'

'That's true.'

The two men stood, their postures ridged, strained, as they continued to peer into the stock crate.

'Should get them unloaded so they have a few hours to settle in before dark,' Ethan said.

'Yup.' Alan jumped to it, helping Ethan unlock the gates to the paddock

Slowly, Ethan opened the back doors of the truck and then lowered the ramp. He held his breath as one by one the brumbies stepped out, nose to tail, each one assessing their new paddock with wide eyes, that was, all but the foal. Huddled into a dark corner of the livestock crate, it couldn't back up any further. Ethan's heart sank. He would have to go in and get him. Grabbing a halter from the fence post he prayed this would go well. He didn't want to get off on the wrong foot with the foal. He knew that his behaviour over the next few minutes would influence how the horse interacted with him in the future, so he remained as calm as possible as he walked up the ramp. Other than what the young horse had been through the past couple of days, which would have been hell, brumbies didn't know hate – living within a firm social structure of law and order in the wild gave them no need to feel such an emotion. So Ethan knew that with the foal being naturally inquisitive, once the animal gained even a smidgen of confidence in him, he would come to Ethan with a willingness to trust him. That, in itself, was the most beautiful thing. It was one of the reasons Ethan loved horses so much. Repay a horse with kindness and it had no reason to kick or bite. Ever. And if it did, it would be the human's fault, not the horse's.

Now with only a couple of metres between them, Ethan took slow steps towards the frightened animal, hands low and palms visible, the halter hanging from his fingertips. From its size he guessed it was nearing one year old, or thereabouts. Keeping his voice low and calm, he assured the animal that everything was going to be okay. With ears pricked forwards the horse pawed at the floor of the truck. Ethan stepped nearer, slowly, gently. The foal reared and Ethan took a slow step back to give it some space. Then, when it had calmed, he began slow steady steps forwards once more, stopping just shy of it – he had every faith this timid young horse would come the last few steps to him. The foal sniffed his outstretched hand, and then the halter. It was a breakthrough moment. Surely, but calmly, Ethan placed a hand gently on its withers, and it twitched beneath his touch. He stood like that for what felt like an age, but was not even a minute, before he looked at the foal's injuries once again, and the sight of the deep gashes made him turn away and close his eyes. There was so much blood and puss in the wounds that Ethan would have to call the vet to come and stitch him up. When he opened his eyes again, the young horse's ears were open and forwards, his head low and turned so he could look at Ethan. A very good sign. Raising the halter, he allowed the foal to sniff it again, before gently starting to pull it over the animal's nose. Five seconds later, it was haltered and Ethan felt as if he could draw in a decent breath.

He gave the lead rope a gentle tug. 'Come on, buddy, let's get out of this damn truck, huh? It's much nicer out there.'

The horse obliged, hobbling behind Ethan and into the brightness of the glorious summer day. His dark-chocolate coat shone in the sunlight, the bright white star with a long tail in the centre of his forehead in sharp contrast to the rest of his coat.

Ethan slowly led him towards the stables, aware the movement would be very painful with his back legs the way they were. He needed the foal in there to tend to his wounds over the coming weeks. 'I'm going to call you Shooter, after a shooting star,' he said softly over his shoulder.

Shooter gave Ethan's shoulder a nudge with his muzzle, as if in total agreement with his new name. And just like that, with simple kindness and a genuine love for such a magnificent creature, horse and man were bonded. Ethan's heart swelled. There would be a lot of groundwork to be covered before he could climb into the saddle, but that most important thing was there – trust.

CHAPTER

8

Standing under the awning of the empty cottage, Ethan hunched his shoulders against the howling wind, his lower back aching after sleeping alongside Shooter throughout the night. There was no way in hell he would have slept a wink in his own bed knowing that the little horse needed his care. Swagging it on the stable floor was the only way he could keep a close eye on his newfound friend. And he would be doing so for the next few nights, if need be, just until he was confident Shooter was settled. All of his brumbies were special, but there was something extra special about this young horse. He was one Ethan wouldn't be selling off, no matter what he was offered. Shooter was his for keeping.

The deafening sound from the last ten minutes of the hail hitting the awning's roof eased off, and then stopped completely. Peering up at the sky from beneath the brim of his hat, Ethan wiped drops of water from his face and shook his head in disbelief. Talk about a downpour coming out of nowhere. At least it looked as if it were safe to make a move. Thank Christ. Time was ticking, and as per usual he still had loads to do, including checking in on Shooter to make sure the dressings were still clean and not chewed off – the bugger was making it impossible to keep them on.

Ethan's wet clothes now clung to him, uncomfortably so, his trusty old boots squelching with every step – there was nothing he hated more than wet socks. He wasn't a dancer, but step in a puddle of water on the bathroom floor in socks and he could tap dance for all of Australia. Striding from where he'd dropped tools and made a run for it to the protection of the awning, he stopped to pick up a piece of the ice that had just fallen from the sky. In awe he swore beneath his breath as he held it up, the quickly melting ice the size of a fifty-cent piece. He had only ever witnessed hail once before in his life, and that was with his childhood buddy, the spirited Alexis Brown. It felt like a lifetime ago since he'd seen her, and in the scheme of things, it was. So much had happened, good and bad, since she'd left. He was reminded of her often, each and every time he was around Wild Thing. She'd loved that horse more than life itself, but sadly her grandparents weren't able to accommodate him, so his grandad had kept the horse as his right-hand man, and Wild Thing had never missed a beat.

Alexis Brown ... her name rolled off his tongue as a smile claimed his lips. With her imaginative mind, fearless nerve and wild spirit, there was always an adventure to be had when she was around – she'd been a true tomboy at heart. Now thinking back, it surprised him that he could remember clear as crystal the day it had hailed. They'd been out riding when the sky had opened up, pummelling them with ice the size of golf balls. They'd galloped for broke, homeward bound, both of them in fits of laughter. They were almost back at the homestead when Alexis had slipped from the saddle and landed on her arm, breaking it in two places. Although he'd kept his cool for her sake, Ethan had been mortified to see her forearm hanging at an impossible angle. But, true to her nature, Lexi had been strong and not shed a tear. Her plaster cast was like a proud achievement and she'd had all her friends at school sign it. He'd quietly revelled in the fact that he'd been the first to do so, and he still remembered word for word what he had written on the bright blue plaster.

Hurry up and get better, Lexi-Loo.

She used to act like she hated him calling her that, but he'd known deep down that she loved it. They were always bantering, stirring each other up, that was all part of their impenetrable bond. He wracked his brain to recall what her nickname had been for him. *Boof,* yeah that was it. He smiled. Two kids, without a care in the world, enjoying each other's company ... little did either of them know how much their lives were going to be turned upside down that fateful night.

Two months after she'd broken her arm the unthinkable happened, and her grandparents took Alexis and Katie down to Townsville. He'd never heard from her again. He'd written her a few letters back in the day but never received a reply, and although it had sent his heart to his boots he'd taken his grandfather's stern advice and left her be. After what had happened, Ethan couldn't blame her for wanting to leave her past behind. He could remember watching the dust swirl out behind the Holden Statesman, Lexi's face pressed up against the back window as she'd tearfully waved goodbye. It was then he'd realised she was more than just his buddy, and he'd acknowledged for the very first time how much of a crush he'd actually had on her. If only he'd had a chance to kiss her, just a quick peck would have sent his heart whirling. Would it have changed their fates? As the car had slipped out of sight, he'd felt an ache in his heart he'd never experienced before, and had only felt again the day he'd lost Jasmine in the accident.

If only Jas hadn't been looking down at her phone, she would have never driven through the stop sign. The only consolation was the driver she'd hit, a tourist passing through town, had survived, miraculously, with only minor cuts and bruises. But it was too late for *if onlys*. After three years, he had to find a way to move on and fall in love again without feeling guilty. He wanted children, and he couldn't do that without a woman to love. He'd made a pact with himself, though, that until he met a woman with a soul as free and deep as his, a woman who wanted to share life and not control his, who would love him for the man he was, who would enrich his life as he would hers, that didn't want to replace his wife but forge a path of her own in his heart, he was happy to stay single.

After wiping his hands on his jeans to dry off the melted ice, he knelt down and gathered his gardening tools and forcefully turned his thoughts to Lexi. He didn't want the haunting images of his wife's body bloodied and broken in the twisted wreck to consume him today. Today, he wanted to be grateful for the good in his life. He wondered if Alexis still had the same addictive laugh, the long chaotic white-blonde hair that always looked as if it had never been brushed, if her freckles that dusted her rosy cheeks, the ones that she hated so much, had faded or become more prominent, if she were happily married with ankle-biters vying for her attention, and if she had ever got over losing both her parents. His heart squeezed painfully with the thought – how anyone could ever come to terms with something so devastating was beyond him. Hell, he still hadn't come to terms with the fact that a man as nice as Mister Brown was capable of cold-blooded murder. Their tragic deaths had shattered his seemingly perfect world and made bad stuff seem so much closer to home. Like his grandmother, God rest her soul, had always said, what Mister Brown had done went to show you never truly knew someone. This was why people had to work hard to earn Ethan's trust. On the night of the killings, he had gone from a boy to a man, way before his time.

Stealing a few moments to admire how the new coat of paint had brought the old worker's cottage to life, he tried hard not to think about what had gone on in there. The last couple of months had been hard work; spending countless hours renovating the old place, sometimes well into the night, and the creaks and groans of the weatherboard home had made the hairs stand up on the back of his neck. Nobody had lived here since, and the sense of spirits lurking had brought goosebumps to his skin on quite a few occasions. He was a realist, though, and put it down to just feeling overtired and his mind playing tricks on him, rather than it being anything from the afterlife. Still, just to be sure, he'd had the local priest bless the place before he'd finally listed it on the holiday site. He didn't want any bad karma, or juju, or hocus pocus, or whatever it was, to ruin his chances of making some money from renting it out to tourists. Hopefully, the cottage's dark past was not known among the city-siders he was aiming for. Ethan put his grandfather's declining health down to partly being an after effect of what he had gone through following the shootings. Neither the property nor his grandpa, Charlie King, had ever really fully recovered. Now, Ethan wanted nothing more than to move forwards, to bring the property that had been in his family for generations back to its former glory. And nothing was going to stop him achieving that. His grandfather's passion and drive may have faded over the years, but Ethan had gallons of it, and he couldn't wait to see the fruits of his labour.

With his shovel slung over his shoulder he made his way down the pebbled path, whistling a tune as he walked. He admired how much better the garden looked now he'd trimmed it all back, bar the mulberry tree that was laden with ripe, juicy fruit – the purple stains on his fingertips proof of that. The hail had knocked some of the berries to the ground, and if he'd had time he would have gathered them up to eat. With a few more jobs to do before sunset, and not sure what the time was after forgetting to put his watch on this morning, he glanced up at the sky to get an idea of roughly how many daylight hours he had left. As quickly as the ominous black clouds had thundered in, commanding attention as lightning had danced across the darkening sky, they had been blown off into the distance, leaving a vast expanse of blue dotted only with the odd grey cloud.

Stepping through the new wooden gate he'd made, Ethan tossed his tools into the tray of his grandfather's beat-up but forever trusty old Landcruiser, and then slid into the driver's seat. Firing it to life, he rolled his eyes when he remembered he had to go home to pick up Elvis. A year ago they'd been arch enemies, with Elvis being very protective of his grandfather. But since taking him under his wing so Elvis didn't end up at the pound, the fluffball of a pooch had grown on him, and now Ethan felt bad whenever he left him alone at the homestead for too long.

The things you do for family ...

Fifteen minutes later, now in dry clothes and with one highly excited toy poodle retrieved from the house, Ethan headed down the bumpy dirt track. He'd had to avoid numerous doggy kisses to his face as he'd lifted the little guy into the passenger's seat. Ethan loved this time of the day, when the earth was quietening, cooling, and stillness hung in the air. Up ahead, the sun was just beginning to disappear behind the mountaintops, and like a match to a wick it set the twilight sky aflame with deep hues of red, gold and orange – soon the stars would ignite the wide night sky in glimmering glory worthy of an ovation. He was in awe of the sight. Views such as this were one of the many reasons for his deep-seated love for this land he had called home for most of his life.

With one arm draped casually over the steering wheel he drove slowly, swerving here and there to avoid the massive potholes the storm had left behind. The ones that were big enough to swallow a small dog would all need filling – just another job he would have to add to his never-ending to-do list. Not that he minded working from sunup to sundown – Diamond Acres was worth every drop of his blood, sweat and tears. After moving out from under his mother's suburban roof at fifteen – because he couldn't stand his stepdad a minute longer – he'd devoted every spare minute to helping his grandfather around Diamond Acres. His move had broken his mother's heart, but it just had to be done.

Biting back hot tears Ethan gruffly wiped his face. His mother had endured almost twenty-seven years beside a man who had a heart of cold steel – but soon now she would be free of him. A devout Catholic who didn't believe in divorce, death was a cruel way for her to be annulled from a marriage that hadn't brought her joy for many, *many* years. After having a front-row seat in his parents' lives Ethan was sure of that. Although it would be a relief to see her free of the constant suffering, the thought of her being laid to rest squeezed his heart so tight he almost couldn't draw a breath. Fuck cancer.

Elvis gave a short, sharp yap, snapping Ethan from his thoughts, and with his focus back on the dirt road he jerked the steering wheel sideways, barley missing a fence post as the four-wheel drive skidded before regaining traction. Tossing the toy poodle a thankful glance he couldn't help but smile at his canine mate, the dog's jowls appearing as if he were grinning back at him. Reaching over, he gave Elvis a ruffle behind his floppy ears and the tiny pooch responded by wagging his tail so fast it looked like a mini chopper blade.

'Thanks, mate, that was a close one.'

Elvis yapped an eager reply.

Although always excited – it was a trait of the toy poodle to forever remain a puppy in nature – Ethan could tell his canine buddy missed his grandfather as much as he did. The times he would find Elvis laying beside his grandfather's empty bed were heartbreaking, but there wasn't much he could do to remedy that. There would be no coming back from where Charlie King was going – dementia didn't give that kind of leeway. It was just something they all had to come to terms with.

A lover of kelpies and cattle dogs, Elvis wasn't the type of dog Ethan would normally choose to have by his side, but fate had made that decision for him, so now he was determined to make the little guy feel as loved as his grandfather had made him feel – which had been one hell of a lot. Ethan, towering over the six-foot mark and solid as a rock, knew that he and Elvis were the epitome of the odd couple. He copped a lot of flack off his mates and acquaintances whenever he rocked up in town with the mini-dog as his sidekick, but he didn't give two shits. This bundle of fur had given him more love and support then he could measure, and that counted for everything in his book.

Humming to distract his thoughts, Ethan tapped his thumb in time to Brad Paisley's southern drawl, the country love song blaring from the beat-up old four-wheel drive's stereo one of his all-time favourites. The breeze whistled through the crack of the window and to breathe the fresh air in deeply, he turned the handle of the window winder, grinning at the way it screeched as he wound it all the way down. Kids would have a fit if they had to manually wind down their window these days – it was unheard of. But true to his grandfather's theory of 'Why fix something that ain't broken' there were many things around Diamond Acres that had survived the years.

Resting his arm on the doorframe he briefly admired the recent handiwork of the local tattoo artist. The ink stretched from his wrist to his elbow – the wild horse rearing up on its hind legs looked so true to life. The man had done an impressive job, not that Ethan would have expected anything else from an Australian champion tattoo artist. Like anything that was going to be there forever, he'd thought long and hard before getting it, each of his tattoos having a reason behind them. With this one he was acknowledging his love of equine majesty and his own untamed spirit, and it was also a reminder not to settle for second best with anything or anyone.

Ethan's gaze was intent as he looked out over the four-hundred acre property. He was still finding it hard to believe it was now officially his. The reading of the will two months ago, at Charlie's instruction (his grandfather wanted to do this before he lost all sense of mind), had created world war three between Ethan and his stepfather. But after what Peter had done all those years ago – cheating on his wife – and with his ignorance about anything to do with horses and farming, what did he expect from Charlie? For Ethan, finding out he was the sole heir had been a shock to the system. Peter had stormed out of the solicitor's office, threatening to contest it, but without a leg to stand on, he'd begrudgingly backed down. Ethan knew he would have just sold it off anyway, and it was over his dead body he would have let that happen. Diamond Acres was much more than a piece of dirt. It had been in the King dynasty for four generations, and Ethan was determined to continue the tradition. It broke his heart that his grandfather had been clinically labelled with dementia, but like a blue sky nudging through dark clouds, Charlie King was fighting hard to stay as lucid and rational as he could for as long as possible. It was a battle he would lose eventually.

With the light fading Ethan took off his sunglasses and tossed them onto the dash among a myriad of random bolts, wire, tools and a few empty cans of Coke – he really needed to clean the old girl out. Then he took a long, satisfied look at the scene ahead of him.

Even at a distance, his befriended brumbies (he refused to use the term 'broken-in') at the top of the paddock appeared large and domineering, their muscles flexing powerfully as they galloped towards him, eager for their feed. The sight of the once wild horses never ceased to fill him with awe. It was going to be tough, selling them off next month, but his work with them was done – keeping them here would only cost more money, money he didn't have. Besides, they were ready to work with riders and to bring joy to new owners – it was time to send them to new homes. He had more wild horses to work with now, so it made the thought of parting with these horses easier to cope with.

Slowing, then backing the Landcruiser up to the fence line, he briefly caught sight of his reflection in the rear-vision mirror. Tilting his chin up he eyed the stubble on his chin that could almost be classed as a beard. His mother would be appalled if she could see him – bless her. He really needed to shave before he went to visit her tomorrow afternoon – he wanted to look his best so she didn't start worrying about him. She needed all her energy to live that little bit longer. He coughed away a lump of emotion that had lodged in his throat. There was work to be done and the only person to do it was himself. Crumbling just wasn't an option.

The CD in the stereo picked up pace and he turned it up, the boot-scooting song just what he needed. Climbing from the driver's seat he made sure to shut the door behind him so Elvis didn't escape.

Scurrying across the seat, the pooch high jumped the handbrake and then placed his front paws on the open window, whining.

'You stay put, you little rascal,' Ethan said, low and warning, wanting Elvis to know he was serious. 'I don't need something happening to you, too.'

Elvis placed his head between his paws, donning the best but-how-can-you-leave-me-in-here eyes beneath his long lashes. At the same time his tail was going like the clappers.

Ethan shook his head. The bugger loved running around the horses, his miniature size not worrying the fearless dog one little bit. But it worried Ethan, because one wrong move and Elvis would be squashed under one of the horse's powerful hooves.

From beneath the shade of his wide-brimmed hat Ethan watched the horses racing towards him, their hooves thunderous as clumps of earth flew out behind them. Reaching the fence, all six of them skidded to a halt, their breathing heavy and their coats slicked with sweat. Warning the other five to back off, the dominant horse of the pack snorted and pig rooted.

Ethan caught his eye. 'Woo up there, Wild Thing. You seriously have to learn some table manners, mate, or I'm going to lock you in the stables and you can watch your buddies enjoy their treat. How would you like that, huh?'

The horse blew air through his lips, as if to say, *Whatever*, before hanging his head so far over the fence in a bid to get to the bail of hay on the back tray, he almost shoved through it.

Ethan gave him a firm push back and Wild Thing responded by flicking his head and then nudging Ethan's hand.

'No wonder the fillies don't take a shining to you, you're way too obnoxious,' Ethan said, giving the animal a quick scratch behind the ears.

Wild Thing neighed and then nibbled at Ethan's sleeve.

'I don't know how many times I've told you, you old brute, you need to show chivalry to the ladies. I give you my word that it will win them over every single time.'

Wild Thing whinnied and threw his head up in the air, as if disagreeing with him.

Ethan laughed. He loved this old horse, for so many reasons. 'Learn the hard way then, not that I think you ever will, you stubborn bugger.'

Pushing up his sleeves Ethan leapt up and onto the back tray with practised ease. Standing behind the large, round bale of hay he shoved it forwards, grunting as he gave it one last push so it rolled off the tray and into the paddock. In true form Wild Thing got to it first, but too busy eating he left the other five horses alone so they could get their fair share. Standing for a few minutes, Ethan drank in the peaceful scene of the horses with the backdrop of the final golden rays of what had been a long but productive day. It was like a scene right out of one of the old western movies he loved so much – but the great thing was that this was real life, his real life. This, right here, was what country living was all about.

CHAPTER

9

With nightfall quickly approaching, the suburban street was quiet, other than a lone dog sniffing at the curb. As Ethan stepped through the front gate the sensor floodlight fired to life, making him squint as he headed down the short pathway. The mouth-watering aromas of the Chinese takeaway wafted from the bag he was holding. He couldn't wait to tuck into it. After not eating all day, and surviving on countless cups of coffee instead, his stomach growled as he climbed the five front steps of the quaint cottage he'd known as his home for the first fifteen years of his life. With all the work he had to do for the horses at Diamond Acres, he didn't get here as often as he would like, but he did his best with the limited time he had and came in every couple of days or so.

Remembering he still had his wide-brimmed hat on he tugged it off, before kicking off his boots. It was a firm rule to never wear a hat or boots inside his mother's home. Peering through the screen door the darkness inside hit him like a slap in the face. His mum would usually have the rooms lit up like a lighthouse. Something was wrong. Fear filled his body with adrenaline. Ready to rush into the hallway he heard a noise coming from the side of the house. In three panicked strides he hurried around the corner of the wide wrap-around verandah, shocked to see his mother on the daybed, a blanket pulled up to her chin, and her face deathly pale. Was she asleep, or was she ...

He stepped forwards, his heart in his throat and his breath held. 'Mum?'

She stirred.

He sucked in a breath.

In utter relief he silently thanked the God he had long ago lost faith in.

But what the fuck was she still doing outside? Where in the hell was his stepfather? It was Peter's rostered day off so he should be home, here, taking care of his wife. Ethan's body clenched in response to his unanswered questions, but he did his best to remain outwardly calm. His mother didn't need any drama between Ethan and his stepfather tonight. 'Hi there, lovely lady ... what are you still doing out here?'

'Ethan, is that you, love?' Once a vibrant woman, filled with so much life and enthusiasm, Joyce could barely turn her head to look at him. 'I didn't know you were calling in tonight, what a lovely surprise.' She noticed the bag that was now clenched tightly in his fisted hand. 'And it looks like you may have brought my favourite too.'

'Sure have, a serve of spring rolls to share, a prawn chow mien for you, Mongolian lamb for me, and a honey chicken for Pete ... ' He peered into the bag, not because he needed to check what was in there, but because he was having trouble meeting eyes that were filled with so much physical pain. 'And, of course, the trusty prawn chips.'

'Oh, thanks, love, you're always so thoughtful. I'm one lucky mum to have a son like you.' She tried to sit up, her discomfort as she did so breaking Ethan's heart. It was as if she were eighty years old. He'd trade places with his mum in an instant if it meant she felt better, but the cancer had laid its claim and there was no bargaining with it.

Placing the bag down he reached out to help her, propping the pillows up behind her back as she sat up. His mother's back all bones beneath his hands, the emotion-fuelled lump in his throat grew to the size of a grapefruit. Feeling woozy, he sat down beside her, at the same time getting a whiff of stale urine. Gut-punching sorrow filled him. Often unable to move about without some kind of assistance, she'd clearly not been able to hold on any longer. Fuck Peter, leaving her to get in this state – watch out when he returned home. And Ethan would be here when the bastard did finally stumble in, because there was no way in hell he was leaving his mum alone tonight. He fought to find the right words. How was he meant to ask his own mother if she'd wet the bed?

'Would you like me to go and run you a bath, Mum?'

'Soon, let's chat first.' Her breathing shaky, she placed her hand over his. 'So, what did you get yourself?'

He'd already told her that. Tears stung his eyes, but he blinked them away. She was not going to see his heartbreak. 'Oh, you know me, creature of habit, Mongolian lamb.' He fought back his stormy emotions. 'I rang yesterday afternoon, to tell you I was going to bring dinner over tonight, but you were sleeping. I asked Peter to pass the message on but clearly he didn't.'

Dismissing it, she waved an arm so frail it looked as if a sudden breeze would snap it in two. 'Oh, he might well have, but you know me, forgetful all the time these days.' Her brows rose to her sparsely covered head of hair. 'Apparently it's just another side effect of the bloody chemo.'

His jaw tightened. She was trying to make light of Peter's behaviour, but Ethan knew she was covering for a man who didn't deserve it, and that angered him even more.

'Yeah, maybe,' he replied through gritted teeth. 'Speaking of the devil, where is Peter?'

As sick as she was, his mother gave him a please-don't-start glower, instantly making him regret his choice of words. His shoulders slumped as though more weight had just been dropped onto them. 'Sorry, I'm just pissed off he's not here, when he should be, taking care of you.'

'Language, Ethan.'

He grimaced as he apologised once more.

She sighed wearily. 'I told him to go and meet his mates down the pub for some lunch and a few beers.'

'A few beers, huh? He would have been able to drink an entire carton since lunchtime. He must have been there for over six hours.'

She smiled at him. 'It really doesn't matter, Ethan. The man needs some time out from me. I take a lot of looking after these days. I couldn't even begin to imagine how draining that is.'

'Yes, you do, which is why he *should* be here, instead of down the pub drinking. Doesn't he remember his vows, for better or worse, through sickness and health? Mum, I told you I'm more than happy to bring you out to the farm, so I can take care of you there.' His voice was hoarse.

She patted his arm. 'Now, now, Ethan, don't go getting yourself all worked up. Like I've told you a hundred times, I want to be here, in my home, where I can say hi to my neighbours, and watch the kids playing in the gardens and riding their bikes down the street. It makes me feel like I'm still somehow involved in the ebb and flow of everyday life. If I were out at the farm I wouldn't have any of that. And besides, you have enough to do out there without having to take care of me as well.'

'You've always put my needs before your own, Mum, so I think it's high time I repaid the favour, don't you?' Knowing she would refute the fact he owed her anything he didn't wait for her reply. 'And speaking of which, did you eat any lunch?'

'No, I didn't feel like any.'

Ethan silently raged against a supposed God that could allow a disease like cancer to exist. Then he snapped back to reality and looked at the small table by the bed. On it sat an empty glass next to the lamp that was providing the only light on the verandah, and a pile of used tissues. 'Would you like me to top your water up?'

'Oh, no thanks ... I'm not really keeping it down anyway.' Her eyes travelled to the bucket on the opposite side of her bed.

Ethan reached across and peered in. It was not a pretty sight, the traces of blood within the vomit breaking him in two. Joyce snatched it off him and then placed it back where it had been. 'Please, Ethan, you really don't need to see it.'

'You need to try and keep your fluids up, Mum. How about I go and grab some ice that you can suck on.'

'No, I'm right, Ethan. Please, just stop fussing over me.' It was said with an irritation he had rarely heard from his mother.

He had no words. Silence hung heavily. A soft, warm breeze played with the wooden wind chimes on the front verandah, the sound reminding him of the family holiday in Bali where his mother had paid three times the amount she should have for them. She had been a terrible bargainer, her empathetic nature making her a sucker to the crafty business owners there, and the many homeless children on the streets. His heart ached even more with the memories.

Tears sprang to his mum's eyes. She tried to blink them away but they rolled heavily down her cheeks. 'I'm so sorry, Ethan, I'm just a little emotional today, that's all. I know you're only trying to help so I shouldn't be snapping at you.'

'Please, don't apologise, Mum, you have every right to be feeling angry, and it's likely you're going to take it out on those you love.' He plucked a tissue from the box and handed it to her. 'You're welcome to use me as your punching bag anytime you need to. I'll take it as a sign of your love for me.' Summoning all his strength among the sadness, he graced her with a smile.

'Thanks for understanding, love.' She blew her nose and wiped at her eyes.

While she gathered herself Ethan stole a few seconds to do the same. Gazing at the blossoming flowers in the garden now lit up beneath the silvery moonlight, his heart ached even more. He found their beauty in such sharp contrast to his dying mother that he wanted to rip them all out from the ground they were growing in. Why could they live when his mother couldn't? The rush of rage he felt at such a trivial thing rocked him to the very core. His usual she'll-be-right attitude had left him when he first found out about her illness. His mum wasn't going to be right. And neither would he be once she left this earth.

'You okay, Ethan?' The gentle, loving voice pulled his gaze back to her.

'Yep, right as rain, Mum.' Leaning in, he kissed a cheek so hollow against his lips his heart shattered further – and it was all he could do to stop from bursting into tears. Holding his mother's hand, he did his very best to smile again. 'So, let's start again. How are you doing today?'

'Oh, you know ... ' Joyce said feebly. 'I was thinking about heading out for a spot of dancing tonight, but then I couldn't find the right outfit to wear, or matching shoes, so I changed my mind and decided to watch the sunset out here instead.'

Ethan chuckled and shook his head. 'Always the joker, aren't you, Mum?'

'My theory is you have to laugh or you'll cry.'

'True that.'

She looked even frailer than she had when he'd last seen her two days ago, Ethan thought. It was a cruel war, fighting an enemy that was armed to the hilt with ammunition, when you had nothing but your desperate will to live to fight back.

'Should we eat?' his mum asked.

Even though Ethan's appetite had upped and left, and he knew his mother would only be able to have a couple of bites of food, he nodded. 'I reckon.' He stood and held out his hands. 'Here, let me help you up.'

She placed the used tissue scrunched in her hand among the others, then reached out to hold his hand, giving it a gentle squeeze. 'I tell you what, how about we eat out here. With the full moon it's a perfect night for it.'

'Shouldn't we head inside now? You could catch a chill out here, or even worse a disease from one of the zillion mosquitos.' Not that he was about to say it out loud, he also really wanted to get her into the bath, but he had an inkling that might be the exact reason she didn't want him to move her. And that would be for two reasons, firstly because she didn't want him to see the mess she would be in beneath the blanket and secondly because he'd actually never seen his mum naked.

'Oh, Ethan, it's not like anything else can kill me, I'm already knocking on death's door.' It was said in jest but there was deep fear in her eyes. 'Besides, I'm feeling hungry now and going inside would take forever with me moving at a snail's pace.' As if reading his thoughts she tugged the blanket in tightly around herself as she sat on the side of the bed, so he couldn't try to persuade her otherwise.

'Okay, yup, let's eat out here.' He moved towards the front door. 'I'll just go and get us some plates and cutlery, and a mosquito coil, and I'll be back.'

'We can just eat from the containers, love, saves washing up.'

'Fair enough, but we can't really eat with our fingers, Mum, we'll need cutlery.'

'Oh, yes, good point. ' She laughed uncomfortably.

Ethan couldn't help but feel she was trying to stop him from going inside. 'I'll be back in a sec.'

'Don't mind the state of the house, will you? I haven't really had the energy to keep up with the housework.'

'Don't stress, Mum, I'm sure it's fine.'

Opening the flyscreen door Ethan switched on the hallway light and made his way towards the kitchen. Looking into the lounge room he noticed the cushions on the couch were tossed onto the floor, and a blanket was crumpled up on the armrest, as if someone had been sleeping there. A quick glance to the coffee table beside the couch confirmed what he thought. Empty beer cans covered it. He walked in and straightened the couch up, placing the cushions just how his mum liked them and then folded the blanket. Snatching the cans from the table, quietly cursing Peter as he did, he gathered them into his arms to throw into the recycling bin. Living there when he was growing up, Ethan knew that everything had a place and his mum always took pride in keeping her home ship-shape. It would be breaking her heart to see it like this. Peter should be making more of an effort to keep the house clean, and just why his stepfather would not be sleeping beside his wife at a time like this was beyond his comprehension.

While trying to juggle the cans in his arms Ethan walked in to the kitchen and flicked the light on. He was shocked at the sight in front of him. Dirty dishes were piled high on the sink, and scattered over the benches were newspapers and mail, some letters still unopened. The table that usually had a vase of fresh flowers on it now barely had a clear space to sit down at it to eat. It was covered with Peter's upended lunch esky, empty chip packets, a half-eaten sandwich and crushed energy drink cans. No wonder his mother wanted to be outside. Kicking the recycling bin open with his foot, Ethan dropped in the cans. He would clean the rest of this up later, first he needed to try to get some food into her. Opening a drawer he took out the cutlery while cursing beneath his breath. Peter had a lot to answer for, and answer he would. Ethan had been raised to respect the man, as hard as it was most of the time, because he was his elder and his mother's husband, but he was not going to stand by and allow her to be treated like this. No. Bloody. Way.

*

Almost three hours later Ethan was standing beside his mother's bed, her gently rising and falling chest letting him know she was finally in a deep sleep. After only being able to get five mouthfuls of food down, she'd finally allowed him to help her into the bathtub, a towel wrapped tightly around her as she'd sunk into the lavender scented water. The dripping wet towel was now slung over the clothesline. Then, while she'd enjoyed a twenty-minute soak, he'd busied himself taking the sheets off the daybed, relieved to see there was a waterproof topper on the mattress, chucked them in the washing machine and then conquered the mess in the kitchen. It had been a struggle, trying to give her some kind of privacy while also helping her get into her pyjamas – but they'd got there, both of them laughing by the end of it. The gratified look on his mother's face as she'd joined him for a bedtime hot chocolate had been well worth his efforts. He'd been chuffed to see her empty her cup. At the very least there was something in her stomach, and she was keeping it down.

Stealing a few moments to appreciate the loving soul that lay beneath the gauntness of her shell, he finally allowed a few tears to fall. And then as much as he tried to fight it off, the wall he'd built around his heart began to crumble. His legs went weak and his chest tightened, making it almost impossible to draw a breath. How was he ever going to watch her coffin being lowered into the ground? He knew the sheer agony of it, after watching Jasmine's coffin entering the earth, that he just couldn't bear to think about it. Sinking to the floor, making sure not to let his sobs wake her, he allowed himself to grieve for the mother he had already lost, her addictive vitality and vigour that had been cruelly taken away before death. He grieved that she would never see him get married again or have children, and he grieved because she had lived in an unloving marriage for all these years. If only his father hadn't died from a heart attack when Ethan was two, and Peter hadn't been the one to come and deliver the news to her, how different her life, and his own, would have been. She didn't speak of his dad much, but when she did it brought a light to her eyes that the mention of no other name would.

The sound of the front door being slammed shut snapped him out of his thoughts and brought him to his feet. It was close to midnight and Peter was finally home. Ethan quickly wiped his face, drawing in a few deep breaths to try to steady his pounding heart before tiptoeing out of the room, his footsteps getting heavier as he approached the kitchen, not that Peter noticed him walking in. He was standing at the sink on wobbly legs, trying to get a glass of water from the tap, but the stream of water was missing the glass entirely. Anger coursed throughout Ethan.

'Where the hell have you been, Peter?' The venom in his voice was palpable, but Ethan didn't give two hoots.

Dropping the empty glass in the sink, Peter spun around to face him, his chubby cheeks covered in the red blotches that came out whenever he'd been drinking heavily. The tap was still running at full force behind him. 'I was out having a few beers with my mates. Us coppers need a reprieve sometime, you know.'

Leaning against the table, mainly to put some distance between Peter and himself while he tried to calm down, Ethan did nothing to hide the disgust he knew was written all over his face. 'Yeah, righto, I can see you enjoyed more than a few, as usual ... you just can't help yourself, can you?'

'So what? Everybody has their vices. It's my way of dealing with all the stress at work.' Peter shrugged. 'What does it matter how many I had anyway?' He waved an arm at Ethan. 'Your mother said it was fine for me to have some down time, so what's it to you?'

Every word was slurred, almost impossible to understand, and to most it would have been, but Ethan had learnt to decipher Peter's drunken lingo many years ago. Alcohol had always been Peter's escape, from anything and everything. Ethan clenched his jaw tight as he fought back an explosion of expletives – that would do him no favours.

'What's it to me? Are you serious, Peter?' Ethan's eyes narrowed. 'My mum was laying in her own urine, without any food or water for the entire afternoon, while you were out getting yourself rotten drunk. A bit of a lowlife act, don't you think?' In an effort not to leap across the table and give Peter what for, Ethan straightened up and then folded his arms.

Peter shrugged again and then leant on the kitchen counter, clearly to hold himself upright. His movements were unsteady but he tried to pretend he wasn't drunk. 'Just calm down, would you? I knew you were coming over, Ethan, and I was enjoying myself, so I thought she'd be right.'

'Yeah, but not until late afternoon, I told you that.'

'No, you didn't.'

'Ah, yes I did.'

'Shit, my bad, the footie was on when you rang so I probably wasn't taking everything in.' He belched, loud and disgustingly.

'Clearly,' Ethan growled.

'Mmhhmm.' Peter went to flick the tap off that was still running behind him but he stumbled to the side, crashing into one of the chairs by the table and bringing it to the floor with him in one almighty bang.

'Oh come on, Peter.' Groaning, Ethan went to help him up but Peter waved his arms around to try to stop him.

Grabbing him by the collar Ethan reefed him to standing, making sure to keep hold so he didn't tumble back over. At five-foot four-inches, it was a cinch to yank him up. There were smudges of tomato sauce all over the front of his shirt and he stunk to high hell of stale alcohol, and cigarettes – a habit Peter had tried to hide for years, even though Ethan and his mother both knew he smoked. Beneath his coiling anger, Ethan somehow felt sympathy for the man. How could he not when Peter had tried to fill the shoes of a father figure, not very well, pathetically even, but at least he'd tried? 'For Christ's sake, Peter, Mum's asleep.' Taking the tumbled chair with his free hand he stood back up and then shoved Peter into it. 'Now, just try and sit there, will you, and I'll make you a strong cup of coffee to try and sober you the hell up.'

Peter eyed him dolefully. 'Okay.' Then, as if all the wind had been let out of him, he slumped forwards and hung his head in his hands. 'I'm such a drunken arsehole at times. I really need to start giving a bit more of a shit, don't I?'

With the kettle on the boil Ethan dumped two heaped teaspoons of coffee into a mug. There was usually a point during each intoxicated episode when Peter would own up to being an arsehole, and in the midst of it promise to do something about it, and they'd reached it relatively quickly tonight. 'I have to agree with you there, Peter. You do need to start giving a shit about people other than yourself.' He spooned in three teaspoons of sugar, deciding to ditch the milk and leave it black. 'It's never too late to do something about it, though, huh?'

'Yeah, well, I'll look into it.'

The spoon clinked against the side of the mug as Ethan stirred for all of Australia. 'You say that every single time.'

'I know, just call me a broken record,' Peter said. 'I'm so sorry, I know I should've been here, but I just don't know how to cope with it all.'

'You could start by focussing on taking better care of Mum.'

'I try, I really do, but I'm not used to having to juggle work and the house, and on top of all of that taking care of her as well. I honestly wish I could just run away from it all, you know, pretend it isn't happening.' Peter began to sob, each one deeper and more anguished then the last.

As much as part of him wanted to relish the breakdown, Ethan also wanted to go and comfort the man, but knowing Peter hated closeness of any kind he stood still and gave his stepdad a few moments to regroup. 'Don't we all, but this is real, Peter. Mum is dying and you have to put your needs on the backburner and be here for her.' Even as the words slipped from his lips, Ethan felt his heart recoil, as though trying to somehow believe they held no substance, no truth.

Peter rubbed his face, his sobs quietening. Leaning back, he nodded. 'Yeah, I know. Easier said than done, though.'

'Sorry, but I don't agree with you.' The coffee now made, Ethan joined him at the table. He placed the cup down and then pulled a chair up, spinning it around so he was straddling it, his forearms resting on the chair back. It was time for some cold, hard facts. 'In my eyes, if you love someone, you'll do anything for them, no matter what. This really isn't a time for you to be selfish, but more of a time for you to be selfless. You reckon you could do that?'

Peter's face scrunched up and Ethan didn't know if he was about to cry again or get angry. He folded his arms defensively. 'Are you saying I don't love her?' He took a large gulp from his cup, wincing from the heat of it.

'No, not at all ... I'm saying that after all the years she's been there for you, through thick and thin, after all the times she's picked you up off the floor without judgment and sobered you up, the entire time loving you through it all, I think it's high time you did the same for her ... don't you think so?' Ethan held Peter's glassy gaze, his own steely. Before he could think about his next sentence, he spat it out, 'And after what you did to her, all those years ago, I think you owe her a hell of a lot.'

'What are you talking about, Ethan?'

'I think you know exactly what I'm talking about, Peter.'

Realisation and fear flashed in Peter's eyes. 'No, I don't, which is why I'm asking.'

'Two words ...' Ethan paused for effect. 'Peggy Brown.'

Peter's sucked in a sharp breath and then his eyes crinkled into angry slits. 'Other than the fact I investigated her murder, that name means nothing to me.'

'Really? That's interesting.'

'Why?'

'Because you and I both know it should mean much more than that.'

'I have no fucking idea what you're talking about, Ethan.'

'Cut the crap, Peter, yes you do.'

'No, I fucking don't.' As though he had just been struck Peter flinched, then slammed his hands down on the table, splashing coffee over the sides of the cup.

'You had an affair with her. Admit it. I saw it with my own eyes so you can't back out of it, and just for the record, Grandad saw it too.'

'You did, do you?'

'Yes.'

'Well, good on both of you for keeping your traps shut. You shouldn't have been spying on us in the first place.'

'Spying?' Ethan shook his head. 'Trust you to fucking turn this around to be someone else's fault. You've never taken responsibility for your actions, and you never will.'

'Who gives a shit what I did or didn't do almost twenty years ago? I've fucking been there for your mother throughout our marriage, don't you bloody worry about that. Joyce has never wanted for anything.'

Peter clearly wasn't going to own up to what he'd done, and after all these years, why would he? There was nothing to be gained from it, and it would only cause deep heartache for his mother, so Ethan let it slide. The guilt Ethan carried for never having told Alexis what he saw remained as strong as it did way back when, and would for his lifetime – it was a cross he had to bear. 'Oh, come on,' he said to his stepfather. 'Do you really believe that?'

Peter shot up, the chair scraping along the timber floorboards. Wobbling, he grabbed the sides of the table to keep his balance. 'How dare you.'

'How dare I what, Peter? Speak the truth? Hurts, doesn't it?'

'Your opinion is the furtherest thing from the truth.'

'Really? Come on, it's me your talking to here. Yes, you're the bread winner and Mum has never had to worry about where the next dollar is coming from, but when was the last time you gave her a hug or told her you loved her?'

'Are you bloody kidding me?' Peter said uncomfortably, and his eyes dropped to the floor. 'Just lay off, will you? I'm not cut out for all the soppy stuff … you of all people should know that.'

'Yeah, I do, all too well, but this isn't about you anymore, Peter, it's about Mum. She hasn't got a lot of time left, and I want her to go knowing how much she means, to all of us.'

'I don't need to say it out loud for her to know how much I love her.'

'Okay, when was the last time you really went out of your way to do something special for her, so she knows you appreciate and love her?'

'I made her a cup of tea this morning.'

'So you should, she's too frail to make her own.'

'Jesus, I can't win, can I?' Peter threw his hands up in the air in defeat.

'Sorry, Peter, but I mean things like buying her a bunch of flowers, or even picking her some from the front garden – you know how much she loves them. Or even giving her a foot rub would do the trick. Anything to bring a smile to her face.'

'Oh for Christ's sake, are you kidding me? I'm too tired to think about all this right now.' Slumping back down in his chair, Peter huffed, as though the conversation was getting old. 'I shouldn't need to do anything more than I do already. I bring home the dough, and in my eyes that's enough to show my love, end of story.'

'But ... '

Peter held his hands up. 'Just stop, Ethan. I've heard enough. I'm a man's man, and I'm never going to change the way I think about all this bloody lovey dovey stuff. I'm just not cut out for it, and as they say, a leopard never really changes his spots. After twenty odd years of marriage I reckon your mum would have clued onto that, don't you think?'

Ethan scowled. He was a man's man too, but that didn't give him an excuse to be a cold-hearted bastard. It was beyond him how Peter could so blatantly refuse to shower his beautiful wife with love, especially at such a heartbreaking time. Reaching his limit, Ethan stood, tucked his chair back into the table and then shoved his hands in his pockets. If he stayed any longer, he and Peter might end up coming to blows. His mum didn't need that kind of behaviour, from either of them. 'Please, just for the time she has left, try and make her as comfortable as possible.'

'I'll try, Ethan. That's all I can do.'

'Good, because otherwise I'm going to have to move her out to the farm, where I can take care of her, and she really doesn't want that.' Checking his car keys were in his pocket, he remembered the takeaway in the microwave. He gestured in that direction with a tip of his head. 'Your dinner is in there, if you want it.'

'I had a pie back at the pub, but thanks.' The tone in Peter's voice let Ethan know in no uncertain terms he wasn't grateful in the slightest.

'I'll give Mum a call in the morning.'

'She'll like that.'

Ethan headed out the doorway. 'Catch ya.'

'Yup, catch ya.'

CHAPTER
10

Sunshine poured through the picture window, bathing the four-seater dining table in golden light, the warmth of it helping to melt away some of the tension twisting Alexis's insides into knots. Out of character, Katie had got up early to join her for breakfast because she hadn't worked at the club last night. Alexis knew she had to do this before she talked herself out of it. Now. So, sculling the last of her coffee, she sucked in a breath and took a metaphorical leap. 'Pebbles ... '

'Yeah ... ' Katie sounded miles away as she stared down at her mobile phone, her fingers going hell for leather as she typed a text message.

'I'm going to go back to Blue Ridge, to see what I can find out.' There, she'd said it, although she couldn't quite believe it herself.

Katie's eyes were wide as she looked up. 'Oh, Lexi, you've got to be kidding me. We always swore we would never go back to that place as long as we lived.'

'Nope, I'm serious.' Alexis was determined not to change her mind, even though the look on her little sister's face was rattling her resolve. It had seemed like the perfect idea at three this morning, after a night of no sleep, but in the light of day, was it?

Katie placed her phone down beside her half-eaten plate of bacon and eggs. Folding her hands on the table, she looked at Alexis as if assessing her sanity.

Alexis felt the knots in her stomach tighten. 'Come on, Pebbles, say something.'

Katie sat back in her chair, her folded hands going to her lap. 'I can kind of understand why you want to do this, but I really don't think you should go back there. You're not on some detective adventure, you know. You wouldn't know the first thing about investigating stuff, and this is way too close to home for you. It might just stir everything up again, Lexi, and send you back to where you were all those years ago.'

'Yes, I'm very aware of the risks, but they are risks I'm willing to take for the sake of Mum and Dad.'

'Don't you think it would be wise to get the forensic results back from Henry before you go doing anything stupid?'

'I'm not being stupid, Katie.' Alexis heard the defensiveness in her voice, but she couldn't help it. 'And yes, in a perfect world it would be better to wait for the results, but he said it could take up to a week, and I don't want to wait that long.'

'What about the wedding? Mel will lose a section if you're not here to help out with it all.'

'I will be back here with plenty of time, don't you worry.'

Katie eyed her questionably. 'Okay, fair enough, but what if it ends up being a big waste of time?

'Argh, Katie, you're such a nego ... you always succeed in seeing the bad side of everything.'

'No, Lexi, I'm not a nego, I just like to see the reality in everything so I don't allow myself to be vulnerable and susceptible to being taken advantage of.'

'Fair enough, but what if it isn't a big waste of time and it turns out my instincts were right, and Mum and Dad *were* murdered? What if I find out who it was who shot them and I can finally put that person where they belong, behind bars? Then I might actually be able to move on in my life.'

Katie leant forward. 'Okay, let's say you're right and the note is for real, and they were murdered, don't you think it's endangering your life to go back to the town where the killer might still be living?' She sucked in a sharp breath. 'Come to think of it, what if it was the killer who wrote the note, and they're trying to lure you back to kill you?' Her eyes widened with fear.

After lying awake that night, weighing up every scenario, this wasn't news to Alexis. 'Yes, there is all of that, but ... ' She sounded as if it didn't worry her in the slightest, while in fact it scared her to death. 'Like I said, I just have to take that risk.'

'No, you don't, Lexi,' Katie shot back. 'I've already lost my parents and my grandparents. I really don't need to lose you too. You're all I've got left, other than Zane.'

Katie's words struck Alexis in the chest like a lightning bolt. 'I'm not going to get hurt, Pebbles. I promise you I'll come home safe and sound.'

'Yeah, right, because you're a master at being able to defend yourself, Miss Black belt in macramé.' Katie finished the cynical statement off with raised eyebrows.

Sighing, Alexis shook her head slowly. 'There's really no need to be like that. This hasn't been an easy decision for me.'

'Isn't there? Someone has to be upfront with you, and if that has to be me, then so be it. You wouldn't know what to do if someone tried to physically hurt you.'

'And you do?'

'Actually, yes, I do. I have plenty of guys putting the heavies on me at work, and some of them don't like being told no, especially when they're drunk, but I put them in their place. You, on the other hand, are nice to everyone and hate stepping on anyone's toes. Sorry to say, but you're a very easy target.'

'I can't help that I'm an empathetic person.'

'No, you can't, and it makes you the wonderful person you are, but it's not really the right quality to have when you're on the hunt for a potential murderer.'

Staring down at her uneaten hash browns and poached eggs, Alexis drummed her fingers on the table. 'I'm so sorry, sis, but I have to go. I can't just sit around here and wait. It's driving me insane already.'

'It hasn't even been twenty-four hours though, Lexi. You really need to learn some patience.'

'Yes, I'm well aware of that, but I don't want to go to bed tonight just to lie there trying to figure everything out. For my own peace of mind I need to take action. I have to go back and see if something jogs my memory.'

'So there's no talking you out of this?'

'Nope.'

'Have you told Henry?'

'Nope.'

'He's not going to like it one little bit when you do.'

'Well, it's not his decision, is it?' Alexis picked up her knife and fork, not because she was about to eat, but because she needed to do something to avoid Katie's suspicious stare. Damn it, why did her sister have to know her so well?

'You *are* going to tell him, aren't you, Lexi?'

Busting the runny yolk and then cutting a piece of the hash brown, she paused momentarily to answer. 'Yes, I'm going to tell him, when he rings to give me the results of the test.' She almost whispered the last half before shoving the food in her mouth.

'Alexis?'

'What?' Katie's use of her full name and her strict tone reminded Alexis of how her nan sounded when was telling Alexis off when she'd got into some kind of trouble.

'I think Henry should know what you're up to before you head off.'

'Why? It's not going to change anything.'

'I know it's not going to stop you going, but at least that way he could ask the local police there to keep an eye on you.'

'I don't want the local police keeping an eye on me. And it will only worry him if he knows, he has enough on his plate with the wedding just around the corner, so don't even think about telling him yourself.' Alexis pointed her fork in Katie's direction.

'I might just accidentally tell him.'

'Don't you dare, Katie. I'll be extremely pissed off if you do.'

'Bloody hell, you're as stubborn as a mule when you want to be.'

'Who are you to talk?'

'Oi, what's that supposed to mean?'

Alexis grinned. 'You're one of the most stubborn people I've ever met.'

'Can't help it if my big sister taught me bad habits.'

Alexis's grin turned wide.

Katie rolled her eyes and groaned. 'At least let me come with you?'

'No, you have to work.'

'I can ask for some time off.'

'I said no, Katie.'

'Why the hell not?'

'Because I want to do this on my own.'

'They were my parents too.'

'I know, Katie, I just think it will be better if I do this by myself. If you come I'll be too worried about making sure you're safe, rather than focussing on what I'm going there to do.'

'You don't give me enough credit, Lexi. I'm a big girl and I can take care of myself.'

'Good, do that here while I'm gone.'

'What if I just jump in the car with you and lock the door?'

Alexis shot her a warning glance 'You'll do no such thing.'

'All right then, little Miss Get-My-Knickers-in-a-Knot, where are you going to stay?'

'I don't know yet, I've got to look into it. Maybe at the pub in town.'

'You hate even walking into a pub, so how in the hell are you going to stay in one?'

'I'll manage.'

Katie gave her a look as if to say, *Yeah right.*

With her already tangled nerves becoming even more frazzled, Alexis tried to shrug off Katie's lack of confidence in her. 'I'll sort something.'

'It's not like there's endless accommodation options in Blue Ridge, Lexi.'

The rubber band that was her nerves pulled taut and then snapped. 'I'm well aware of that, Katie. I'm not a bloody idiot.'

Closing her eyes Katie drew in a slow, steady breath, blew it away, and then repeated the process.

'What in the hell are you doing?'

Katie cracked open one eye. 'Calming myself.'

'Right, good for you.'

'Maybe you should try it.'

'Maybe I should, but then again maybe you should just try and understand this is something I need to do.' Alexis could hear the irritation in her voice, and although she didn't like being narky to her sister, she couldn't help it. 'You apologised for not supporting me last night, Katie, so this is a time you can prove your apology meant something by supporting my decision to go back there.'

Katie flicked her eyes open and nodded. 'I'm sorry, you're right. I'm being selfish, not wanting you to go. I'm just scared of something happening to you, that's all.'

'I know, and I can completely understand that.' Alexis made an effort to soften her tone. 'But like I said, I'll be fine. I'm not going to turn up there and start pointing the finger at everyone. I'll just keep a low profile. Promise.'

'That's a good idea, sis.'

'I'm always full of good ideas.' Standing, Alexis went over to the kettle and flicked it on. At just shy of nine o'clock, she had already downed three cups of coffee; one more wouldn't do any harm. 'You want a top up?'

'No, thanks, any more than two cups of coffee and I get the jitters. And yes, you are an ideas woman. And you're a champ at following through with them too, not like me.'

'You can't help that you're a side tracker, Katie.'

'Am not.'

'Oh, look at that pretty butterfly.' Alexis looked over Katie's shoulders.

'Where?' Katie said, her eyes darting around the kitchen.

'Case closed.' Alexis smirked.

Katie gave her the finger. 'Smart arse.'

'Thanks, Pebbles. I like to think I'm clever so I'll take that as a compliment.'

CHAPTER

11

Not usually a big drinker, Alexis was feeling tipsy after enjoying two glasses of wine, the weight that had been bearing down on her since reading the note yesterday afternoon lighter now. She didn't condone drinking to drown one's sorrows, but just for tonight she didn't want to adhere to her ethics. Not only was she drinking to numb the emotions of the past twenty-four hours, but also in the hope that it may help her get some much needed sleep – she had a long drive ahead of her in the morning. After rescheduling two photo-shoots she now had five days off – not much time but she was grateful she could at least swing that with her clients. She tried not to think too much beyond getting into her car because the thought of where she'd be heading made her stomach summersault nauseatingly. There were so many *what ifs* that she was driving herself insane trying to come up with answers.

She balanced her MacBook Air on her lap and flicked it open. While waiting for it to fire to life, she finished the last of her Pad

Thai straight from the container, with the plastic fork it had come with – a cardinal sin in her eyes, to eat from plastic cutlery, let alone from a plastic container. Not only did she hate the environmental impact of plastic, but also, in her opinion, food always tasted better when eaten from plates and silverware. Usually she would have gone to the trouble of pouring it into a bowl and dressing the top with peanuts and coriander from the small container that came with it, but tonight she couldn't be stuffed. Peeling herself from the couch had been strenuous enough when the delivery guy had arrived at the front door, her emotion-fuelled day zapping every bit of her get-up-and-go – after the conversation at the breakfast table this morning it had all but got up and left. Tonight all she wanted to do was tie up the final details of her trip and then climb under the comfort of her doona. Her bag was packed, her car was fuelled up and she was biting at the bit to go, but that would be silly before she'd figured out just where she was going to stay. Crawl before you walk, and all of that stuff.

Rain pitter-pattered against the windows. The refreshing scent floated through the open French doors that led out to the generously sized verandah. Alexis breathed in deeply, loving how the rain could make her soul feel soothed and somehow restored. It was the prefect night to stay in. The flicker of candlelight filled the lounge room nicely, the country music playing softly in the background helping her to relax even further into the couch – or was that the effect of the wine? She shrugged as though answering herself. Either way, she was enjoying the sensation.

With her homepage now open, she typed in *Accommodation options other than the pub, Blue Ridge* ... it paid to be precise with Google. Choosing one of the links that read *A holiday home to get away from it all* she impatiently waited for the page to open, delighted she may have found a better option than the dingy old pub. Watching the timer swirling, the damn thing taking its own sweet time due to the stormy weather, she thought about Katie and hoped she'd made it to work before the rain had closed in. How her sister could go to work at a time when most people were getting ready to hit the sack was beyond her, but then they were like chalk and cheese – she was a morning person, Katie was a night owl; she liked tomato sauce, Katie liked barbeque; she loved tall dark and handsome men, Katie liked the blond, blue-eyed surfer types, exactly like Zane. She had noticed they seemed to be getting extremely close of late, either Zane staying here or Katie over at his place, and she was happy for her sister, finding love. She just wished she could have it herself with that special man, whoever he was.

Dragging her eyes from where the curtains were floating in the evening breeze, the image conjuring up a long ago feeling she couldn't quite remember or explain, Alexis looked back at the glowing screen. Her jaw dropped and her eyes widened. No freaking way. It wasn't possible. Like a startled horse, her heart took off in a gallop, its hurried beats feeling as if they were pounding at her ribs to break her heart free of its cage. Crossing her legs up under her and with her almost empty glass of wine in hand, Alexis leant in closer, as though doing so might make her see something different. But there it was, clear as crystal, the cottage she'd spent the first thirteen years of her life in, the cottage her parents had lost their lives in, staring right back at her. An immense sense of loss overcame her and she had to take a moment to let the shock and emotion ease. This was the first time she'd laid eyes on it since the day her grandparents had driven away with Katie and her clinging to each other in the back seat as Ethan waved goodbye. She recalled how much it had hurt, watching him fade away.

Holding her breath, she clicked on the gallery tab, dismayed to see there were only two photos and a note at the bottom of the page saying the website was still under construction. The first picture was the homepage shot of the front of the cottage and the second was of the backyard, the view over the valley as magical as she remembered. Taking in the finer details, her heart sank as she noticed that the cubby house her dad had built was gone. But then, after so many years, what did she expect?

Ever so gently she reached out and placed her hand against the screen. Time stood still for the briefest of moments before she was heaved back to the past, to a time when she and Katie and her mum and dad were a happy family. The images were so vivid and so real, it stole every puff of air from her lungs. They were sitting around the dinner table, eating her favourite, spaghetti bolognaise. Her parents were laughing as she and Katie raced to see how quickly they could suck a piece of spaghetti into their mouths. Of course, she'd let Katie win, as she did every time, and then they'd all cheered Katie's victory. Her mum would always give her a loving and knowing glance to silently say thank you for doing such a kind thing for her little sister. Then, like rising bubbles, more memories surfaced, in speedy succession – with Katie riding their bikes down the rutted driveway, or with her dad out feeding the brumbies, Ethan and her riding their horses at break-neck speeds across the paddocks, her mum cuddling her to sleep, her dad cupping her cheeks and telling her how much he loved her ...

It was all so unexpected, so beautiful and heart crushing at the very same time.

Wrapping her arms around herself as if to stop from breaking into tiny pieces, Alexis closed her eyes and sucked in a few shaky breaths. After years of wondering how she would feel if she ever saw her childhood home again, she now knew. She could only imagine what it would be like to actually step foot inside. But she didn't want to think too much about that right now, for fear that she'd cower from the challenge ahead of her. As she fought to bring her mind back to the present, another wave of emotions overcame her, sucking her in as if she'd been pulled into a rip. She felt as if she were falling, as if the room were spinning. A memory fought for her to take notice, the niggling feeling making her all the more edgy. She struggled to yank it free of wherever it was stuck on, but try as she might it wouldn't budge.

She flicked her eyes open, hoping it would give her a sense of steadiness.

What am I meant to remember?

Staring at the photo on the screen, at the paddock that stretched out beyond the cottage, at the way the distant mountains rolled into each other, Alexis could almost feel the dampness of the earth beneath her feet as she ran. Breathless. Terrified. Katie was running alongside her, crying. It was dark and soft rain fell. She could hear that the horses were restless in their paddocks, their hooves stomping and their whinnies agitated. There was a great sense of urgency, but for what she didn't know. She shook her head slowly, trying to piece the fragments together. Was this memory even real, or just a trick of her imagination? She looked to the glass gripped tightly in her hands. Maybe she was more drunk than she thought. A sharp pain shot through the back of her head. Reaching up she rubbed where it had hurt, the scar left from her bad fall down the steps in the Kings' house still faintly raised beneath her hair. Then, as quickly as the pain had started, it stopped, leaving her questioning if she'd even felt it at all. As she had many times before she gave a few seconds thought to having survived such a terrible fall. She'd certainly had an angel watching over her that night, unlike her parents.

'*Mum, Dad ... who did this to you?*' It was spoken in a whisper, in between sobs.

Like a moth to a flame her eyes flicked to the photocopy she'd taken of the note now placed on the corner of the coffee table. Come hell or high water she was going to find out who had sent it. And then, without warning, her heart clenched again, tighter this time, as another memory demanded her attention. She was standing by her parents' open graves, the holes seeming to go down forever into the darkness, her small hand grasped tightly within her grandpa's big strong one. Then she was looking up at him. He was trying so hard not to cry as he stared at something off in the distance. He'd always been their rock, their confidante ... she missed him so much. The priest was saying something, people were crying, she was finding it hard to see through her tears. The utter heartache and devastation she'd felt as she'd watched each of the coffins being lowered into the ground, of watching Katie bury her head into her grandpa's chest and sob her heart out, of seeing her nan drop to her knees as she cried out to God, asking why he'd taken them both, still tortured her heart and soul as it did all those years ago.

Landing back in the present, Alexis punched the cushion beside her as a fierce anger claimed her – one she'd never felt before. Damn whomever it was that took her parents from them all. They needed to repent their sin.

How dare they have a normal life when her parents were ...

She choked back more sobs.

Dead.

Gone forever.

She would never, ever see them again.

Still to this day it was a hard reality to swallow.

Bile rose, but she fought the urge to heave her noodles up. Gripping the arm of the couch she tried to catch her breath. More hot tears stung her eyes and rolled heavily down her cheeks. The image on the computer blurred. Reaching out, she slammed the laptop shut. She really needed to get a grip if she was ever going to be able to do this.

Even though every part of her screamed she was stupid to have another glass, she grabbed the bottle of merlot from the coffee table and refilled her glass. Gathering courage from who knew where, she sat up straight and tried to disentangle herself from her past, even if only for a few minutes. There would be plenty of time to delve into that terrible night, to dissect it and put it back together, piece by tiny heartbreaking piece, but tonight she needed to see the cottage for what it was now, a holiday home she could rent for the five days she was planning to stay in Blue Ridge, and that led her to the question of who owned it. Was it still in the King family? Or had it been sold? Were Mavis and Charlie King still alive? Would Ethan still be in Blue Ridge, and if he was, did he still live at Diamond Acres? Would she recognise him now? And even more importantly, would he recognise her? Her curiosity to know more now overrode everything else.

Bracing herself, Alexis slowly opened the laptop up again, while trying to stay focussed on the present. She drew in a few steady breaths. She could do this. She took a sip of wine, and then another. Dutch courage.

On closer inspection the cottage was the same but different. It was still small and charming, there was no doubt about that, but it looked as though it had received the care it had so desperately needed when they'd lived there. The verandah she'd spent many happy times on was now longer and wider, surrounding the entire front of the house. The garden her mother had taken such meticulous care of still encircled the house like a warm embrace, although it was lusher now. The apple and citrus trees that were only as tall as she had been back then were tall and heavy with fruit in the photo on the computer screen. Memories of eating her mum's apple pie and enjoying lashings of lemon butter on her toast for breakfast made her mouth water.

Although still feeling emotional, a smile claimed her lips when she spotted the big mulberry tree at the corner of the cottage, the branches heaving with juicy, finger-staining fruit. She and Katie had loved that tree – their faces and whatever they were wearing at the time would be covered in purple by the time they had finished gorging on its berries. Much to their mother's dismay, as she had to try to get the stains out, usually to no avail. The garden gate that had squeaked wearily every time it was opened and closed had been replaced with a rustic timber one. The path was still windy but now paved with pretty coloured pebbles. Although appearing well cared for, without a chicken, duck or dog in sight, or pushbikes tossed on the front lawn, it looked strangely abandoned. And that saddened her. She was now dying to see the inside, but with no photos in the gallery, that would have to wait.

How would she be, staying there? Fear filled her. She minimised the screen and typed in *Accommodation Blue Ridge*. Nothing but the pub came up, and on closer inspection there were no rooms with an ensuite. What to do? She felt as if the universe was leading her back to the cottage, and she needed to put her faith in the greater powers. Maybe it was her parents' spirits showing her the way. She went with that thought. But would she be able to book it at such short notice?

She hoped so. Her desperation to walk around inside the cottage once again was growing by the second now she'd made the decision to do so. Like opening a book read many years ago, she knew there would be parts of her life story she'd long forgotten, or buried, and she couldn't wait to uncover them, page by page, line by line, word by word.

Her eyes travelled down to the blurb at the bottom of the screen.

Cosy three-bedroom cottage in the heart of the picturesque Blue Ridge Valley. Fully furnished with absolute comfort in mind – it will be your home away from home. A place where you can get away from it all, put your feet up and breathe in the fresh country air while you forget about your troubles for a weekend, a week or a month ... the choice is yours. Breakfast baskets are provided, with locally sourced produce where possible. There is a log fireplace for the winter months, and air conditioning for the warmer ones. Click on the link below to make a booking ... you know you want to, or please don't hesitate to contact the owner, Ethan King, on the number provided for further information or if you'd prefer to make your booking the old fashioned way.

Alexis choked on her mouthful of wine.

Not only did Ethan still live there, he was the man she would have to deal with if she wanted to rent the cottage, which she did, without a doubt.

Holy crap!

With her heart in her throat she looked at her mobile phone on the coffee table, and without hesitating a moment longer she snatched it up and dialled the number from the bottom of the screen.

It rang once, twice, three times.

Her heart thudded against her ribs like a boxer's fists.

She dared not take a breath.

She almost hung up but fought off the moment of fear.

'Hi, Ethan King speaking.'

His voice was so familiar, so husky, so ...

She went to respond, but the words jumbled in her mouth.

'Hello?'

She pulled the phone away from her ear, her finger hovering over the disconnect button. She couldn't do this.

CHAPTER
12

A throwback from her favourite era, Alexis's cherished 1971 marina blue VW Beetle held its own as she tore down the highway. Seeing the turn-off up ahead that would take her deeper into the country, she slowed and took it. The dream catcher she'd bought the day she'd left her desk job to pursue her dream of being a freelance photographer dangled from the rear-vision mirror. It was a constant reminder to follow her dreams and to believe in herself. '*Jesus*,' she swore out loud. Her camera was still sitting on the end of her bed. She smacked the steering wheel. Damn it … so much for taking photos while she was out here. She'd been so stressed as she'd run out the door that she'd gone and left behind what she thought of as her right arm.

There was nothing she could do about it now.

Light danced on the windscreen, the midday sun shining like a beacon in the cloudless blue sky. As straight as an arrow, the road seemed to stretch on into eternity, meeting the horizon way off in the distance. Houses were now few and far between and Alexis glanced out on either side of her to see paddocks filled with cattle and horses. The tranquillity she felt looking at the fields was almost as appealing as the serenity she felt when gazing at the ocean. In her opinion, nothing could beat the scent of the ocean and the sight of endless blue. Diving beneath the waves would instantly cleanse her from the inside out ... what she'd give to be able to dunk herself in the ocean right now.

Wriggling in her seat she readjusted her sunglasses, the two painkillers she'd taken half an hour ago thankfully easing the headache caused by the aftermath of an entire bottle of red wine. When the alarm had gone off at six this morning she'd felt as if a freight train was tearing through her head, her mouth had been drier than the Simpson Desert and she'd momentarily felt as if she were about to throw up, that was, until the flash of dizziness had eased. With two glasses usually her limit, Alexis was disappointed she'd gone overboard. It had felt like a good idea at the time, drowning her fears and sorrows. Hindsight could be an absolute bitch.

Groaning, she leant forward to stretch out her lower back. She was four and a half hours into the trip and itching to get out of the car. From memory she believed the turn-off to Blue Ridge was not far up ahead and a quick check on Google maps, which had got her this far, confirmed she was right. Plucking another smoked almond from the half-demolished packet in her lap she tossed it into her mouth. Although she kept telling herself it would be the very last one, they were so more-ish she couldn't stop eating them. Making an executive decision, she zip-locked the top of the packet and then threw it to the floor on the passenger's side, so she couldn't be tempted to open it again. The wrap she had bought at a drive-through just over an hour ago, although not very nutritious, had filled the hole in her belly. Now she was only eating because she was nervous.

Grabbing the bottle of sparkling water from the cup holder she took a swig, grimacing at the lukewarm temperature as she swished it around in her mouth. Heaven forbid her smiling with food in her teeth when she met Ethan at the cottage. Her belly flip-flopped as she tried to envision what he looked like now, her midnight search on Facebook revealing twelve Ethan Kings in the world but none were *her* Ethan. After braving the nerve-wracking phone call to book the cottage, if his deep husky voice was anything to go by, she was guessing he'd grown into one hell of a manly man. She'd almost turned to a mushy puddle on the couch as he'd explained all the ins and outs of renting the cottage for the four nights, her mind wandering off on a tangent as she imagined what it would be like to kiss him. Her heart fluttered even now as she recalled the phone conversation that had made it feel as if time were standing still.

Yeah, it sure is available for those dates. Can I have a name to put the booking under?

That question had put her on the spot, and she'd stupidly given a false name to save having to play catch-ups with Ethan over the phone while she was drunk. Now in the light of day and with a clearer mind, why she'd gone and done something so stupid, she hadn't a clue. Of course he was going to recognise her from the get go. A quick glance towards her bookcase had saved her at the time – a mixture of her favourite author and favourite erotic book combined to make her alias. *'Danielle Grey,'* she said her new name out loud, then shook her head at her stupidity. Firecrackers exploded in her belly. How in the hell she was going to explain this one without looking like a right fool?

With the sun beating down relentlessly the VW felt as if it were a tin can. Beads of sweat rolled down her forehead and behind her sunglasses, stinging her eyes. Sighing, she reached out for the umpteenth time and tapped the air-conditioner vents, hoping that might miraculously fix whatever the problem was. Yanking her singlet up she tucked it under her bra, giving her sweat-slicked stomach a small reprieve. She'd forgotten just how damn hot it could get away from the sea breezes of the coast. Up ahead, the ripples of heat rising from the bitumen made a mirage of water appear. As much as she didn't want to, with her air conditioning now doing more harm than good, she flicked it off and wound her window down. A furnace of hot air slapped her in the face. Thankfully she was almost there. Looking at first like just a hazy cloud of dust, a road train approached quickly then roared past, the smell of the livestock on board making her instinctively breathe in deeply. The earthy scent yanked her back to her childhood, and the memories of spending her days out in the saddle with her dad made her heart ache.

A computerised voice stole the Led Zeppelin song from the speakers, as Google maps advised Alexis that she was nearing her next turn-off. She hadn't skimped on the cost of a good stereo system when restoring the old girl, shame the same couldn't be said about her air conditioning. Slowing, Alexis put her blinker on and touched her foot to the brake as she took a sharp right-hand turn, the wind blowing through the open window making the flyaway strands of hair flutter in her face. She quickly tucked them behind her ears, her eyes glued to the narrow road. The exhaust pipes rumbled low and throaty as she accelerated once again. Passing a large sign, she read it out to herself, '*Blue Ridge. Population 4532.*'

Her belly back-flipped.

Not long now.

A few minutes down the road and she was on the outskirts of the pretty inland town. Slowing to fifty kilometres per hour, she rested her arm on the window frame. Apprehension filled her as she tried to divert her attention from her inner battle and instead take in the chocolate-box charm that brought tourists to the long-ago goldmining settlement of Blue Ridge. Driving through the main street, it was as lovely as she remembered. The well-kept shops with their display windows made her smile – the butcher, menswear shop and bakery didn't appear to have changed much in all the years she'd been away, other than having a recent lick of paint. A well-dressed elderly couple, arm in arm, were standing at the side of a pedestrian crossing. She drew to a stop, liking the way both acknowledged her doing so with a nod and a smile. Pulling the woman closer to him, the man supported her with each and every step, his fingers entwined with hers. It was heart-warming to witness the affection between them, as subtle as it was. Alexis wondered if they were lifelong partners and hoped to be lucky enough to find her very own one-in-a-million man.

As they shuffled across the road, she looked to the hardware store, memories of going there with her dad and scouting the shelves for supplies tugging at her heartstrings. Life had been so simple back then, drama free and filled with sugar-coated dreams. Little had she known her life would be turned upside down before she'd even celebrated her fourteenth birthday. The very thought fuelled her determination. She had to get to the bottom of the message in the note. Her father was no murderer. And she had five days to prove it.

With the elderly couple safely stepping onto the footpath, she accelerated and in less than a minute she left the shopfronts behind and was driving past streets lined with colonial-style brick homes, well built for the heat. Most were surrounded by colourful gardens and neatly mowed lawns with leafy trees for children to play beneath and fences to keep treasured pets from wandering. Two boys rode past on their bikes, without a care that they were on the road, their laughter loud and infectious. Such a different pace of life from what she'd become accustomed to, and in a way she felt cheated that she hadn't been able to experience this life for longer than she did.

Taking a left-hand turn she followed the navigator's directions while at the same time still breathing everything in. An old man stood out the front of one of the houses, a hose in his hand as he tended to a flower-filled garden. She flashed him a friendly smile and he acknowledged her with a wave. A few houses down a middle-aged man hauled his wheelie bin down the driveway. As she was only a few metres from him as the VW rolled past, Alexis said a quick hello out her window, and he flashed her a gold-toothed smile in greeting. Familiarity flickered within her, but she couldn't for the life of her put a name to his face. Looking in her rear-view mirror she observed him parking the wheelie bin as he watched her drive away and then it hit her. He was Ethan's stepdad, Peter King. The very man who had headed the police investigation into her parents' death. Oh he'd gotten it so damn wrong, and she was about to prove it so. And she really didn't care about showing him up. She'd never taken a shining to him.

Heading out of town she hit the hundred kilometre zone and accelerated. Half an hour and she would be at Diamond Acres. Far from feeling serene as she drove past the tranquil scenery, Alexis began to stress over absolutely everything; the seriousness of what she was doing now felt all the more real and all the more daunting. Deep in thought, the chiming of her mobile phone sitting in the centre console made her jump. Pressing the answer button on the hands-free before she'd even looked at the caller ID, she jumped even higher when she heard the stern tone in the caller's voice.

'What in the hell do you think you're doing, Lexi, going all the way out there on your own?'

Even though she couldn't blame him for being upset, Alexis's grip on the steering wheel tightened as she drew in a calming breath. 'Well, hello to you too, Henry.'

'Sorry, hello.'

'That's much better.'

There was a measured sigh. 'I've just called around to your place to check in on how you and Katie are doing only for Katie to tell me you took off this morning.'

'Damn her, I told her not to tell you.'

'You expected her to lie to me?'

'Yes.'

'Well, for a someone who hates lying, that's very contradictory of you.'

'Yes, I know, I'm sorry, but I just didn't want to stress you out. You've got so much happening at the moment.'

'You're not the impulsive type, Lexi. This would be something I'd expect from Katie, not you. What's got into you?'

'That note has bloody well gotten into me.' Her words were sharp, and she knew it was because Henry was right.

'The same note you asked me to do a check on, the one I told you to do nothing about until I had a chance to talk to my mate in forensics?'

'No, my shopping list, of course the note I asked you to do a check on.' Alexis instantly regretted her harshness.

'I know that, Lexi, I'm just being a smart arse.'

'So am I.'

'Well, stop it. It doesn't suit you – that's my job.'

'Did you really expect me to just sit around twiddling my thumbs? These are my parents we're talking about, and your aunty at that. Of course I'm going to jump at any chance to prove Dad's innocence.'

'Lexi, please don't take the note as gospel. As much as I know you want to believe your father had nothing to do with your mum's death, or his own for that matter, there's a big possibility he did. As you know, I've looked over the case notes and the police did a thorough investigation, there's no doubt in my mind that ... '

Alexis couldn't take any more. 'Stop, just stop…' She sighed. 'Please, don't start this right now, Henry. I don't need another lecture, especially from you. I'm stressed out enough as it is.' A sob escaped before she had a chance to hold it down.

'Shit, don't cry. I'm so sorry, Lexi, I'm just really worried about you, that's all.'

She wiped tears from her cheeks and sat up straighter. 'Well, thank you for worrying about me but I'm a big girl and I can look after myself.'

'Uh-huh.'

'Thanks for the vote of confidence. You're as bad as Katie.'

'Am I now? Don't forget I've known you for almost all of your life, Lexi, and although you can hold your own, you're not emotionally equipped to investigate two deaths, especially when they were your own flesh and blood.'

'I'll just have to suck it up … I've got no other option.'

'You have the option of involving the police.'

'I have by talking to you, haven't I?'

'I'm not a police officer, I just work alongside them – so you know what I mean.'

'I don't want to get the police involved yet. And what are they going to do anyway, other than tell me what you can for now. There's no evidence for them to take any action. The case is closed in their eyes, with no need to reopen it.'

'Yeah, okay, fair point. But still, I'd feel better if you weren't out there by yourself.'

'Who do you suggest I bring out here with me?'

'Me.'

'You have to work, and your wife-to-be would throttle you.'

'Another fair point ... She's certainly not herself at the moment. I think the stress of the wedding is making her a little loopy.'

'You think?'

'Like I said, being a smart arse doesn't suit you.' He chuckled lightly. 'Anyway, I've rung to tell you I've got some of the forensic results back.'

'And?' She held her breath.

'There's no fingerprints, Lexi, whoever did it was extremely careful.'

'Oh, bugger it.'

'Yeah, it's a let down, but don't lose all faith just yet. I've sent it off to see if there is any DNA evidence. Although I'm guessing that if there aren't any fingerprints, that's going to come up negative too.'

'So what you're saying is that we're no better off.'

'I'm afraid so.'

Alexis smacked the steering wheel. 'Damn it.'

'So, are you going to turn around and come home now?'

'No.'

'Why not?'

'Because I've booked accommodation for four nights, so I'm going to use the time I'm here to sniff about.' She wasn't about to tell him which cottage, and she'd chosen not to tell Katie either.

'I don't think that's a good idea, Lexi.'

'You may not, but I do.'

'Bloody hell, you're stubborn.'

'No more than you are.'

'At least promise me you'll keep in touch, and that you'll answer my calls when I check in on you.'

'Scout's honour.'

'Good.'

'Thank you, Henry, for always having my back.'

'Of course I do, and always will.' A muffled voice sounded in the background. 'I've got to run, the big boss is giving a briefing in five minutes and he's a total arse if you're late.'

'Righto. Talk soon.'

'Yes, we will. Catch ya.'

'On the flip side,' Alexis replied before ending the call.

The conversation, although uncomfortable, had been a good distraction for the final part of her journey. Now travelling along a road only wide enough for one car, a road that she had been down many times before, Alexis kept her eye out for the landmark Ethan had explained in detail but that she already knew well. Spotting a letterbox made from an old milk churn and one beside it made from an old microwave she slowed to a crawl and turned. Her teeth rattled as the VW bounced over a cattle grid and then onto a bumpy dirt road. Out of the blue a feeling of missed opportunities and a paradise lost swept over her, engulfing her in a flurry of emotions. She pulled to a complete stop, the motor still running, as she tried to catch her breath. She needed to get a grip, to arrive cool, calm and collected, but to do so she needed a few moments to really grasp the fact that she was about to see her childhood home for the very first time in seventeen years. Her hand going to the tree-of-life pendant at the nape of her neck, which her mother had been wearing that fateful night, Alexis closed her eyes and silently asked her mum and dad to be with her now, more than they ever had been before. And she swore she could feel their presence strengthen. This gave her the courage to open her eyes, grip the steering wheel and drive on.

'I've got this,' she said to herself with conviction.

The road veered off in two different directions. She knew that the road to the left led to the neighbouring farm, which was only a hop, skip and jump away, so she took the one to the right. Reaching a rustic timber sign with 'Diamond Acres' etched into it, hanging from the branch of a big old gum tree that stretched over the road, she passed beneath it and into a world of neatly slashed and fenced paddocks dotted with stunning horses. The picturesque view stole her breath away, as too did the sense that this had been her homeland. She fought back the tears. This was not the time to break down – there would be another time and place for that. The dirt road twisted past impressive stables and a few more horse paddocks, and then led up a rise. The grand homestead with its graceful verandah and lush gardens finally came into view.

Pulling up in the shade of a towering jacaranda tree that was flowering in its full purple glory, she switched off the ignition, drew in a desperate breath and then hopped out before she lost all courage. Now all she had to do was force her legs to walk to the front gate, down the path, up the stairs and to the front door where she would knock and see Ethan King.

Simple.

Her stomach twisted into knots, confirming otherwise.

'Howdy.'

Alexis jumped, her hands going to where her heart had just tried to leap out of her chest. With the sound of his voice Alexis felt the years drop away. Drawing in a deep breath, she plastered a smile on her quivering lips and turned, in no way ready to explain her way out of lying to him about who she was on the phone. Her pulse fluttered and her stomach felt as though she were peering over a thousand-metre drop as her eyes fell upon the most gorgeous hunk of man, all strapping six-foot something of him. His gait was sexily confident as he strode towards her. Sweat glistened on his creased brow, and his breathing was ragged. The spurs wrapped around his dusty boots jingled with each step and his jeans told of the many times they'd been worn. It was undoubtedly him. Her Ethan. She ached with memory. Her legs almost buckled beneath her and she placed her palms on the bonnet to stay upright. Unlike the image of the sixteen-year-old boy she'd held onto so fondly over the years, his face was now all sharp-set angles, his jaw chiselled with a five o'clock shadow. She wanted to run to him, to fall into his strong arms and apologise for not trying harder to keep in touch with him all these years, to ask him why he hadn't tried to keep in contact with her, but she remained glued to the spot. She looked to his wedding finger, and her heart sank when she spotted the gold band. He was spoken for. The lucky woman, whomever she was. And then she tried to speak. To say anything but stand there, mute. Even a simple hello, but her heart and thoughts twisted into a tangle as her nerves increased, tenfold.

'Miss Grey?'

It was like a slap to the face. Did he really not recognise her? Seventeen years *was* a long time, and in that time she'd grown very much into a woman. Her freckles had thankfully all but faded and even her hair colour was drastically different – now black instead of blonde with her chaotic curls habitually ironed straight. It was possible, she half-heartedly supposed. Even so, it hurt her beyond words that it appeared he didn't. Maybe she should run with it, save face explaining she was a drunken idiot who'd stupidly lied to him in the heat of the moment? There was always tomorrow, when she'd gained some footing and calmed her nerves, when she could speak without stuttering, to open up and explain everything. Now just didn't feel like the right time. Taking her sunglasses off she finally found her voice. 'Hi, Ethan.'

'Nice to meet you.' He acknowledged her with a tip of his wide-brimmed hat as he walked up to her.

She searched for a flicker of recognition from him, but there was nothing. Now within her reach she was met with a wall of chest that seemed to block out the sun. He exuded the aura of a man who could handle anything, or anyone, that came his way. The muscles in her belly quivered, but she kept her voice steady. 'Nice to meet you too.' The lead rope slung over his shoulder added to his appeal and she had to fight to drag her eyes from where his broad chest pulled his button-up shirt taut. She held out her hand and his came to hold hers. His grip was firm but at the same time gentle, his hands calloused from the years of hard work. His touch sparked her inside like a match to a flame. She wanted to brush his cheek, to look into his eyes and ask him how the last seventeen years of his life had been, ask if he missed her at times like she had missed him at times, ask him how married life was treating him, but common sense won over. As if reading her thoughts he looked at her a little longer then she was confortable with and she found herself glancing away, hopefully not coyly.

Clearing his throat Ethan looked over her shoulder. 'I was up the back paddock, trying to rein in one of the horses when I seen your trail of dust. I only just got the bugger in time to make a dash down the paddock to meet you.' He glanced down at the state of his mud-splattered jeans and grimaced. 'Sorry, I'm not really dressed for the occasion but he got out of one of the yards and I had a job getting him back in,' he said. 'He's a stubborn old brute when he wants to be.'

'A case of the grass is always greener on the other side of the fence, huh?' Her voice was shaky.

'Apparently, but it's not always the case.' He flashed her a knee-buckling smile, his dimples dancing on his cheeks.

It was a dazzling smile, one Alexis had never forgotten. Her breath stopped for a split second as he stood now only inches from her. She could smell his scent, a heady mixture of leather, dust, horse, lingering aftershave and something she could only describe as a real man. It made her want to throw her arms around him tightly so she could breathe him in deeper.

Lifting his sunglasses so they rested on his hat, their eyes met and locked as sparks fizzed between them. His blue eyes zeroed in on her and a strong twitch rippled over the muscles of his jaw, bringing a flush to her cheeks. Her fingers itched to reach out and touch him but instead she shoved her hands into the pockets of her denim shorts.

'Did you find the place okay?'

'Yup, it was a cinch thanks to Google maps.'

'I thought it might have been from my awesome directions.'

She giggled, feeling like a lovesick teenager. 'Oh, yeah, and that too.' His country drawl made her insides tumble as an image of him stark naked, wearing nothing but his hat and leather chaps, flooded her mind. Silently chastising herself, she mentally tried to slap the image away.

Get a grip. He's a married man ...

Silence settled between them.

She shrugged and smiled gently.

He gave her a look that made her feel as if she'd just been caught with her hand in his biscuit jar. 'Rightio, well, I better take you down to the cottage so you can get yourself settled then, hey?'

Alexis nodded a little too eagerly. 'Oh, yes, that would be wonderful, thanks.'

He thumbed over his shoulder. 'I'll just go jump in my Cruiser.' Then, turning on his heel, he wandered towards where an old Landcruiser was parked in an open carport.

Frazzled, she went to follow him.

He paused and turned, a cheeky grin plastered on his delectably kissable lips. 'Probably best if you follow me down in your car.'

She shook her head at her stupidity. 'Oh, yes, sorry, wasn't thinking.' Feeling her cheeks flame even brighter, she spun around and made a mad dash for the VW, cursing under her breath. She really needed to get a grip because there was not going to be any hanky-panky with her and Ethan. As hypnotically gorgeous as he was, he was completely unattainable.

CHAPTER
13

What in the hell was happening here?

Ethan almost slapped himself to make sure he wasn't dreaming. Reeling from the shock, and with his heart in his throat, his head was spinning so badly he was having trouble piecing everything together. Was it really her? Or had he imagined it? What in the hell was she playing at, coming back here parading as some stranger when they had no reason not to pick up from where they'd left off, no matter how many years it had been? She should know he would welcome her with open arms, shouldn't she? They'd shared a unique bond, or so he had thought.

With a combination of emotions swirling through him, Ethan shook his head as he strode towards the four-wheel drive. He fought the urge to turn right back around and ask her these questions, and more, his burning need to hear the answers growing by the second. Why would she choose to lie to him? Nothing about this made any sense. The girl who had stolen his heart all those years ago, who had made him believe in true friendship, was here and had stood only inches from him, her sweet perfume luring him, as too did the very essence of her that made Alexis so special. Yes, she looked very different from the teenage girl who had left here, but he knew without doubt that it was Alexis. It tore him to pieces not being able to take her into his arms for a welcoming hug hello. He'd sometimes imagined what it would be like, running into her again, but he'd never imaged it to be so, cold, so aloof, so ... fake.

Climbing in and then pulling the door shut more firmly than necessary, he revved the old girl to life. His breath was shakier than he realised as he drew air deep into his lungs. Until this moment, he hadn't realised he'd been holding onto it. The sweat glazing his brow and chest wasn't from the heat. It was from her. From the fire he'd felt just being near her. He stole a few moments now he had some privacy to somehow come to grips with his feelings. Standing in front of her, he'd held his tongue and bit back the hurt while trying to maintain a poker face, while at the same time her presence was twisting him up inside. He'd felt drawn to her from the second she'd stepped from the car, and he'd at first thought it was because her physique was so deliciously curvy, yet toned in all the right places, but then the curl of her full lips as she'd turned and spoken to him with that same enchanting smile he'd grown accustomed to as a teenage boy explained why. It was so powerful that it had jerked him back to the days when it was easy to live in the moment, and not worry about tomorrow or regret the mistakes of yesterday, when they just *were*. Alexis and him. Him and Alexis. Beautifully raw and real. That's how they'd been. He'd never really understood just how much she had meant to him until she'd left. And now she was back.

Alexis Brown, the name swirled in his head and made his heart canter out of rhythm. Glancing down at his wedding ring, he tried to curb the guilt by reminding himself that Alexis had been a huge part of his life before Jasmine, *way* before. He honestly didn't know how to feel – pissed off, hurt or disappointed that she felt she needed to be dishonest. They were best mates way back when, so why the secrecy? Why lie to him? And how stupid of her to think she could fool him into believing she was someone else. How could he not remember her when they'd spent almost every spare second together?

Although she'd sounded confident, Ethan thought she also seemed vulnerable and fragile, as though she'd been to hell and back, which he knew all too well she had. There were shadows over her captivating eyes and he wished he could shine some light on them and help her heal. It had taken every bit of his resolve not to take her into his arms and kiss those enticing full lips so he could distract her from her worries, if only for a few moments. But then she might have slapped him in the face too, especially considering he was wearing a wedding ring. And just because he remembered her fondly didn't mean she thought that way about him. She had ignored all the letters he'd sent her, fifty-two to be exact, and if that wasn't a sign she wanted to forget he existed, what was? Why the hell come back here, other than to stir up a past she should leave behind? And how was she going to feel stepping foot in the cottage after all these years? If she'd told him who she was when they'd talked on the phone he would have done anything he could to make her return easier.

He drove slowly as he headed down the dirt driveway, so he didn't stir up too much dust. He didn't want to cover her spunky little car in it. In her tight denim shorts and silky black singlet, she was a heady mixture of class and casualness. She had certainly grown into one hell of a woman, and had got under his skin within seconds, without even seeming to try.

Glancing in his rear-vision mirror he caught a glimpse of her black locks flying around her pretty face. Dark hair suited her, as too did the blonde hair he remembered from her teenage years. A strange sensation of heat, like firecrackers being set alight, sparked in his stomach when she caught his eyes and flashed him a smile worthy of falling to his knees. And what normal red-blooded man wouldn't feel like that beneath her scorching smile? With her long black hair, blue–green eyes and blush coloured glossy lips, Alexis Brown was startlingly beautiful. And those long, smooth legs that just seemed to go on forever and ever, although she was still easily a few inches shorter than him – not surprising at his height. She honestly had to be one of the most stunning women he'd ever laid his eyes upon. Jasmine had been attractive, in a girl-next-door kind of way, whereas Alexis would give a model a run for their money. He hoped she had a very good excuse for acting like a stranger because already now he so wanted to forgive her for her stupid mistake. There had to be a plausible reason, didn't there? He wanted to ask her outright, but then part of him wanted her to come to her senses of her own accord and tell him the truth. That would mean a lot more than him drawing it out from her.

Reaching the cottage he pulled to a stop, gesturing with a wave of his arm to Alexis to park in the carport. She gave him a nod to let him know she understood. Then stepping out, he reminded himself to keep his cool as he made his way over to her, just in time to stop her dragging a suitcase from the boot that would have weighed more than she did.

'Here, let me grab that for you.' He almost said her name, but stopped just short.

'Oh, that's okay, I got it in there so I certainly should be able to get it out,' she said as she tried to haul it up and out, grunting and groaning as she did.

Her determination was as strong as he remembered, and very adorable, but he couldn't stand by and watch her lift something so heavy. 'Please, let me do it before you cause yourself an injury.' Not waiting for a reply, he reached out and took hold of the handle. As his hand brushed against hers a bolt of energy shot up his arm, spreading heat throughout his body. The sparks he had felt when standing near her before were now more akin to a blaze.

As if mirroring what was going on inside of him, her cheeks flared a bright shade of red. 'Okay, yup, sure.' She stepped away from him. Well away. 'Thanks.'

'Welcome.' He couldn't help but notice how she'd quickly put her hands in her pockets. It was then that he knew that she could feel whatever he was feeling. He wanted to say, *Come on, I know who you are. Come here and give me a hug.* But he zipped his lips. She needed to be the one to speak about it first.

Suitcase now in hand, he carried it towards the cottage, Alexis close behind him. 'Wow, have you got the kitchen sink in here? You're in the country now, you know, you don't need all the vices to get through out here.' It was said in jest and he laughed, expecting her to do the same. They'd always shared healthy banter.

'I know I don't need all my vices out here.' She huffed loud enough for him to hear her and he turned to see her fold her arms defensively as she marched behind him. 'And just for the record, it has wheels, you know, so there's no need to carry it.' The curt tone of her voice let him know in no uncertain terms she didn't find his light-hearted comment even remotely funny. Boy oh boy, she needed to lighten up.

'Yeah, I can see that, but I don't want to drag it through the dirt.' Reaching the pathway just outside the gate, he stopped and placed it down. 'Considering how smicko this suitcase looks I was gathering you'd appreciate that.'

She stepped in beside him, her citrus-infused perfume provoking his senses again. A few faint freckles still dusted her cheeks and her small, perfect nose – they'd certainly faded to almost nothing over the years, but they were so familiar that he wanted to brush his hands over her face and kiss her.

'Thank you, Ethan, it's an expensive bag so that was very thoughtful of you.' There was no sign of a smile as she tucked a stray strand of hair behind her ear.

Fighting to drag his gaze from the faint line of a scar on her left cheek from when she'd fallen out of a tree and landed on the handle of her bike (she'd always been accident prone), he nodded towards the front door and said, 'Welcome to your home away from home for the next five days.' He felt nervous for her, the memories of what had happened in there almost too much for his own heart and soul to bear. Alexis's presence made it all the more real. He could only begin to imagine what it would be like for her. He wanted to comfort her, tell her he knew what she was going through right now.

'It's very ... ' she paused. 'Lovely.'

He noticed the tremble in her voice and his heart sank to his boots. Her pain was his pain, just as it had always been. As much as he was pissed off and hurt by her deceit, he still cared for her. For as long as he could stand it, he kept looking forward, then he turned ever so slowly towards her. He could feel her anxiety; see it in her ridged posture and her tight-lipped smile. Maybe she was upset that it didn't look the same as she remembered? 'I promise it's very quaint on the inside.' Not what he was aching to say, but he had to say something.

She shook her head, her hand going to her chest. 'Oh, sorry, please don't think I don't like it. You've done the place up, so I wasn't expecting this, that's all ... ' She lightly touched his arm. 'It looks very nice, very homely.'

He wanted to soothe her anxiety away. But he stood firm, pretending he didn't know who she was. 'I don't understand what you mean, it's exactly like the photos on the website. Isn't it?' Maybe this was an opportunity for her to open up and tell him who she really was, so he could do what he wanted to. He silently begged her to.

Her face paled and she bit her bottom lip before smiling. 'Oh, yes, sorry, I meant it looks different to what I was envisioning ... ' She was stumbling over her words now and he almost saved her by telling her he knew who she was, but she stole the moment away and continued, 'What I meant to say was that the renovations have done the place wonders.' As if realising she was digging an even bigger hole she sucked in a sharp breath and turned away from him, pretending to be engrossed in something way off in the distance.

'How do you know what it looked like before I renovated it?'

She turned back to him, her face now a brighter shade of red. 'I beg your pardon?'

He almost didn't repeat himself. 'I said, how do you know what it looked like before I renovated it?' He fought hard to keep the frustration from his voice.

'I don't. I, ah ... ' she said. 'I just guessed that you'd recently renovated it because the paint looks so fresh, that's all.' She ran her finger along the top of the new white picket fence as though confirming her observation.

'Oh, right, yeah, I only just finished the renovations a few weeks back.'

'Well, it looks great.'

'Thanks. It's been a labour of love over the past twelve months. The home means a lot to me. A very close friend of mine used to live here, and I wanted to do her and her family justice by bringing the old place back to life.'

'Oh, how sweet of you. She's one lucky friend.' She was looking down at the ground now.

'I was lucky to have known her. Haven't seen her for years, but would love to cross paths with her again some day, you know, catch up on old times.' He tried to feign nonchalance by shrugging.

'You never know, you might.' Alexis's voice was trembling.

'Maybe, maybe not ... that's in fate's hands.'

She remained silent as she rocked back and forth on her heels, her eyes still staring at her feet.

He took his sunglasses off. He wanted to look her in the eyes and tell her it was okay, that whatever the reason she had lied to him it was going to be okay, but with her dark sunglasses back on he couldn't capture her pretty eyes to do so.

'Has anyone lived here since your friend did?'

'Nope, it's been empty for years.'

'Oh, why's that?' She finally turned to him again.

'No reason really, it just turned out that way.'

'So I'm the first guest to enjoy the cottage since your friend lived here?'

'You sure are.'

'Wow. I'm extremely honoured.' She smiled gently, and this time it appeared genuine. 'I hope it's not haunted or anything.' She laughed, but it sounded forced.

'Nah, of course it's not. Why would you say that?' He knew exactly why, and also believed she wouldn't care if her parents were the ones haunting it, but he couldn't let a comment like that slip by—worried it would seem unnatural in the flow of the conversation to ignore it. This was getting more and more awkward, and he hated it. They used to be so comfortable together.

She tilted her head to the aside. 'I dunno, just the fact it's been empty for years, and it used to be an old farm house, I suppose.'

'Oh, right, well, I don't believe in ghosts, so I can't say there's any in there.'

'How can you not believe in ghosts?' She gave him a flabbergasted look.

'Easy as,' he said. 'I just don't.'

She nodded as she took her sunglasses off, finally allowing him a glimpse into the mesmerising windows of her soul. Then his heart squeezed tight with pain. She looked terrified, the depth of her fear reminding him of the look in the eyes of the horses when he saved them.

'Do you want me to show you in?' He really wanted to be there if she crumbled when she walked through the doors.

Her lips parted softly as if she were about to say yes, but then she inhaled a quick breath before smiling. The curl of her lips was in sharp contrast to the war raging in her eyes. 'No, I'll be fine to let myself in, but thank you.'

Again he had to fight the urge to take her into his arms and soothe her fears away. 'Righto, I'll just pop your suitcase near the front door then.'

'Okay, that would be great, thanks.'

'You staying out here?' he asked with a forced laugh, and he hoped she didn't pick up on it.

As if oblivious to his inner turmoil, she waved him forwards. 'No, you go, I'm still admiring the view from here.'

Stopping mid-step he dug in his pocket and then handed her the keys to the cottage. 'There's a carton of milk in the fridge, local I might add, with cream that sits on the top, and the basket of breakfast goodies for the next few days is in there too. When you need a top up of any of it, just let me know and I'll be all too happy to bring it over.'

'Thank you, Ethan, I'm so sorry if I'm coming across as frazzled, I'm just tired from the long drive.' She reached out and gave his arm a gentle squeeze. 'I really appreciate your warm welcome.'

'My pleasure, all part of the job,' he said with another strained smile before heading down the garden path, the entire time feeling as though an invisible cord was pulling him back towards her.

CHAPTER

14

Alexis's mouth went dry. Her heart beat madly. She struggled with all her might to remain cool and composed on the outside; holding it together right now was her only option. Had Ethan just cottoned on to who she was? The suspicious look in his deep blue eyes told her he might well have.

Should she open up and tell him the truth, and apologise for being such an idiot for not saying something in the first place? Her internal voice of reason screamed at her to do so, but she stood fast. She couldn't deal with that as well as walking back into the cottage for the first time in seventeen years … it would be too much for her. So she fought the urge to tell him. Tomorrow. She would do it tomorrow. One thing at a time.

Watching him carry her bag to the front steps as if it were as light as a feather, Alexis tried to force herself to follow him, but it was as if her sandals were lead weights and her feet just wouldn't move. She knew she must seem like a fool, stuttering and stumbling on her words, but she felt as if the way she was acting around Ethan was out of her control. As much as she tried to rein in her stupid slips of the tongue, she only seemed to make matters worse and her story seemed to grow more and more unbelievable. She'd always been a terrible liar, and giving him a false name over the phone had been a really bad idea. Damn the bottle of wine that had made her do something she never would have done sober.

She shook her head, disappointed with herself. Ethan was right here, in the flesh – gloriously so. She wanted to hug him like crazy, tell him how much she'd missed him and then reminisce over the good times. But what would his wife think of that? Was she a jealous type of woman, or would she welcome her in with open arms? Like a weight bearing down upon her, the guilt of not telling him who she was crushed Alexis to the point of not being able to draw a decent breath.

Keep it together, just for now. You can tell him later ...

Ethan glanced back at her as he placed the bag near the front door, his smile so warm and tender it touched her soul. In that brief moment the world seemed to fade away and time stood still. She sucked in a much-needed breath and tried to smile back. The pull she felt towards this man was indescribable, out of this world. It was shocking, overwhelming – she hadn't expected this at all. It was a connection that had lasted almost her entire lifetime and was as strong as ever. How she wished he wasn't married.

As much as she wanted to run to him, she remained frozen to a spot just inside the gate, hesitant to enter her childhood home. The home where she'd gained so much and then lost almost everything. She now wished Katie was standing beside her so she didn't have to do this alone. Her body felt strained and no matter how she fought to be in control of this situation, it was slipping out of her grasp at an alarming speed. Using a coping mechanism that Doctor Jacobs had taught her, she tried to imagine what she'd do for a friend in her shoes, and she knew without a doubt that she'd tell that friend to be gentle on herself, to not feel bad for not being as strong as she felt she needed to be and to allow each moment to pass into the next, step by step, slowly does it.

Breathing in, she pulled back her shoulders, stood up straighter and decided she would follow her own advice. She needed to be strong when she walked back into her old home, stronger than she had ever been, but at the same time she should be easy on herself. She had no idea what memories were held captive in that little cottage or how she was going to react if and when they surfaced, and she didn't want Ethan to bear witness to that if it happened as soon as she walked through the door. Their conversation about who she was and her apology for lying to him on the phone would have to wait.

With her renewed courage, time sped up to more of a normal pace. Ethan was heading back towards her now, tall, tanned, but certainly no mystery to her. Another smile lit up his handsome face, his dimples deepening. It was an easy, welcoming smile, but it made her all the more nervous because all she wanted to do at that very second was claim his lips with her own in a hungry kiss. What a pleasant diversion from her inner battles that would be. But there was the matter of him being spoken for. Thank goodness he couldn't read her thoughts, but even so heat rose to her cheeks and her belly filled with butterflies. Damn it, he had a power over her that she'd never expected. A shiver ran down her spine, sending her legs weak.

Stopping just short of her, he stood with his thumbs hooked through his belt loops. She couldn't help but think he was looking not just at her but right in to her heart. She ached to fill the silence.

Now. 'Okay, well, thank you for showing me to the cottage, Ethan, I can take it from here.'

'No worries at all. But just a couple of things before I head off ... '

'Yes, and what are they?' Her voice sounded strained as her eyes travelled from the fine scattering of hair peeking out of his shirt up to his eyes, which had captured hers once again. His lips curled ever so slightly, as if he knew she was perving.

'You don't have to lock the doors out here but whatever you do, don't forget to keep the front and back screen doors shut. '

'Why?

'You don't want any uninvited guests coming inside.'

She wanted to tell him he was welcome to sneak into the cottage at anytime, but ... married! 'You mean snakes?' That sounded better.

'I do mean snakes, and the odd possum ... and if that isn't enough you've got plenty of insects that like to make their way inside too, especially if there's a light on.'

'Insects I can live with but snakes ... ' She shuddered. 'I hate them. I lost one of my dogs to one once, when I was a kid, and it broke my heart.'

'Yup, me too, and I've lost a couple of good horses to them as well. That's why I hate the bastards.' He shook his head, his jaw clenching as though recalling the terrible memories. 'Do you know what sort of snake it was, that got your dog?'

'I think it was an inland taipan.' She wanted to suck the words back into her mouth as soon as they had left her lips. Damn it.

'Really? An inland taipan? I thought you mentioned on the phone last night you were from Townsville?'

'Oh, yes, I am.'

'An inland taipan on the coast? Well bugger me dead, that's a first.' He shook his head, a smirk claiming his lips. 'Are you sure that's what it was?'

Was he playing with her? 'No, not one hundred percent sure.' She shrugged indifferently. 'Maybe it was a coastal taipan. Being a bit of a city chick I'm clueless with all that kind of stuff.' With her dad having taught her from a very young age what snakes were what, that was a far cry from the truth.

He suddenly looked very serious, and it was a look she fondly remembered from the times they would playfully banter – which were many.

'Oh, right, that'd make more sense,' he said before clearing his throat.

'What makes more sense, that I'm a naïve city girl or that it was a coastal taipan?'

He laughed along with her. 'Bit of both maybe.'

Far out, he looked even sexier when he laughed. 'You cheeky bugger.' She gave him a playful shove. Even though she was in turmoil on the inside, his lighthearted talk helping her to relax. This was how they used to be, all those years ago, and the connection, as fleeting as it was, was really, *really* nice. 'I do find possums cute, though, so they're more than welcome to visit me.'

'You might find them cute, but they can pack a punch with their bite, and they have long claws that will slice your skin like a knife ... ' His brows shot up. 'So whatever you do, don't let their cuteness fool you.'

'Wow, really? Thanks for the head's up.' She knew he was right, but she'd had a pet possum they had handfed for years at the cottage so she had a soft spot for the nocturnal creatures. Like anything, the combination of love and a gentle approach could work wonders.

He lifted his hat and ran his forearm across his brow.

Silence settled between them, long enough for Alexis to start to feel uncomfortable.

Ethan cleared his throat again. 'And one last thing, the water can sometimes come out brown when you first turn on the taps, but just give it a few seconds and it'll run as clear as crystal.'

She gave him the thumbs-up, shocked at doing so. She never gave the thumbs-up. 'Okay, gotcha.' She felt really out of her depth in this strange situation and wished she'd never given a false name.

'Great, just give me a holler if you need anything, day or night. I'm only a two-minute drive away, or a minute on horseback in an emergency.' He grinned cheekily. 'I love having a good excuse to go for a gallop.'

'Ha-ha, there's nothing much better then feeling the gait of a galloping horse beneath you, is there?'

'You can ride?' He didn't look as shocked as his voice conveyed.

'A little.' She wanted to say, 'Hell yeah, I can ride, and I'll bloody well prove it to you,' but she held back.

'Well, then, you and I will have to go for a ride sometime so I can show you some nice spots to relax while you're here.' His deep voice washed over her like a glass of whiskey on a cold winter's night. But her breath caught in her throat. What would his wife think of him out riding with another woman? She wanted to drop her gaze, but his eyes held hers spellbound. She wondered if he could see the quiver in her lips. 'That would be lovely, thank you.' She recalled all the times she and Ethan had gone riding as young teenagers.

'Great, you just let me know when you'd like to go and I'll saddle Wild Thing up ... he's a bit of a stubborn old brute with men but he's a true gentleman with women. His first owner taught him well.'

Her heart stopped and she fought to hide her shock. Tears threatened to form but she blinked them away. 'You have a horse called Wild Thing? How old is he?'

Ethan beamed. 'He's about twenty-two years old now. He's the stubborn bugger I was trying to get back into the paddock when you arrived.'

'You were?'

'Yup.'

She wanted to say that Wild Thing hadn't changed a bit, by the sounds of it. 'Oh, right, well there you go.' It was her turn to clear her throat. 'That's a really cool name, Wild Thing. I like it.'

He scanned her face, and then as if satisfied with what he saw, he smiled. 'Sure is, but I can't take the credit – a friend and his first owner named him.'

'He sounds like a right character, I'm looking forward to seeing how he rides.' She fought the urge to jump up and down on the spot as she imagined seeing her beloved Wild Thing after all these years. She wondered if he'd remember her.

'Yeah, as frustrating as he can be at times, he's loveable too. You'll fall in love him from the get go, everyone does.' A beeper sounded. He glanced at his watch and pressed the side of it. 'I better be off, still got loads to do and not enough daylight hours to do it.'

She nodded. 'I'm hearing you, loud and clear. If you need any help around the place while I'm here, just give me a shout ... I'm more than happy to lend a hand.' She couldn't help herself, the thought of working out in the saddle or alongside the brumbies was so appealing and filled her with warmth.

'Oh, thanks, but I wouldn't do that to a lady.'

'Do what?'

'Put you to work when you're here to have a holiday.'

'Why? And I hope it's not because I'm a *lady* ... ' She raised an eyebrow as she emphasised the word. 'Do you think I wouldn't cut the mustard in the saddle?' She flashed him a sassy grin – he had a way of bringing out the playful side in her.

'Nooo, not at all.' His smile told her otherwise. 'Thank you, but in all seriousness I can't expect you to arrive as a paying guest and then put you to work.'

'Oh, don't be silly. It would be a nice change of pace from what I usually do.'

'And what might that be?'

'I'm a freelance photographer.'

'Holy shit, really?'

'Yes, really.' She grinned. 'Why do you sound so shocked?'

'Oh, sorry, just ... nothing ... ' He waved a hand through the air. Now he seemed to be hiding his own thoughts. 'Good for you, following your dreams.'

'My dreams?'

'Yeah.' He looked at her like she was speaking a foreign language.

'How do you know being a photographer was a dream of mine?' She was just about to blurt out she was sorry she'd lied about her name on the phone, but ...

'Oh, dunno, wild guess I suppose. Don't all artists dream of being one from a young age?'

'Not always.'

'Rightio.' He pointed to the set of keys in her hand. 'The gold one is for the front door and the one with the blue tag is for the back.'

'Okay, got it.' She pushed them into her pocket. 'Enjoy your afternoon. I'm sure I'll be seeing you again soon.'

'Well, we *are* neighbours now, so I dare say sooner rather than later.' He turned and gave her a wave over his shoulder. 'Have fun settling in and don't be shy to shout out if you need anything.'

'Will do, thanks.' Alexis watched him climb into the Landcruiser, rev it to life and then spin around and head back towards the homestead, and to his no doubt stunningly beautiful wife. He flashed his charming smile as he drove by the cottage, the gesture warming her heart and soul.

Now on her own, Alexis suddenly felt overwhelmed with fear. Spinning back to face the verandah she drew in a deep breath, and then slowly blew it away, imagining all her fears dissipating with her outward breath. As much as she wanted to, she couldn't just stand there all day. She shifted her laptop bag to the other hand. Her palms were damp and her fingers trembled, as too did her heart. Another deep breath and she repeated the process three times before she felt a calming wave wash over her mind. Emotions bubbled up from deep within, but she pushed them back. If she had to cry, she would do it later.

She could hear Katie at the back of her mind saying she had this.

Curling her fingers tighter around the laptop bag she took a step forwards, and then another, and another, until her strides were long and confident. The path she followed was as she remembered, winding between bright green citrus trees and a lush, colourful garden. Her mouth watered with the thought of tucking into a juicy bush lemon. Sprinkled with a bit of salt, it had been one of her mum's favourite treats. Climbing the front steps, she reached the screen door that had replaced the old one, which had been patched in a number of places to keep the flies out. The new door was more heavy duty and burglar proof. Without any further hesitation she opened it, resting her knee against it to stop it from closing, and then pushed the key into the lock of the timber door. She rolled her eyes when she realised she'd locked it rather than unlocked it. So different from suburbia out here, and she loved the freedom and simplicity of it – who wouldn't?

Stepping inside, the first thing she noticed was the lingering smell of paint beneath the faint scent of vanilla. Closing her eyes she breathed in deeper, trying desperately to catch a hint of her past, but there was nothing. Long gone were the scents of her mother's frankincense perfume, Nag Champra incense burning and the mouth-watering aromas of goodies baking in the oven. Focussing on the room once more, her hands went to her chest and instinctively her fingers clutched tightly at her mother's tree-of-life pendant hanging from her necklace.

'What happened that night?' she whispered. 'Who did this to you?'

A gust of wind blew the sheer curtains at the side windows and a crash sounded from the corner of the lounge room. Her heart in her throat she spun around to see a simple candlestick lying on the floor, a broken candle beside it. And then as quickly as the wind had filled the room, the curtains were now deathly still. Goosebumps prickled her skin. Was this a sign that her parents' spirits lingered here? With what felt like icy fingers tracing up her spine she almost retreated back into the safety of the bright sunshine outside. Her heart quickened and she tried her best to soothe it by breathing deeply. She reminded herself they were dead, gone, buried ... her mind had to be playing tricks on her. Pushing the unnerving feeling away she took a few cautious steps forwards, her eyes darting from left to right. Where had it happened? Where had they found her mum's and dad's lifeless bodies? Her heart squeezed tightly with the thought. She had always wondered what room they'd died in, but now she was standing here, looking into the heart of the cottage, she was thankful for not knowing. It was something she didn't need to know. Not now. Not ever. Her parents were dead. Someone had killed them. She needed to find out who pulled the trigger. That was all she needed to know.

With her eyes now adjusted to the dim light, she waited for a memory of that night to hit her, to rock her already unsettled emotions. But there was nothing and she was disappointed – not a good start. Five steps forwards and she was standing in the lounge room on a cow-skin rug. Alexis placed her laptop bag down on a cream three-seater lounge chair with scattered cushions and a matching throw rug slung over the armrest. It was mirrored by two armchairs placed on the opposite side of a long, rustic coffee table. Desperately wanting to get rid of the shadows, she walked over to the windows and flung open the curtain. Light spilled into the room, sprinkling the timber table with golden warmth and igniting the few flecks of dust into a shimmer. It was charming in here. Ethan had done a wonderful job.

Alexis began to scan every inch of the room as if beneath a microscope. The wall that had divided the kitchen and the lounge room, which had been decorated with framed photographs of her family, had been knocked down, making the cottage appear a heck of a lot bigger than she remembered. Gone was the worn linoleum, and in its place she saw the timber floorboards that must have been lying beneath, the wide boards brought back to life by shiny varnish. The seventies colour scheme of orange and lime was gone, and the walls that were once covered in hieroglyphic wallpaper were now painted cream, as too was the ceiling. The glass louvres in the kitchen and dining room, which her mother had always cursed having to clean, had been replaced with big sliding windows, all open to allow the breeze in but screened off to stop the insects Ethan had warned her about.

The kitchen, too, had changed. The contact-covered cupboards were replaced by glossy timber ones with stone bench tops – very country chic. The lino had been ripped up in there as well, and replaced with shiny white tiles that made the room appear larger than she remembered it. A skylight had been put in, allowing the sunlight to spill into every nook and cranny. She could imagine spending lazy Sundays in this room. How nice would that be, to be back living in the house she'd spent such treasured moments of her life in, ready to raise a family of her own? She stole a moment to imagine standing at the impressive new AGA stove, her hair still damp from a shower and her feet bare, Ethan's arms wrapped around her waist as he gently kissed her neck and nibbled her earlobe. She could almost hear her soft laughter as she tipped her head back to kiss him, then watch his lips move as he told her how much he loved her, before whisking her off to spend the entire day between the sheets. Her heart ached as she imagined how blissful that would be, to be loved by a man who, in turn, would be so very easy to love. Her entire body was filled with a yearning she hadn't felt for a very long time as she envisioned him, naked, on top of her, kissing her like he meant it.

Too late – the man was married.

She sighed. A girl could dream ...

Turning, she walked over to the fridge, remembering how theirs used to be covered in paintings she and Katie had done at school, and tugged the door open. A smile momentarily stole her anxieties away. She picked up a bowl, admiring the huge eggs that she guessed must have come from Ethan's chooks. There was nothing better than cooking with farm-fresh produce. She placed it back near a paper-wrapped parcel she guessed was the bacon, a bowl of shiny purple grapes, a block of cheese, tomatoes and in the door was a glass bottle of the creamiest looking milk she'd ever seen. She had planned to go back into town this afternoon to buy a few groceries but happy with the prospect of bacon and eggs for dinner, she decided otherwise. There was always tomorrow.

She wandered over to the large window where her mother used to have pots of herbs on the windowsill. Sun catchers used to hang from thumbtacks above the sink, dancing a kaleidoscope of colours over the room. She and Katie used to have so much fun trying to capture the colours. It was quaint in here, but there wasn't the strong sense of home, of family, that used to be. Her already straining heartstrings tightened. Alexis sucked in a breath, feeling dizzy. Leaning on the sink she looked out to the backyard, memories of playing there with Katie filling her mind. The shed her father had built was still out there, standing strong despite the years in the elements. She remembered that it had been filled with her dad's garage sale collections, hardware and tools, and she couldn't help but wonder, even after all this time, if maybe there was something in the shed that would remind her of years gone by.

She hoped so.

After a few moments she turned around and scanned the room once more. So many memories, but none of the night she so badly needed to recall. Deciding it was time to go down the hallway, she walked with cautious steps. The first door she reached was where her mum had had her sewing room. It had been cluttered and colourful and filled with fabrics. A Singer sewing machine had taken pride of place on a table surrounded by racks of pretty clothes that her mother used to sell at the local markets. When they were little, she and Katie would play in there as their mother worked. They were such wonderful times. Now it was furnished simply, with two single beds, a small table between them with a lamp atop it. Leaning against the doorframe she tried to remember her mum in here, humming to herself as she tended to her passion of dressmaking. By closing her eyes the memories became more vivid and more poignant.

Next was her parents' room. Memories of tiptoeing in and crawling into bed with her mum and dad filled her mind, and brought tears to her eyes. A few fell before she sniffed and wiped her cheeks. Her father would play the tickle monster and her mum would hide Katie and her under the blankets to avoid the tickling, their laughter contagious. It was strange looking at the room now, with no trace of her parents ever having been here. The dressing table that used to be covered with her mum's make-up, perfume bottle and hairbrushes was gone, as was the old bed with matching chipboard tables, replaced with a very impressive timber bed that looked as if it would have cost an arm and a leg, made up with linen that was crisp and white. As inviting as the bed looked, she wouldn't be sleeping in this room.

She headed back out the door and down the hallway, passing the toilet and bathroom along the way. Glancing into each room she saw that they too had been renovated beyond all recognition. She bit back a swear word, almost mad at Ethan for erasing any trace of her life here, of her parents' lives here, of Katie's life here. It was as if they had never existed. Part of her felt ripped off, cheated that she couldn't walk back into the cottage and pick up where they had all left off, but as with anything in life, progress was inevitable and she couldn't hold it against Ethan for moving forwards. The world had just kept on turning, regardless.

At the end of the hall was the bedroom she had shared with Katie. Unlike the rest of the cottage, for some reason the door was shut. She stood still, her hand coming to rest on the door handle. It felt cold beneath her fingertips. Drawing in a shaky breath she turned the handle, taken aback to find it was locked. She wriggled it, and then gave the door a bit of a shake. Stepping back she eyed it curiously. Ethan hadn't mentioned anything to her about not having access to the entire the cottage. Maybe one of the keys he'd given her fitted it. She took the keys out of her pocket, only to realise there was no keyhole and no lock. Confused, she tried the handle again, and this time it opened with no trouble. The chill that had crept through her before returned. The door creaked halfway. She nudged it with her foot until it was wide open, and her eyes instantly went to where the window was ajar.

A cool breeze lifted the sheer curtains with a flutter. The branches of the big old oak tree brushed against the side of the house, sounding like fingernails scraping down a blackboard. Something about it all felt strangely familiar, and it gave her a glimmer of hope. Trying to dive deeper into her past, she concentrated as everything around her seemed to blur. A crack of thunder made her jump, but a flick of her eyes confirmed it was still summer perfection outside. Somewhere, a dog was barking, but it was so distant that it felt dreamlike. A rush of adrenaline claimed her, enticing her heart into a canter. She shook her head slowly, confusion bearing down upon her. What in the hell was happening? Panic and fear clutched at her and made her heartbeats quicken so much that she found herself gasping for breath. The wall gave her support as she collapsed against it. She shuddered, her hands trembling as she fought off a wave of nausea. Suddenly, a force greater than she'd ever felt before pulled her into a void, a space in time she was instinctively afraid to be in, and then as if gripping her, a memory seared into her consciousness. She was on her bed, clutching Katie, and her parents were yelling. It was dark. Their bedroom door was closed. Rain fell outside. Her camera hung on the doorknob. She was scared now, so very scared. Katie was sobbing and she didn't know what to do.

Wrapping her arms around herself Alexis sank down to her knees against the wall as her past claimed her with ruthless potency. She felt vulnerable, like any young teenager would feel in a terrifying situation. Why was she so frightened when it was just herself, Katie and their parents in the house? Was she right in believing someone else had been there that night? She looked around the now unrecognisable bedroom, the queen-sized bed and timber furnishings were posh in comparison to what she and Katie had in here. For a fleeting moment she was back in the present, but then *Bam*. She was back in her past again, trying to remain calm for Katie's sake.

'What do I do, what do I do?' The words escaped in a whisper so soft she could barely hear it herself.

Her eyes darted upwards. The window, she needed to climb out the window. The necessity to do so was urgent. But why did she want to escape from the safety of the cottage and into the dead of night, especially when it was raining? Were hers and Katie's lives at stake? She recalled the yelling getting louder, her mother's cries heartbreaking. Her father was so angry. It was not something she was used to hearing. Present time claimed her once more and she begged it not to. She needed to stay in her past. Something was itching to reveal itself. She closed her eyes, encouraging the memory to come to the forefront, to reveal what was lurking in the shadows of her mind, when she was slammed back to that horrible night again. She remembered getting up from bed and then helping Katie to climb out the window. Hand in hand they ran for the cubby house, the earth sodden beneath their feet. Their dog was quiet now. Eerily so. A gunshot echoed, the boom so frighteningly real she covered her ears. Was it her father who had pulled the trigger? Had she been wrong to believe his innocence all these years? A stab of guilt pierced her already aching heart with the thought as she remembered she and Katie running for their lives across the paddocks. But that's where the memory came to a grinding halt, and as much as she begged for it to continue, there was nothing more.

Her mind was now blank.

Exhausted, as though the life had just been drained out of her, Alexis slumped and drew in some slow, deep breaths. This was a massive step forwards. As scary as it was, climbing back into a life she'd long ago left behind, she couldn't wait to see, and feel, what else the ghosts of the past had to show her.

CHAPTER

15

Placing the feed bucket down, Ethan carefully assessed Shooter's injuries while the young horse started to eat. In response to his gentle touch Shooter lifted his head and nudged Ethan's shoulder softly. Satisfied the bandages were still in place, and clean, Ethan leant back. One boot up against the wall, he folded his arms. Highly intelligent, alert, patient and intuitive, and with the kindest eyes Ethan had ever seen in all his years of doing this, Shooter was going to make one hell of a horse when he grew older. Ethan was sure of it. He felt blessed to have crossed paths with such a magnificent creature, and took satisfaction in knowing he'd never sell him off. Born into the wild, Shooter already had a strong sense of family structure, the strict law of the pecking order giving each horse a definite place in the mob, and Ethan could tell that Shooter knew his place, even at this young age. By building on this, tuning into Shooter's natural abilities and showing him how to lead without domination, he would quickly become Ethan's best mate, bonding with him in a way that a domestic horse, in his opinion, rarely achieved. It drove him mad that close-minded people thought brumbies were inbred, and even disease ridden. His extensive experience with them proved otherwise. Free-ranging horses instinctively knew what they needed in terms of nutrition and foraged for it. As for the inbreeding, that only occurred when large numbers of horses were confined to small areas for grazing, and it was still very unusual, even in a domestic situation, let alone a wild one.

With the bucket licked clean, Shooter lifted his head and neighed. 'You're welcome, buddy.' Ethan pushed himself off the wall. He ran his hand through the mane that had taken him over an hour to tame, and then over Shooter's back, savouring his horsey scent. In his opinion, it should be bottled and sold as men's aftershave. He was yet to meet a woman who didn't like the smell. 'I'll be back a bit later to bunker down for the night with you, okay, buddy?'

The horse nuzzled him again, and he ran his hand gently over Shooter's velvety nose and then down his neck. 'You're certainly a lover, and not a fighter, Shooter. I reckon you and me are going to make a good team. See you soon.' Grabbing his hat from where he'd left it on a tack hook, Ethan tugged it on and stepped back out into the sunshine. Next job was rounding up his girls and locking them away for the night.

A short stroll down a rutted dirt track and he started to call out, 'Come on, you lot, in you go. I haven't got all bloody day, you know.' Ethan shifted from boot to boot as he waited for his chickens to dawdle into the coop for the night. Rebel the Rooster, a name given to the bird by Ethan's grandfather, was the last one in, his strut as cocky as his attitude. Job done, he latched the gate shut and tapped the corrugated-iron roof lightly. 'Night night, catch you all bright and early tomorrow, hey?'

Picking up the old ice-cream container from the ground, he admired his collection for the day. Eight eggs in total. There was something so satisfying about harvesting his own food – such a shame he didn't have the time for a veggie patch. He'd make sure to drop a few of the bum-nuts off to Alexis in the morning, or maybe it would be a good excuse to call over there tonight? How nice would that be, to see her twice in one day. He wouldn't be able to hold his tongue much longer. Maybe he should bring it up next time he talked to her? Yeah, he nodded as if answering himself, that was exactly what he was going to do. Would it be out of line for him to say something? He tried to shrug off the concern. When had he ever cared before about stepping out of line, or over the line? She needed to explain herself, so they could get past this bullshit.

All the horses tended to, wild and tamed, and his day done and dusted other than a few bills he had to pay later with money he basically needed to scrounge up from thin air, Ethan crossed the front lawn and then cleared the steps two at a time just as nightfall closed in. He paused for a moment on the wide verandah, watching the first star emerge. He said a silent hello to Jasmine as he did so often when he looked up at the night sky. Part of him wondered if that was where he'd look to see his mother, too, after she left this earth. The thought almost sent him crashing to his knees. He didn't want to let her go, and even thinking about it cracked his already broken heart a little more. Sighing, Ethan hung his hat on a hook between his oilskins and odd bits of tack on the back verandah, and kicked off his boots. It felt good to be barefoot. Then he turned to head inside. As if mirroring his aching bones the flyscreen door squeaked as he gave it a shove with the toe of his boot. He flicked a switch and the kitchen glowed with cold, iridescent light. Up on his hind legs, Elvis was immediately there to greet him, his tail wagging a million times a minute.

Chuckling, Ethan gave his furry mate a quick scratch behind the ears. 'Hey there, buddy, I'm lucky I've got you here to welcome me home. Otherwise it would be pretty lonely.' His heart squeezed as he recalled how, if Jasmine had made it home from her teaching job before him, she would always run to greet him. They'd been staying with his grandparents, saving up to build their own house at Diamond Acres, but now that wasn't to be. He'd put all of the money back into the running of the farm and the renovations of the cottage.

Elvis shadowed him, nipping playfully at his ankles. Shaking his head, he leant over and scooped his canine mate up, fruitlessly trying to avoid doggy kisses while also trying to keep a firm hold on the container of eggs. His belly rumbled in anticipation of the meal he was about to pull from the freezer, salvage from the box and then shove in the microwave. Tucker stuffer, he liked to call the microwave, because that's what it basically did. He missed home-cooked meals, nothing could beat them and he loved cooking, but when he was on his own, he couldn't be bothered. With his chosen butter chicken and rice dinner heating up, he opened the fridge and grabbed himself a nice cold beer along with a paper bag containing two chicken wings.

'Here you go, buddy.' He leant over and tipped them into the bowl, only to have Elvis whip one onto the floor beside the bowl before Ethan even had time to straighten up. 'Hungry then?' he said. 'I wish you'd learn some table manners and not drag your food all over the floor.'

With Elvis hell-bent on chewing his dinner into oblivion, he only graced Ethan with a quick sideways glance, his paw protectively on top of the wing.

'Trust me, I ain't going to be stealing that anytime soon. I like my meat cooked.' He shook his head and smiled. 'Might see what's going on in this crazy world of ours, what do you reckon, Elvis?'

After giving his hands a thorough scrub at the kitchen sink, Ethan retrieved the remote from where he kept it on the top of the fridge and switched on the television that sat on the corner of the bench. The local news was on. He took a swig from his beer as he leant against the sink, sighing in pleasure when the golden ale washed away the day's grit from his throat. The newsreader was reporting the murder of a woman in Melbourne, apparently a crime of passion, and the prime suspect was her husband. Ethan swore beneath his breath. How a man could do such a thing to a woman, and a woman he loved at that, was beyond his comprehension. In his opinion, the son of a bitch should be locked in prison, with the key thrown away. How Alexis's father had killed his wife in cold blood, no matter what she'd done, was still something that turned his stomach.

With an ad break, his thoughts went to Alexis's beautiful face and the way she made him feel so acutely alive just by being near him. His eyes shifted from the television to his wedding ring, and then to where he could see the warm glow of the lights from the cottage rising into the sky. He wondered what Alexis was doing right now and if the ghosts of her past were haunting her. He really wished she didn't feel the need to lie to him. He could be there for her otherwise. What was she hoping to achieve, coming back here parading as someone else? He now ached to call over to the cottage to check in on her, to make sure she didn't need his support in some way or another. Should he?

The microwave beeped, saving him from his indecision, and his belly growled in response. He leapt to action, stepping over Elvis who was finishing off the last of his second chicken wing. Reaching into the nuker Ethan regretted not using the oven mitts, the container now gripped in his hands. Cursing as his fingers were almost burnt to a crisp, he tap-danced across the kitchen floor, half tripping over Elvis, and saving himself just in time before he hit the deck, then plonked the scorching container on the placemat that was permanently at the head of the table. There was something about sitting where his grandfather had sat that made him not feel so alone here. Pulling up the chair he slumped down and tucked in, the manufactured taste doing nothing for him, but at least it filled the gap.

With the news now finished and the theme song for *Home and Away* starting up, Ethan leant back in his chair and decided to drop the eggs over tonight. Spending most of his nights hulled up at the homestead because he was too worn out to do anything else, it would be a nice change to have some company, as fleeting as it might be, and especially with a woman as amazingly beautiful in every way as Alexis. But first things first, he needed to run through the dip, shave, freshen up with aftershave and put on some nice clean clothes that didn't smell of the day's work. Walking out of the kitchen and then padding down the hallway, his eyes skated over the framed black-and-white photographs of his forbearers. Everything was exactly as his grandparents had left it, a mixture of nostalgia and lack of time had stopped him from making the place more his own. That would've meant finality and he hated goodbyes. There were too many of them to give in the near future for his liking.

The floorboards creaked beneath his socked feet as he strode towards his bedroom.

*

After a simple dinner of the most delicious bacon she'd had in a long time and eggs so vividly orange she'd *Oohed* and *Ahhed* when she'd cracked them into the pan, Alexis poured herself a small glass of the tawny port Ethan had left on the coffee table beside two Ferrero

Rochers. Picking up one of the chocolates she peeled it open and popped it into her mouth, her eyes rolling back in pleasure as she bit into it. While indulging herself in her chocolate obsession, she re-read the note that she'd found beneath the bottle, inviting her to enjoy the local drop. A flutter went through her belly as she admired Ethan's neat handwriting. It was typical of him to put so much thought into the holiday house. He'd always been the one to bring a packed lunch when they went out riding for the day, not only for himself but for her too. Even back then, when boys were the farthest things from her mind, she could see he was a catch. And by golly, he had been caught. Part of her didn't want to lay eyes on the woman who got to sleep beside him every night, but that would be inevitable. Alexis couldn't help but wonder if *she* would have caught him if she'd stayed here, or if they would have grown up more like the brother and sister they'd acted like as youngsters. She sighed. It was too late to find out now.

With a heavy heart she made her way outside where the air felt cooler, crisper – such a welcome change from the heat of the day. If only she hadn't forgotten to pack her camera in her mad rush, she would have brought it out here to capture some of the magic of a country night sky. She pulled the shawl her nan had knitted her a few years back tighter around her shoulders, enjoying the comfort it brought her. Easing herself into the swing chair on the verandah she listened to the sounds of the country – crickets, the distant gentle call of cattle and the soft whinny of horses – the most alluring sound of all being the ear-ringing silence. Taking a sip of the sweet liquor and rolling it around on her tongue, she looked up at the black velvet sky sprinkled with dazzling stars – stars her mother had said were fairies flickering their wings. The memory tugged at her heart. Her mum had always been magical like that, describing things in a way that made the world an enchanted place.

But it wasn't so enchanted anymore. Being an adult could really, *really* suck.

Hot tears pressed at her eyes and the emotions she'd pushed down earlier threatened to choke her. Feeling it was time to allow them to surface, she gave way to her tears, which were heavy and in some way cleansing. The breeze picked up, sending leaves flying across the floorboards and sending a *whoosh* through the trees near the cottage. A curlew cried out, mimicking the sounds of a woman screaming. Instinctively, Alexis tugged her shawl in even tighter. Suddenly, the scent of roses filled the air and she quickly scanned the garden for sight of the striking flowers, not recalling seeing any as she'd made her way to the front door. And then she remembered how her mother had loved a perfume called Chloe Rose, and for a second her heartbeat stalled.

The scent became stronger, almost overpowering.

'Mum, are you here?' She whispered it so very softly, almost afraid of getting an answer.

The wind blew again, stronger this time. Leaves brushed over her bare feet and she lifted her legs, curling them up beneath her. The curlew called out once more. Goosebumps pricked her skin. She felt the pull she'd experienced earlier, her instincts telling her to go for a wander over to the shed. She gazed to where the corrugated-iron walls were shining beneath the silver of the half moon, and she suddenly had an urgent need to know what was inside.

As if on autopilot she placed her empty glass down on the floor and then padded across the verandah, down the steps and onto the lawn, instantly feeling herself earthed as her bare feet pressed down the blades of cool grass. She took a wide berth around where the cubby house used to be, as if she were avoiding a gravesite, finding her need to do so strange. Reaching the shed, she went to tug open the door and was instantly dragged back to that night again. To where she felt like she was thirteen years old, and terrified to her very core. Her heart pounded. Her breath caught in her throat. And then she could see it, feel it. That night, it was all around her. She and Katie were holding hands. Rain was hammering the roof of the cubby house. And then her mother's blood-curdling screams echoed, along with the sound of the gun firing in succession. She cried out, unsure of what she said. The shock of it stole her breath away as her hands went to cover her ears. And then as quickly as it had happened, the memories ceased, the heart-wrenching sounds stopped and she returned to the present with the silence she'd enjoyed only moments before now feeling unnerving.

A deep sob escaped her, and then another, until she was crying so hard it was difficult to breathe. With her shaky legs giving way she collapsed to the ground, not caring about the grit that dug into her knees. Burying her head in her hands, her tears dripped through her fingers. She couldn't remember ever crying like this. Grief overcoming her, she folded into a ball, the memory of her mother's spine-chilling screams still echoing through her head, tormenting her. She covered her ears even tighter as though back there, trying her hardest to block it all out. She didn't want to remember anything more, not for tonight anyway. But as hard as she tried, she couldn't erase the sickening sounds. The screams. The gunshots. Katie's sobs. Their feet pounding the ground as they'd run sounded like drum beats. It all twirled around and around as if on repeat. Like sharp claws the noises cut into her, tearing at her heart and soul, drawing more pain-filled sobs from deep within. So engrossed in her own world of heartache and fear, she didn't hear the four-wheel drive pull up.

*

Showered, shaved and wearing his best cologne, Ethan stepped from the Landcruiser with a wriggling Elvis in one arm and the container of eggs in the other. A quick thought as he was heading out the door, he'd scooped his fluffy friend up as an icebreaker. Every woman loved an adorable little dog to cuddle, didn't they? Heading through the cottage's front gate and down the path, his breath caught in his throat when heard Alexis's cries. Had she hurt herself? Panic fuelled his already heightened adrenaline. Quickly placing the little dog on the ground, he ran hell-for-leather to the backyard, Elvis at his feet. Sliding around the corner of the house he spotted Alexis on the ground in front of the shed, huddled up and crying her heart out.

And his heart bled with the sight.

'Lexi,' he called without thinking.

Her sobs stopped short and she sat up, her face as white as a ghost as her fear-filled eyes met his. 'Ethan.' She pulled the shawl around her trembling shoulders. 'What did you just call me?'

'I, ah ... ' He stumbled on his words. With a new person to shower with his limitless doggy love, Elvis went tearing past him like a bull at a gate. Then, leaping just short of Alexis, the bundle of fur landed in her lap, instantly lighting her face up with a smile.

'Oh, hi there, you gorgeous thing,' she said tenderly, tears still rolling down her cheeks. 'What's your name?' She gave the wriggling bundle a scratch on the belly.

'His name's Elvis ... and just like them possums I warned you about before, don't let his cuteness fool you.' Ethan stopped by her side and knelt down. Reaching into his pocket he pulled out a clean handkerchief and handed it to her, the appreciative smile on her kissable lips as she took it warming his heart. The mud on her cheek only made her more adorable. He ached to reach out and wipe it away.

She wiped at her tears and then turned back to gaze lovingly at Elvis. Stupid, but Ethan longed for her to look at him the same way.

'Oh, look at him. How could he not be all sugar and spice?' Glancing up again she caught Ethan's eyes. 'So, are you going to tell me what you just called me?'

Ethan released a heavy sigh. 'You heard exactly what I called you. Did you really think, after how we were joined at the hip as kids, that I wouldn't recognise you, Lexi?'

She just stared at him as though the cat had got her tongue. 'No, of course I didn't.'

'Why did you do it?'

'When I booked the cottage, I'd enjoyed a bit too much wine, and in a panic I gave you a false name.' Elvis was now cuddled into her neck as if he were a scarf. 'And then when I arrived you acted like you didn't know me, so I went along with it. I promise I had every intention of telling you the truth tomorrow, once I'd got over the shock of coming back here.' She wasn't about to make him privy to the fact it had annoyed her that he hadn't seemed to recognise her when he first saw her again.

'Why would you panic about telling me your real name?'

She faltered. 'Because I've always had a crush on you, and it felt weird hearing your voice after all these years.'

Reaching out, Ethan lightly brushed her arm. 'I have thought of you often over the years, too, Lexi.'

'You have?'

'No word of a lie.'

'But ... ' She shook her head slowly as though dazed.

As if reading his thoughts and sensing his longing for her, she looked away from him and towards the blackness of the night, her jaw clenching. 'I'm so sorry I lied to you, Ethan. I didn't plan to, it was just a slip of the tongue when I was drunk ... I panicked when

I heard your voice and as soon as I lied I regretted it. I shouldn't have done it.'

The fact she was being open and honest, and apologising, meant a lot to him. Gently touching her chin he turned her face back towards him. 'Shh, it doesn't matter right now ... we can talk about it all later, if you like.' He placed his hand on her cheek, her skin cold against the warmth of his. Gently, he wiped away the smears of dirt. The softness of her skin beneath his fingers sent currents of desire rushing through him and he allowed himself a few brief moments to imagine pressing his lips against hers, claiming her in a hungry, passionate kiss. 'What matters right now is if you're okay?'

She didn't answer him straight away, but instead looked into his eyes, wanting to soak in all that he could offer her, all that he already felt for her. Ever so slightly her lips curled, as if she knew everything he was thinking. Something indescribable passed between them, the depth in her sea-green eyes making him feel as though he were about to fall into her soul.

Her eyelids fluttered and she pulled herself together. 'I'm all okey-dokey.'

'You sure, because you don't really look okey-dokey?'

She bit her bottom lip, nodding. 'Mmm, I'm sure.'

'This is me you're talking to, Lexi.' He pushed some stray hair from her face, and tucked it behind her ear. 'So tell me, what happened?'

'Well, we just lost contact because life got in the way, I suppose.'

'True, but that's not what I meant. I meant what happened now, tonight, to make you so upset.'

'Oh ... ' She heaved a heavy sigh, her shoulders slumping. 'Coming back here has brought up a lot of stuff, and much quicker than I expected it to, that's all.'

'It certainly would.' His knees starting to ache from kneeling, he sat down beside her, both of them now looking at the star-studded sky. A snore escaped Elvis, who was asleep in Alexis's lap. They had a little chuckle at Elvis's expense before turning their attention back to the breathtaking beauty that was a clear country night sky.

After a few minutes of sneaking sideways glances at her perfection, his affection for her only deepening with every stolen look, Ethan broke the silence. 'Is there anything I can do to help make this easier for you?' He stretched his legs out and leant back on his palms.

'Not really, but thanks. It's something I have to do if I'm ever going to get to the bottom of it all.'

'The bottom of it all?' He couldn't hide the confusion from his face as he turned towards her. 'In what way?'

'I don't believe my father killed my mother, and I intend to prove it so he can finally rest in the peace he deserves.'

Ethan bit back the words that nearly escaped his lips. He remembered how fastidious his stepdad had been when he'd investigated the case along with the city detectives. For nights on end Peter had worked into the early hours, and days would go by without seeing him around the house, the police station becoming his home over the weeks when the case ran hot and heavy. But it would do neither of them any favours for Ethan to express his difference of opinion. Not right at this moment, anyway. Instead he said, 'Righto, and just how do you plan to do that?'

Frowning, she looked back towards the sky. 'I'm not completely sure yet.'

'That's a really good plan of attack, if I've ever heard one.'

She gave him a playful shove. 'Get stuffed.'

'And there's the old Lexi-Loo I once knew.'

Her face lit up. 'Oh no, I had forgotten about that nickname.'

'How could you forget about your favourite nickname?' he said in jest.

'Ha-ha, true.' She sucked in a breath and then pointed at him. 'And I used to call you Boof.'

'Yup, you sure did, and I loved it.'

Gently shifting Elvis to the ground beside her so as not to wake him, Alexis pulled her legs up and wrapped her arms around them. Resting her cheek on her knees, she regarded him with glistening eyes. 'You know what, now that we're older and wiser I'll let you in on a little secret.'

'I like the wiser bit, but what do you mean, older? I'm still a spring chicken.'

Alexis rolled her eyes. 'Yeah, whatevs.'

Ethan shook his head. 'So what's the secret?'

'I used to love you calling me Lexi-Loo.'

'I know you did.'

She sat up straight, her eyes wide. 'You did?'

'Yeah, of course I did. Do you really think I would have called you that if I knew you hated it?'

'Honestly, yes.' Her eyes were wickedly mischievous now.

He laughed. 'That's a bit harsh.'

'Let me guess ... ' Alexis cut in before he could finish. 'Because you've got feelings?'

'Yes, because I've got feelings ... you used to always finish my sentences.'

'And you used to always finish mine.'

'We made a good team, you and I, didn't we?'

'We sure did.'

Her hair hung long and loose over her shoulders, and she sighed in a way that made his heart pound. She went to say something, but then looked as if she couldn't get the words out.

'What are you thinking, Lexi?'

'I hadn't realised until now, just how much I've missed you, Ethan,' she said, her voice scarcely above a whisper. 'And although this is going to be a tough gig, being back here and rehashing everything that happened on the night of my parents' deaths, I'm glad we're going to get to spend some time together.'

'Yeah, me too, it'll be nice to hang out like old times.' Ethan's heart soared as if he were on the wings of an eagle, flying high above the mountaintops. 'I've really missed spending time with you.'

They stared at one another in a comfortable silence, a lifetime passing between them within a matter of seconds. If passion could have been seen with the naked eye, Ethan was sure as hell there would have been sparks flying left, right and centre. Alexis leaned so close he thought she was about to kiss him; but instead she laid her cheek against his shoulder and wriggled in closer to him. It was such a small gesture, but it touched him deep down within his soul, in a way that only Alexis ever could. Bringing his arm around her, he held her close, hoping he was easing some of the turmoil she was feeling by being back here. He could feel the warmth of her breath against his neck, and the slight tremble in it. If only he could make her feel safe like this forever – this woman deserved so much love. Subtly, he breathed her in, closing his eyes so he could savour the depth of what he was feeling for her at this very second.

'Thank you.'

His heart beat faster with the softness of her voice. 'What for?'

'For the cuddle. I needed it. I don't feel so alone now, so scared.'

'That's good, I'm glad I can help.'

'I feel like we've picked up right where we left off, Ethan.' She looked up at him. 'And I really like that.'

'I like it too.'

Would this be a bad time to kiss her?

Every inch of him craved to.

He looked down at his arm slung over her shoulder. The moonlight ignited the gold band on his wedding finger, and his heart kicked as he became painfully aware this was the first time he'd even considered kissing a woman since Jasmine had passed. He was still a married man. The harsh reality kicked in and he mentally slapped himself for his moment of weakness. He couldn't do this. As if he'd been sitting on a thorn, he moved away from her, stood, and then held out his hands. 'Here, let me help you up before we both get eaten by the mosquitos out here.'

Although she eyed him with bewilderment, she did as he asked. The feeling of her hands in his was electric, and for a brief moment, he froze, riveted by the sensation. Now she was on her feet their eyes met again, and neither of them moved. Without a moment's hesitation he took her into his arms so he didn't have to look into those beautiful eyes any longer. He gave her forehead a peck, more as a sign of mateship than anything else, and then stepped back, finally letting her go. 'I'm glad you've decided to come back for a visit, Lexi. It'll be nice to catch up on old times.'

'It will be.' And then she tipped her head to the side and asked, 'So why did you call over at this time of the night anyway?'

'Oh, just to drop off some fresh eggs.' Remembering where he'd put the container just before he'd run to Lexi's aid, he strolled over and picked it up and gave it to her.

'Aw, that's really nice, thank you.'

'I'm a nice kind of guy.' He laughed at his own expense.

But Alexis didn't smile, her eyes intent on holding his. 'Yes, you are Ethan, and always have been.' Fresh tears welled in her eyes. She blinked faster, successfully ridding them as she straightened her shoulders. Her gaze then veered away from his, at something beyond him.

Elvis came tearing in beside him, running full pelt for Alexis. Chuckling, he plucked a dancing Elvis from the ground. 'I should head back home and leave you to get some sleep.'

Drawing in a broken breath she looked to her watch and nodded. 'Yes, it's getting late,' she said. 'Hope you have a nice night's sleep.' She reached out and gave the dog a quick scratch on the head. 'That goes for you too, Elvis.'

'There's no doubt Elvis will sleep like a log, but as for me, I doubt it. I'm actually crashing in the stables tonight.'

'You are, why?'

'I've got an injured horse I want to keep my eye on.'

'That's so kind of you, Ethan.'

He shrugged off the compliment. 'All part of the job.'

'No, it's all part of you.'

That made his heart ache. Why did she have to be so damn loveable? It would be so much easier right now to dislike her for lying to him. But he couldn't bring himself to do so. For a heartbeat, and then two more, he actually considered following her into the cottage and making love to her. Invisible flames flickered and danced between them. 'I really have to get going.' He needed to move, to get away from her, before he did something he might regret. Stepping back, he took her by the hand and gave her a quick peck on the cheek. 'It's nice to see you, Lexi-Loo. Catch you tomorrow sometime.' Giving her hand a gentle squeeze he let it go.

'It's nice to see you too, Ethan ... ' Reaching out she grabbed hold of his arm, stopping him from walking away. 'Thank you for not being mad at me for lying to you ... it really means the world.'

He smiled. 'I've never been able to be mad with you, so it's not like I'm going to change now.'

'Lucky me.' Her hand dropped away. 'Night then.' She hesitated for a moment and then turned and headed towards the front door.

'Night.' He finally answered as he watched her climb the steps, feeling as if part of him was leaving with her. At the doorway she turned and glanced back at him. He saw the shimmer of tears in her eyes. But before he could lose all sense of reason and go to her, and comfort her, and love her the way he ached to love her, she thankfully closed the door, leaving the cottage shrouded in darkness. Had she seen the wedding ring on his finger? If she had, he found it strange she hadn't asked about Jasmine. Maybe she already knew his past and didn't know how to broach the subject. It certainly wasn't an easy one. He couldn't really blame her if that were the case. He found it hard enough to talk about, let alone expecting others to. Closing his eyes, he drew in a slow steady breath. Alexis Brown was here and he couldn't wait for the sun to rise so he could see her beautiful face again.

CHAPTER
16

Dawn had stolen the night away over two hours ago. Streaks of sunlight pierced through the corrugated-iron roof, spearing the dusty floor and bouncing off the wooden doors. With weariness claiming his every muscle, the stable floor not the best place to sleep anyway and especially not beside a restless horse, Ethan felt ten years older than his thirty-three years. He'd spent most of the night tossing and turning as he'd thought about Alexis and what it would be like to be *with* her, and then feeling guilty for doing so when images of Jasmine filled his mind. He knew it was fruitless, holding onto the memory of his wife, but try as he might he couldn't help but feel like he was somehow cheating on her, or betraying his love for her by acknowledging his feelings for Alexis. He'd found the strength last year to pack up all Jasmine's belongings and give them to her parents, the ring on his finger and a few keepsakes now the only things he had left that had been hers or that Jasmine had given him. Maybe, if he found the strength to finally take off the ring?

He groaned. He'd tried many times before and just couldn't bring himself to do so.

He looked through the doorway in the stables and down to the cottage. There was no sign of Alexis yet, and as much as he didn't want to feel it, he couldn't wait to see her again. He plucked his favourite bridle from the tack hook and walked out.

Ten minutes later the clip clop of the horse's hooves broke the silence of the morning as he and his stockhorse, Waylon, headed up the rise. Now at the highest point of Diamond Acres, Ethan turned in his saddle and looked out over the valley. Focussing on the paddock below where the few cattle he kept for his own supply of beef grazed on lush grass, their red coats and broad backs aglow beneath the rising sun, he smiled. He was a lucky man to call this place home. The distant cry of Rebel the Rooster made him chuckle. It looked like it was going to be a glorious day, the mountains off in the distance were a brilliant mirage against the endless blue of the sky and the few pure white clouds. He let go of a satisfied breath, his skin prickling with goosebumps. The vastness that was Diamond Acres dwarfed anything man-made, and the beauty of it all made his heart sing.

And then his thoughts went back to Alexis. She was so beautiful, inside and out, but he loved how she didn't try to flaunt her looks either. It was as if she were unaware of the magnetism she possessed, and that made her all the more appealing. Then it struck him, with his emotional battle of feeling tied to Jasmine, he hadn't even stopped to wonder whether Alexis might be in a committed relationship. She wasn't wearing a ring, but that didn't mean she wasn't spoken for. The very thought made his heart tighten. And then his thoughts went to whether she had children, or not, gathering the latter must be the case as she was here on her own. Or maybe they had a tribe of ankle biters and her doting, loving partner was back home taking care of them while she did what she needed to do. When the moment was right, he would ask her all these questions, but for now he wanted to erase the outside world and pretend it was just Alexis and him, here, at Diamond Acres.

The urge to see her was now too intense to ignore. With a subtle command, the horse did as he was asked and opened his stride, and within seconds they were galloping across the paddock at full throttle, clearing fallen tree trunks with practised ease. The cottage came into view, the iron roof gleaming in the glare of the morning sunshine. Just at the thought of being able to say good morning to Alexis, Ethan's heart soared to unbelievable heights.

*

Alexis's head felt as if it were about to explode, the throbbing behind her eyes most certainly from stress and lack of sleep. For the past hour and a half she'd laid longing for sleep to take her, a pillow over her head, as she thought about everything that had happened since she'd arrived here only eighteen hours ago. Snippets of that horrible night had stormed to the forefront of her mind, and she was keen to find out what would be revealed today. She'd also tried to fool herself into believing she was over the shock of seeing Ethan, that the quiver in her belly whenever he was near her had been nothing but nerves, and the warmth in her heart whenever she pictured his handsome face had nothing to do with an emotional connection, but she knew she was lying to herself, and that in itself terrified her. Yes, she'd harboured a crush on him since she was thirteen, but never in her wildest dreams had she imagined feeling so powerfully drawn to him, as though she had finally arrived back home. But he was married and she had to push all these thoughts aside immediately.

Donning her favourite fluffy robe and matching slippers, she shuffled down the hallway, her hair in absolute disarray and her eyes as weary as hell. Thoughts of her parents' deaths, combined with memories of her and Ethan as kids, made the perfect fuel for sleeplessness. She was finding it hard to comprehend that one minute he was cuddling her, making her feel as though nothing could harm her while she was protected in his arms, and the next he couldn't seem to get away from her quickly enough. Had he thought she was making a move on him? Is that why he'd pulled away from her? She hoped not. She would never do that with a married man. Ever. No matter what. She was just taking comfort from his support, like good friends do. Maybe he'd felt her inner desires for him, and she could do nothing about that – but it wasn't as if she was going to try to act on them. Perhaps she needed to make this very clear the next time she saw him.

But the attraction wasn't only coming from her ...

To find out that he'd thought about her all these years had been shock enough, but then to feel the chemistry between them and the irresistible pull she'd felt by his side had left her head spinning. And the way he'd looked at her, his dazzling blue eyes drawing her in and sending heat coiling low within her stomach had been almost overwhelming. It saddened her to think that as a married man he would allow such feelings to be noticeable, but then, like her, maybe he just couldn't control them. It was up to both of them to somehow ignore it all. Even so, there was something to be said about how comfortable she felt around him, and how she felt so deeply connected to him. They had spent almost a lifetime apart but the bond between them was still strong. It was something that many people wished for and never had the chance to enjoy. This made her extremely thankful for his friendship, if nothing else. What if they'd been given a chance to make a life together, would they have? Too late now.

Although she'd been sucked into the magical moment last night, and couldn't deny how deep her feelings ran for him, in the light of day she felt stronger and ready to ward off their connection. Besides the fact that he was married, her life and Ethan's were so far apart now, so different, that even if things were different it wouldn't be all roses. Rubbing her temples she tried to stop rationalising everything. She was being ridiculous. She'd come here to step back into her past, and that was it. Coffee, she needed coffee, and the stronger the better. She really hoped there was a jar of it in the breakfast basket.

On a mission to fulfil her craving for a stand-your-spoon-up kind of cuppa, something stopped her as she passed through the lounge room, as if a hand had come down to rest upon her shoulder. She paused, mid-step, and the hair on the back of her neck stood on end. She swore she could feel a presence in the room and took comfort in the thought that it could be either of her parents, or even better still, both of them. She dared not think it could be anyone else lingering in the afterlife. Alexis walked across the room to where the curtains were open, the glare of the sunshine making her squint while her eyes adjusted. Staring out the window, the same window she'd stood at while waiting for her grandpa to arrive back from town so they could start their journey to Townsville, Alexis could feel the deep sense of loss that she'd felt that cold, misty morning seventeen years ago. In a blink of an eye, the only life she had ever known had been ripped out from beneath her. What she'd give to rewind time and take her and Katie back to a day when their lives were simple, and filled with their parents' love.

Nothing would ever be able to replace that. Damn the person, or people, who had taken them from her.

Turning away from the glorious view, she tried to keep her emotions in check as she headed down the hallways and into the kitchen. A few minutes later she was walking out with an extra-strong coffee in hand, in search of some of the wonderful sunshine she'd seen filtering through every window of the cottage. Her stomach growled in protest against her liquid breakfast, but she would make something more substantial later ... first she needed to breathe in the beauty that was Diamond Acres.

Yawning, she stepped out onto the verandah. Her breath caught in her chest, the sight before her one to behold. The landscape rolled out before her, illuminated by golden warmth, the majestic horses grazing in the paddocks were entrancing. In her opinion, this was the best part of the day, and she smiled as she thought that Katie would definitely disagree. And then, just when she thought it couldn't get any better, her view was made even more captivating by the man and horse galloping at full pelt towards the cottage. The first thought that came to her mind was that Ethan was her knight in shining armour and he was coming to whisk her off into the future. She rolled her eyes at her train of thought, but then how could she not think of him in this way, at this moment? He rode tall in the saddle, his broad shoulders and his wide-brimmed hat silhouetted against the sunrise, all six foot of him bent into the wind and flowing with the horse's wide gait. Her heart gushed. He was the epitome of the manly man. Nearing the gate now, he slowed his horse to a walk, the harness jingling as the animal tossed its head and then came to a complete stop, its coat slick with sweat.

She pulled away from where she leant against the bannister and hastily tried to tame her hair. Glancing down at her ugly fluffy slippers she quickly spun around, opened the flyscreen door and kicked them off down the hallway. She turned back around just in time to see him swing down from the saddle with a sexy ease, his steps towards her assured and his swagger affecting her more than it should. So much for her being strong enough to ward off her attraction to him. She felt the touch of his stare, partly hidden by the shadows cast over his face by his hat, his magnetism so potent she couldn't look away. It was as if they were made for each other. Old souls who had spent many lifetimes together. He took off his sunglasses and flashed her a charming smile, his dimples deepening. Time stood still as their eyes met and melted into one another's. The sun chose that moment to come out from behind a cloud, lighting his handsome face in the most striking way as he strolled towards the cottage. Crinkles formed at the corners of his eyes as he reached her. And then his full, firm lips parted into another knee-buckling smile before he leant in and brushed a kiss across her cheek, leaving heat where his lips had been. She knew she was flushed now and couldn't do a damn thing about it.

'Morning, Lexi, how'd you sleep?' His tone was low, casual and so damn sexy.

'Pretty crappy, to be honest.' Holy heck, he smelt so good she was fighting not to bury her head in his chest so she could breathe in more of him. She wanted the scent of him on her, wanted to feel his breath on her ear as he whispered sweet nothings, wanted to feel his lips upon hers so she could feed on his soul as he took her to places filled with sheet-gripping ecstasy. She *really* needed to get a grip.

He took his hat off and ran a hand through tousled hair. 'Oh, bugger, that sucks. Was the bed uncomfortable?'

'Oh, no, nothing like that. It was more me, not being able to turn my bloody mind off, that's all.' Embers kissed her skin wherever his gaze rested, and if he were a single man she would have pulled him into the cottage right then and there, stripped him naked and had her wicked way with him. Almost a year without the sensual touch of a man was making her irrational.

'Anything you want to talk about, to take the load off?' He held her eyes, a long, silent moment suspended between them, one where anything felt possible.

Her heart jolted, stealing a breath from her. She suddenly felt stupid and wondered if she should raise the subject of not wanting a married man. 'Nope.' Pressing her lips together she shook her head to emphasise the fact.

'Okay, well, if you change your mind I'm all ears. Sometimes it helps to get things off your chest.'

'Thanks, Ethan, I appreciate the offer.' She eyed him steadily as her heart hammered. 'Have you had breakfast?' She swallowed over a dry throat. Breakfast between friends – there was nothing wrong with that.

'No, not yet, are you offering to make me some?'

'Well, if I wasn't, I sure as hell am now.' She matched his cheeky grin as she slowly pushed herself off the wall he'd unwittingly backed her up against, stepped inside, held the flyscreen open and invited him in with a wide sweep of her arm.

'Why, thankya,' he said as he kicked off his boots and stepped in beside her. 'So what's cooking, good looking?'

A bit forward for a married man, she thought, but then again, friends said that too, didn't they? 'Ha-ha, you crack me up ... a good old-fashioned, Sunday-style fry up, what do you reckon?'

'Sounds bloody good to me.'

Why wouldn't he be sharing a Sunday breakfast with his wife? Maybe things weren't all rosy back at the homestead. 'Yeah, me too. I'm starving.' She rubbed her grumbling belly.

'Ditto.' Ethan followed her into the kitchen. 'You want a hand?'

'Nope. You'll only get in the way ... ' She pulled a frypan from the cupboard. 'And as I recall, other than being a mean sandwich maker, you couldn't cook to save your life.' She flashed him a mischievous grin. 'So probably safer if I do it.'

'Hey, fair crack of the whip. I'll have you know I'm a brilliant cook these days.' He rested up against the kitchen bench, one leg crossed over the other, his expression playful and challenging.

'Are you now?' She took out what she needed from the fridge and placed it all on the bench.

'At least let me make us both a cuppa ... do you want a top up?'

'Yeah, please.' She glanced over her shoulder, liking the feeling of them working together. She knew she shouldn't feel this way, but as long as she kept these thoughts to herself she wasn't actually doing anything wrong.

A few minutes passed and a comfortable silence settled as they both focussed on their tasks at hand. Then brushing in beside her, Ethan placed Alexi's steaming cuppa down next to her where she was standing at the stove. There were only inches between them, and she enjoyed the way his aura seemed to dance with hers, lifting her spirits even higher, making her heart feel even warmer.

Grabbing his cup he made his way to the dining table, and spinning a chair around, he sat on it as if he were in the saddle, his forearms resting on the back of it.

He took a sip from his coffee. 'So, Lexi-Loo, what have you been doing these past seventeen years? Have I missed much?'

'Oh, you know, just living ... trying to make ends meet and at the same time make the best of everything life throws my way.'

'I wish I could have been there for you after everything happened, but that was a bit hard with the miles between us.'

'Thanks, Ethan, that means a lot.'

He cleared his throat. 'So have you got yourself a boyfriend, or husband? Any kids?'

Her heart stalled. She turned to face him. 'Why?

Looking at her over the rim of his coffee cup, he smiled. 'Just showing an interest in my friend's life, that's all. Why so defensive?'

'Nope, no partner, or kids, I'm afraid. ' She looked away from him and down to the frypan as she flipped the bacon and then cracked in three eggs, two for Ethan and one for her. 'How about you, I see you've got a wedding ring on?' Her heart took off in a wild gallop as she waited for his reply.

'Oh, yeah, um.' His voice cracked. 'My wife Jasmine died in a car accident three years ago.'

Alexis's heart almost exploded in her chest and she spun around to face him, one hand over her chest and the other covering her open mouth. 'Oh, I'm so sorry. I had no idea.'

His fingers touching the ring, his eyes looked everywhere but at her. She could see the glisten of tears, but blinking fast he held them at bay. 'I've been trying to take this off ever since, but just haven't been able to bring myself to.'

She flicked off the gas under the frypan and hurried over to him. Pulling a chair up beside him, she placed her hand on his arm. 'I can understand you not wanting to. It's a kind of closure that would be very hard for you.'

He finally looked at her. 'Yes, it is,' he said softly. 'I'll know when the time is right, and so far it hasn't been.'

'Oh, Ethan, I hate knowing you've been through such terrible heartache.'

'Thanks,' he said.

She sniffed back tears and stood up. 'Can I give you a hug?'

He stood too and opened his arms, inviting her to him. 'I reckon we could both use one, so why the hell not?'

Leaning in, they squeezed each other tight, no words needed to convey their support for one another. As much as she didn't want to allow her feelings to surface, it was out of her control. She genuinely felt for him, losing a loved one to such tragic circumstances. She knew all too well what that felt like, and she understood the amount of time it took to heal from such a loss. One never did completely. But, within his arms, it felt as if the future she'd dreamt of was promised within them, and this was exactly where she needed to be, where she belonged. If only life were that simple. She tried to ignore the voice of reason in her mind as she felt his warmth, and his strength, appreciating the way he made her feel safe and cared for, and loved. Ethan had always made her feel this way. But now, with the wisdom of life behind her, she knew exactly what this was. This, right here, was soul-deep love, the kind of love you fought for and fantasised about. She also understood that his heart, although reaching for hers, was also still with Jasmine, and she knew that until he really let his wife go, he would never be able to truly love again.

She glanced up at him. Even though his eyes conveyed a deep sadness, he remained her pillar of strength, soothing her with his tender touch. Then his arms loosened, but only a little. Not wanting him to let her go just yet, she breathed sigh of relief that he remained holding her. Placing a tender, lingering kiss on her forehead he hugged her for a few moments longer before he brought his hands to cup her face.

'It makes me so mad that you lost your parents the way you did, Lexi. Life can be so fucking unfair.' His voice shook and he closed his eyes for a moment as if he were squeezing back tears. 'I know now what it feels like to have a loved one taken from you way too soon. So please remember that I am here for you any time you need me, okay?'

The moment so very poignant, tears rolled down her cheeks. 'As I am for you, Ethan.'

A rush of love filled her, her heart breaking for this man. It was then she realised that something deep and buried in her was also deep and buried in him – they were kindred souls, always had been and always would be. No matter what came of her visit here, Ethan would always be special to her, like no one else ever could be. Emotions swarmed her but she swallowed down a sob, not wanting to distress him any more than she already had. 'I'm so sorry, Ethan. I should be the one comforting you here, not the other way around,' she whispered, wishing she could rest her cheek on his chest.

'Don't apologise. I know your heart breaks for what I went through, and that's enough for me. I want to be here for you now that I can be, because I so badly wanted to be there for you when your ... ' He stopped as if afraid to say the words out loud for fear of hurting her. 'It's just ... ' He shrugged. 'My mum, she's ... ' His hands dropped from her face and he spun around.

'Ethan?' The fall of his shoulders as he buried his face in his hands told her he was fighting other battles she didn't know of. Placing her hand on his shoulder she gently coaxed him to turn around and face her. 'Is your mum okay?'

'No, she's ... ' He cleared his throat. 'She's only got a few weeks to live.'

'Oh, Ethan, I'm so sorry.' She wrapped her arms around him. 'Cancer?'

She felt him nod. Her hug tightened. 'I'm so sorry ... ' What else was there to say? 'Would you mind if I went to visit her while I'm here?'

'Of course not, she'd actually really like that, Lexi. She's always had a soft spot for you.' Ethan stepped back, his arms still loosely around her. 'I'm heading over there this arvo, if you want to come too?'

'I'd love to, thanks.' She sniffled, and as much as she tried to fight it back, a tear ran down her cheek. 'It's so sad. I've always loved your mum. She was so kind to me.'

Perhaps trying to snap himself out of it, Ethan sucked in a deep breath and leant back from her. 'Sorry, Lexi, I don't mean to put all my shit onto you.'

'Don't be stupid. You're my friend. I want you to talk to me so I can help you through it.'

'Thanks, that means the world.' He sighed as he raked his hands through his hair. 'I'm usually not a big sook like this. I think I'm just overtired. What with Grandma dying two months back and Grandad in the home now, and ... '

She sucked in a noisy breath, stopping him midsentence.

He shook his head as though confused. 'What?'

'Is Charlie still alive?'

'Yeah,' he said. 'Oh, you thought because I had this place, that he was ... ?'

'Uh-huh.'

'It's a long story, but to cut it short, he's been diagnosed with dementia so he's had to go into a home, and because he knows it won't be too long before he can't make rational decisions, he asked for his will to be executed now.'

'Oh, poor Charlie. That's horrible.'

'Yeah, it's been a pretty rough couple of months.'

'Sounds like it, no wonder you're emotional.'

'Believe me, I don't like being like this.'

'Well, sometimes you just have to be, Ethan, you can't be rock solid all the time, it's not good for you.' She reached out and gave his hand a squeeze. 'Please feel safe to let it all out around me. You know I'm not going to judge you for crying. I lost Grandpa to cancer, so I know what if feels like to watch a loved one fade away from that terrible disease.'

'Oh, Lexi, I'm so sorry. Is your nan still alive?'

She shook her head sadly. 'Nope, she passed away two weeks later from a heart attack. I reckon it was because she was heartbroken losing Grandpa. They loved each other so much.'

'Wow, that's beautiful and sad at the same time.'

'Sure is.' She graced him with a tender smile.

He returned it, the gesture in sharp contrast to the deep hurt in his eyes. 'You're the most generous soul I've ever met, Lexi, worrying about me when you're here to fight your own battle. I just wish there was something I could do to make it easier for you.'

She placed her hands over his, her tears now from the depth of care this man had for her, the tenderness in his eyes melting her heart. 'Just by being near you, you're helping me.'

'Good, I'm glad. It's just a shame it's only for a few days.'

'It sure is.'

He wiped at her tears. 'It breaks my heart seeing you cry.'

'It does?' Her voice was barley audible, the intensity of the moment stealing it away from her.

Then, without warning, he brought his lips to hers. They felt even better than she'd imagined they would, his kiss hard but tender. With a growing intensity he clutched her hips, closing any distance left between them, every inch of his torso pressing into her. Quivering, she relished the way his body felt hard up against her own, loving the way she could feel the erratic beat of his heart against hers. She wound her arms around him, feeling the muscles tensing in his back. The kiss was sweet and soft at first, but then quickly became deeper, urgent, hungry, their tongues twirling around one another's in an erotic dance. She traced her fingers up his back and then, her hands needy, she clutched at his hair. His low growl made her shiver from head to toe. Grabbing a handful of her hair, he gently tipped her head back and slid his lips down her neck, his teeth grazing her skin in exactly the right way, making her quiver all over. As if a match had just been dropped her desire burst to sizzling life and her connection with this gorgeous hunk of man intensified. This was no longer a childhood crush, a fantasy she harboured to get her through the lonely days; it was more, way more. His hands were back on her hips now, growing more and more possessive of her. He raised his face back to hers and she saw his eyes were intense, hungry, as if spellbound by her. And then he kissed her again, his hands clutching at the nape of her neck, giving more life to their unspoken love. How in the hell was she going to find the strength to drive away from Diamond Acres, and him, again ... this time with her hands on the wheel?

Part of her panicked about the utter heartache she knew she would feel, as well as the fact he still wore his wedding ring – somehow making her feel as though she were cheating with a married man. There was split-second's hesitation in her touch, her kiss, but before she had time to think more about it, Ethan's hands dropped from her waist and he took a step back. He was so in-tune with her, so in touch with her, it blew her away. But this was one moment when she didn't want him to listen to her feelings.

She almost cried out, to beg him not to stop. 'I'm sorry,' she whispered. 'I didn't expect this to happen when I came here, and I'm just scared, that's all.'

He nodded softly. 'Me too.' His eyes filling with anguish, he took her by the hands. 'I don't want us to rush into this, Lexi. As much as I want to tear your clothes off and make sweet, hungry, endless love to you, I also want it to be for all the right reasons. I would rather keep you as my friend for life, than do something stupid we may regret, something that might ruin the strong bond we share. I need to be able to take my ring off, and truly let go of Jasmine, before I do anything like this with you.'

'I understand.' Unable to hold his kind eyes any longer, she looked down at the floor.

He gently tipped up her chin. 'Let's not ruin the good vibes between us with an *amazing* kiss, though, huh?'

'Amazing doesn't cut it,' she said cheekily.

'I agree.' He smiled now, warm and tender. 'How about we go for a ride after breakfast?'

'That's the best damn idea I've ever heard.'

He pulled her into a hug. 'We'll have a great time, I'll make sure of it ... I promise'

She hugged him tighter. She didn't doubt his promise for a second.

CHAPTER
17

'I can't believe you didn't tell me where you'd be staying before you left, Sis.'

'I know, I'm sorry, Pebbles. I just didn't want to worry you any more than you already were.'

'Apology accepted,' Katie said softy. 'So nothing has jogged your memory about anything substantial yet?'

'No, not really. Other than the flashbacks I mentioned, of us jumping out the window and running to Mister King's house, there's been nothing.' Alexis didn't want to tell Katie about remembering their dad yelling or their mother's screams. She was still trying to deal with that herself.

'Bugger, that sucks.'

'Pretty much sums it up.' Alexis wished she had more to tell. Katie sounded as disappointed as she felt. 'But don't give up hope yet, Pebbles, I've still got a few days, and I'm wondering whether going into the homestead might jog something in my memory, seeing as that's where I fell down the stairs.'

'True. When are you going there?'

'As soon as it feels right. I can't really just invite myself to Ethan's house, can I?'

'Why the hell not?'

'Because I'm not as forward as you are, Katie.'

'Well, you're on limited time, Lexi, so you might just have to find a way to be forward.'

'I'll do it in my own time, but thanks for the pep talk.' She sighed. 'Look, I know this might sound weird, but I can feel Mum and Dad around the house, like their spirits are still here waiting for the truth to come out. I have a really strong feeling it will, as long as I don't rush it. If needs be I can always come back again.'

'You sure it's not just your wishful thinking playing tricks, feeling like Mum and Dad are still there?'

'Maybe, maybe not ... all I do know for sure is that I have to follow my gut, and do whatever feels right at any given time while I'm here.'

'Following your gut, hey? Interesting. So, seeing as you now know Ethan is a single man, tell me, have you kissed him yet?'

'Of course not. He is still trying to get over losing his wife.' Feeling guilty for succumbing to the moment this morning, there was no way on earth Alexis was going to kiss and tell. She certainly wasn't going to tell Katie over the phone anyway. She'd fill her in on Friday when she was back home.

'I know he would be, but as you and I know, life also has to go on after losing a loved one. The poor bloke is in his thirties and he hasn't even had kids yet. Maybe you can help him with that?'

'Katie!'

Katie laughed and Alexis couldn't help but laugh along with her. 'You're wicked, Pebbles.'

'I like to think I am. Is he good looking?'

'He's pretty easy on the eye.'

'How easy?'

'Oh bloody hell, you don't give up, do you?'

'Nope.'

'He's extremely easy on the eye.'

'Ooooo, noice.'

A knock at the front door sent Alexis into a mad flurry, the bed behind her now covered in all the clothes she'd tried on and then decided were either too much, or not appropriate for horse riding. Now she was standing there dressed in the first things she'd tried on, over half an hour ago. The woes of being a woman. 'I gotta run, Ethan's here to take me riding. I can't believe Wild Thing is still here.'

'Oh, how romantic. I'm happy you'll get to give your boy a hug. And your horse too, I might add.'

Alexis rolled her eyes. 'Stop it.'

'Never.' Katie's laugh was devilish.

'Bye, Pebbles, chat again tomorrow. Love you.'

'Bye, Lexi, love you too. And don't do anything I wouldn't do now, will you?'

'Ha-ha, that's not leaving me much.'

'Exactly my point.'

'Yeah, I gathered that.'

Another knock sounded, this time louder as Ethan called out her name. She loved hearing it roll off his tongue.

Pushing her face up against the security screen of her bedroom window, she called out, 'Hey. Sorry, come in, I won't be long.' First a phone call to Henry to let him know she was fine, and then the one to Katie, she hadn't got ready as quickly as she'd planned.

'Rightio. Should I make myself a cuppa and put my feet up?' There was a hint of playfulness in his voice and it made her heart flutter.

'You're a smart arse, and no, I'll only be a couple of minutes.' She sat down on the end of the bed to pull her socks on.

That done in record time, she went back to the full-length mirror. She was quietly satisfied with her reflection, although at the same time she wished she had less hips and more boobs. Yanking her hair up into a tight ponytail, she quickly applied some strawberry-scented lip-gloss. While trying not to slip around on the polished timber floors in her socked feet, she picked up her trusty old boots from the floor of the cupboard and hightailed it down the hallway. It had been a couple of years since she'd dressed in her country gear, and that had been for a rodeo passing through Townsville. It felt good to be wearing it for a ridgy-didge reason this time round.

'Wow, you've scrubbed up all right, Miss Cowgirl.' Ethan stood in the middle of the lounge room looking sexy as hell in his faded denim jeans, check shirt and well-worn boots. The appreciative expression in his eyes as he looked her up and down made her heart do a happy jig.

'I've always scrubbed up all right as a cowgirl.'

'True that,' he said with a nod.

'Did you get Wild Thing saddled up?' Alexis asked as she tugged her boots on.

'Sure did, and I even made us some corned beef sangas for lunch.'

'Wow, nice. Fresh or canned?'

'Fresh, of course.' He gave her a grin to say otherwise.

'Onion?'

'Of course, and pickles ... just how you like it.'

'Yes, I sure do, but I can't believe you remember.'

'Of course I do.' He looked at her as if she'd just said the most ridiculous thing ever.

Alexis's heart swelled even more. 'It didn't take you long to do all of that.'

'I'm a doer, I don't muck about. I even packed an icy cold beer each, to wash them down with.'

This man was one in a million. 'You always think of everything, don't you?'

'I try to.'

Boots on, she clapped her hands together. 'Right, let's do this, shall we?'

'Oh yes, we shall,' Ethan said in a very posh English accent, making Alexis laugh with him.

Stepping from the coolness of the cottage out into the heat of the day was like stepping into an oven, the air was so thick and humid it was almost difficult to draw a breath. Putting her sunglasses on Alexis looked to where the mid-morning sunshine blazed fiercely in the wide, sapphire-blue sky. Feeling the rising temperature, she knew it was heading towards one scorcher of a day. She was thankful that Ethan had suggested she wear her swimmers under her jeans and long-sleeved shirt, because a dip in the dam was going to be necessary. It was typical of North Queensland to be so hot in January.

Climbing up and into the saddle with practised ease, Ethan let his legs dangle and then held out his hand. 'Here, let me help you up.'

A hunky man on a fine horse, wanting to whisk her off ... Alexis's heart beat faster. She enjoyed the firmness of his fingers entwined in hers as she put the tip of her boot into the stirrup and then launched up and over behind him, the horse staying rock solid as she did.

'He's a good boy,' she said as she wrapped her arms lightly around Ethan's waist.

'He is, especially when there's ladies about. But he can be a right shithead when its just me and him, likes to push the boundaries.' He pulled Alexis's arms in tighter. 'But that's why I like him, he challenges me.'

She felt Ethan give his horse a subtle cue and they were galloping across the paddock she'd watched him appear from earlier this morning. The thunder of the horse's hooves and the wind whipping past her made her feel so alive, so free, so happy, as too did Ethan's company. Before she knew it Ethan brought the horse to a stop at the stable doors.

'Holy crap, that was quick.'

'Told you I don't muck about.' He helped her slide off before dismounting like he was stepping off a curb. 'You ready?'

'Yup.'

With her heart going a million miles a minute, she walked into the shade of the stables, her eyes taking a while to adjust to the dim light. Ethan stayed right beside her, his presence calming and comforting. She wiped her hands on her jeans as trickles of sweat rolled down her back and between her breasts. And there he was, her best friend, her soul mate in a horse, the animal who had given her so much without expecting anything in return. Her Wild Thing. At sixteen hands high, with a gleaming back coat and strong muscular frame, he was as striking as she remembered, maybe even more so. A rush of love overcame her and she stood glued to the spot, her eyes fixed on him. She felt like she was finally home, back to her roots, back to where she'd once been happy and carefree. She'd loved this horse so much, and like anything in life she'd loved and lost, she'd pushed her emotions to the backburner so she didn't have to deal with the pain of losing him. But now, unlike her mum and dad, her nan and grandpa, she had him back.

'Wild Thing,' she whispered. 'How have you been, buddy?' She stepped towards him, the scent of him earthy and familiar. She noted the grey dusting his muzzle. Like her, her boy had grown older and she felt sad that she hadn't been able to spend the past seventeen years with him. But she was with him now, and that was more than she could ask for.

Lifting his head, the horse looked at her and neighed softly. Then moving forwards he came to rest his head on her shoulder and proceeded to nibble her ponytail, just like he had when Alexis was a teenager.

Her heart soared so high she felt dizzy. 'Oh wow, Ethan, he remembers me.' She smiled from ear to ear as she wrapped her arms around Wild Thing's neck and buried her face into his silky coat.

'Of course he remembers you, Lexi, you're not an easy woman to forget, trust me.'

Alexis couldn't reply, the lump in her throat making it impossible to speak without sobbing. Ethan's heartfelt words made the moment all the more special.

She gave Wild Thing's muzzle a gentle kiss. 'So are you ready to go for a gallop?' Longing to feel the connection they'd always had when she was riding in the saddle or bareback, she couldn't wait to feel the wind against her face as they flew across the paddocks of Diamond Acres and into the rugged bushland surrounding it.

Wild Thing nodded as though understanding every word she said. She smiled, and catching the loving expression in Ethan's eyes as he looked on, she suddenly felt like the luckiest woman alive to be here, surrounded by so much love.

If only she could stay longer than five days.

A few minutes later, with Ethan riding closely beside her, the jaw-dropping landscape demanded all her attention. The horses' breaths were slow and steady, their clip-clops rhythmic, mesmerising. Back in the saddle again after so long, Alexis felt on top of the world. In every direction, for as far as she could see, were lush green paddocks dotted with brumbies and bordered by the spectacular blue-tinged mountain ranges that circled the township of Blue Ridge as if embracing it. There wasn't a cloud in the sky, only the occasional bird against the wide expanse of blue. Off in the distance, two eagles circled as if dancing together above a cliff where she imagined their nest to be. Even at a slow walk she could feel the strength of Wild Thing beneath her, his muscles expanding and contracting with each smooth stride. Reaching down she stroked his neck, marvelling at his magnificence. It really had been way too long.

They rode like this for a good hour, across the paddocks, into the bushlands, and up and down bumpy dirt tracks. Their conversation was easy and free flowing, and the silences were ones that didn't need to be filled. It was only once they were heading back in the direction they'd come that Alexis felt the hunger pains bite and her need to dip her sweaty body in the dam suddenly became insistent.

'You ready to pick up the pace, Lexi-Loo?'

Ethan's deep husky voice broke the silence nicely. 'Only if you're up for the challenge of seeing who gets to the dam first,' she said and flashed him a grin.

'Okay, you're on.' With the flick of the reins Ethan and his horse were off, getting a decent head start.

With hands and heels Alexis urged her mate onward and Wild Thing opened his stride and quickly headed in the direction she was guiding him. Her hips sprung into motion with his steps, the sensation of human and horse moving together making her heart and spirit sing. She pulled her ponytail out and her hair blew into a frenzy, some strands whipping across her face and making it hard to see, but she didn't care – Wild Thing knew the way. The horse's mane blew in the wind, making him appear even more majestic. Closing her eyes, she inhaled the fresh country air, feeling free, unbounded and fully connected to horse and earth, as if they were all one. She took great satisfaction in not needing to know exactly where they were going, the destination unimportant, unlike her usually busy life where her days were run on a schedule. Here, she felt free to live totally in the moment. Exhilaration filled her as Wild Thing jumped a small pile of rocks and, experiencing a split-second of weightlessness as if they were flying, she laughed out loud. Blinking against the breeze, she then opened her eyes and noticed the graceful curve of the long grass as it bent to the wind, reminding her how she had to learn to bend and flow with each moment of life, good and bad, to be able to get the most out of it and move forwards.

Without her needing to encourage him, Wild Thing pressed on even harder, as if in a race with his mate. She couldn't help but admire his grit and determination. Up ahead, a mob of kangaroos paused, all eyes on the two horses thundering towards them, and then they were off, bounding across the paddock in search of safe ground. Windswept, Alexis licked her lips, her throat feeling parched. The glimmer of the dam came into view, the surface looking as if it were sprinkled with diamonds. About ten metres in front of her, Ethan pulled his horse to a stop and then spun around, the victorious grin on his face letting her know in no uncertain terms he'd won the race. She slowed Wild Thing and gave Ethan the finger, her smile brazenly cheeky. He pretended to be wounded by her gesture by clutching at his heart, his lips teasingly turned downwards.

'Bit of a sore loser, hey?' Ethan said as she reached him.

'Nope, I'll have you know I let you win, so I've got nothing to be sore about.'

'Oh, is that so?'

'Yup.' Alexis fought off the smile that begged to dance upon her lips.

'And why would you let me win?'

'Just because I'm so nice.'

'Yeah right, not buying it.'

Reaching down, Alexis pulled her water bottle from the pocket of the saddlebag. Then rode up to the edge of the dam so Wild Thing could have a drink too.

'You know me way too well ... ' She turned in her saddle to flash Ethan a sassy grin. 'I can't hide a bloody thing from you, can I?'

'I do, don't I? So no, you can't hide a thing.' He brought his horse Waylon up alongside her. Taking his sunglasses off, he looked around. 'Gorgeous here, isn't it?'

'It sure is.' She gazed at the mirror-like water that was reflecting the trees surrounding it. A duck landed, causing the clear reflection to ripple. Water lilies flowered in clusters across the surface: red, pink and white. 'And so peaceful.' She pulled her own sunglasses to the top of her head so she could drink in the true beauty of Mother Nature. 'I remember spending so much time here as kids ... so many happy memories. We always stopped here for a dip when we were out riding, and that was nearly all the time, wasn't it? Apart from when we were at school or doing chores.'

'It was our spot where we could get away from the world and just have some fun, hey?'

'Yup.' She nodded slowly. 'And you know what, it still is.'

Ethan gave her a slow smile. 'That's a nice way to look at it.'

'It's exactly as I remembered it, other than the trees being way taller now.' Grabbing her hair tie from around her wrist, she pulled her windswept hair back up into a ponytail.

'Do you remember that day you lost your mum's favourite bangle, and you were terrified you were going to get into big trouble for wearing it in the first place?'

Alexis only needed a few seconds to recall the memory, and her heart cartwheeled when she did. 'Oh, that's right. You spent a good part of the morning diving to the bottom of the dam until you found it.' She caught his eyes. 'You always looked after me, didn't you?'

'I had a massive crush on you, so of course I did.'

'I always thought it was because you saw me more as a sister.' Alexis licked her dry lips, noticing how Ethan watched her do it.

'So did I, until the morning you all drove away ... that's the day I realised just how much you meant to me.'

'Why didn't you ever tell me how you felt about me?'

Ethan looked mortified. 'Because you were thirteen, and not at an age to know things like that.'

'Yeah, very true. Good point.'

'And I was a naïve sixteen-year-old who really had no idea about girls, or what it felt like to be falling for one.'

'Oh, Ethan, that's so sad and so beautiful. '

'Yup, my heart was broken for ages, and to be honest I don't think it ever really healed ... even when I met Jasmine.' He looked away from her and the atmosphere changed around them. 'There was, and still is, a piece of it that you own, Lexi, and you always will, no matter what.'

'I think I can say the same for you, Ethan.'

He went to say something more but then stopped. He seemed so surprised and taken aback that if Alexis weren't sitting in the saddle she would have wrapped her arms around him.

His horse fidgeted and Ethan settled him with a light tug on the reins. 'Are you sure you're not just being nice?'

'Why do you find it so hard to believe that you're very special to me?'

'Because after you left I wrote you letter after letter, every week, for a year.'

'You did ... why didn't you ever post them to me?' Alexis said.

'I did.' His brows furrowed to the point he almost looked angry.

'Well, don't shoot the messenger but I never got any of them.' Alexis held a hand up.

'What?' he said, filled with confusion.

'I never got them.'

'Yeah, sorry, I heard you the first time, it's just ... ' He rubbed at his five o'clock shadow. 'So I suppose that would explain why you never wrote back.'

'I didn't reply to your letters because I never got them in the first place, but I did write you a couple after I left here and I was heartbroken when I never received one back from you.'

'Shit, really? I'm so sorry. I never got them, Lexi. Of course I would've replied to a letter from you. It would have made my day, actually, no scratch that, my fucking year, to get a letter from you. '

'What in the hell happened to them all then?' Now it was her turn to sound confused. 'What address did you send them to?'

'I'm not sure. I gave them to Grandma to post.'

In an instant everything fell into place. 'I always knew your grandma wasn't fond of me or Katie, but I didn't think she'd stoop that low.' Something twinged deep down in her belly and Alexis couldn't shake a feeling of unease.

'Now hang on a minute, we don't know it was her fault they didn't make it to you.' Ethan looked pissed off. 'Maybe they went missing at your end.'

Her grandpa had meant everything to her, so Alexis's defences fired to life. 'Are you saying that Grandpa deliberately didn't post them, and even worse, hid the ones from you to me?'

'Possibly. How do you know for certain that he didn't?'

'Because he wouldn't have done that to me, or to you, for that matter. He's the one who encouraged me to write them in the first place, because he knew how much I missed you.' She knew she shouldn't really say what was on the tip of her tongue, but ... 'Whereas I can't say the same for your grandma.'

'Oh, come on now, that's a bit harsh, Lexi.'

'Sorry, Ethan, but she made it very clear she didn't like any of us, my mum and dad included, so what am I meant to think?'

'Fair enough, if that's how you feel, but to be honest I don't remember her ever being mean to you and Katie.'

'She wasn't blatantly mean, but ... ' Alexis stopped short. This was going to get them nowhere, and she felt bad speaking of the dead. 'Sorry, Ethan.'

'That's okay,' he said, sucking in a breath. 'I suppose we'll never know what happened to all our letters, so we should just let sleeping dogs lie, don't you think? It's not worth an argument.'

'Yeah, agreed.'

Ethan turned his attention back to the glimmering dam. 'Well, then. Let's get our arses in there and have some fun.'

Although she was still curious, and annoyed Ethan would lay blame on her grandpa, Alexis smiled through it. 'Let's.'

With the horses settled under the shade of a tree, Ethan was the first to strip down to his undies in what felt like a matter of seconds, his boots and clothes tossed in a heap beside him.

Alexis swore she could feel her pupils dilate in gratification of seeing him in next to nothing while still wearing his hat like only a true-blue stockman would. 'Keen to have a swim then?' Grinning, she kicked off her boots.

'My bloody oath I am.'

Alexis fought to keep her eyes from the magnificence that was all of him: the bulging muscles of his arms, his strapping shoulders, his burly chest scattered with just the right amount of hair and a tattoo that accentuated its strength, his narrow waist and a six-pack worthy of kissing for hours, and the fine scattering of dark hair just above his jocks that would lead down to his ...

Her body instinctively shivered with the thought of making love to him.

She mentally slapped herself. This train of thought was doing her no favours, other than making her extremely sexually frustrated. Super shy about letting him see her in her bikinis, she turned, and with her back now to him, she tugged off her socks and jeans, and then unbuttoned her shirt. Shrugging it off, she let it drop to the ground. When she turned back around, he was still standing there, staring at her. The desire-fuelled look in his eyes sent heat coursing through her body. Her face flushed. She bit her lip. She wanted to sashay over to him, rip those damn Bonds jocks from him and then have him take her however he wanted to. If only she had the courage, she might have done just that, but instead, she stood there, feeling ablaze beneath his eyes.

As if snapping himself out of his trance, Ethan cleared his throat and then glanced over towards the water. 'How about last one in has to cook dinner tomorrow night?'

'Why not tonight?'

'We'll probably be back late from visiting Mum, so if you like, we can just buy some takeaway on the way home.' He grinned, then took off like a bull at a gate, not even giving her time to answer.

Rising to the challenge Alexis tore up behind him, waving as she overtook him, and then dived into the dam with an almighty splash, almost losing her bikini top in the process.

Ethan followed closely behind, only giving her a second to put her breasts back where they belonged.

When he emerged from the depths of the water she gave him a playful shove. 'What's for dinner tomorrow night then, loser?'

'Beef stroganoff.'

'Oh my gosh, yum. That's my favourite.'

'Yeah, I know.'

'You remember that?'

'Sure do.' He dunked under, disappearing out of sight.

Twenty seconds later, Alexis started to panic when there was no sign of him, and no air bubbles rising to the surface. She called out his name once, twice, three times. Doggy paddling, she spun left and right, just about to call out his name again when there was a tug on her foot and in a *whoosh* she was swept beneath the water. He tugged her to him, hugging her as they rose to the surface.

'You're a shithead,' she said, wiping her eyes and enjoying the feel of his arms that were still tightly wrapped around her waist.

'Don't you mean Boof-head?'

'Yeah, that too.'

'Well, I like to live up to my reputation, you know.'

Their eyes met and held, and just when she thought he was going to kiss her, his arms dropped from around her waist and he flopped backwards so he was floating. 'Do you remember how we used to see who could float the longest before turning into a prune?'

She followed suit and drifted beside him. 'I sure do and from memory, I always won.'

'If my memory serves me correctly, I always *let* you win.'

'Oh, you did not. I'm not buying that for a second.' She turned her head so she was looking at him, and he smiled.

'That's my line, Lexi-Loo.' His hand met with hers, and without saying another word he took hold, his fingers sliding around hers perfectly. And then they just floated, hands clasped, her long hair spread out around her. Time passed blissfully.

That was, until her belly grumbled loudly.

Ethan gave her hand a gentle squeeze and then let go. 'By the sounds of it I reckon it's time to hop out and eat, don't you?'

She lightly rubbed her belly. 'Sounds like it, doesn't it?'

They swam to the bank and climbed out.

'Shit.'

'What?'

'How are we going to dry ourselves?' Alexis remembered she hadn't thought to bring a towel.

Ethan pointed to the glowing sun high up in the clear blue sky. 'That big shiny thing up there should do the trick.'

Alexis rolled her eyes. 'Oh, ha-ha.'

Pulling a blanket from the saddlebag, Ethan shook it out and then spread it down on the ground. And before Alexis knew it, he had their sandwiches and two beers out waiting for them to enjoy lunch. She plonked down beside him, positioning herself so her little belly rolls weren't too visible. He passed her a sandwich that looked like it had half the fridge on it.

'No way. How am I going to get my mouth around that?'

'Easy, watch and learn.' Mouth wide, he took a bite.

Alexis was still staring at the skyscraper of a sandwich. 'I thought you said you'd made corned beef sangas?'

'I have ... with lettuce, tomato, beetroot, cheese, cucumber ... and most importantly of all, mustard pickles.'

'That's mighty impressive.'

'Yeah, I thought so. It's a special occasion, having you here for lunch, so I decided to make the most of it.'

'That's really sweet of you, Ethan. Thanks.' Alexis had had her fair share of expensive dinners bought for her, and they were always nice, but this, right here, was warming her heart in a way no other meal could. She took a bite and after a couple of chews her eyes almost rolled back in her head in pleasure.

'This is the most amazing corned beef sandwich I've ever had,' she said.

'Ain't it ever?'

Then they ate in silence, only chatting again as they washed it down with their beer.

Spotting a familiar rivergum, Alexis's eyebrows shot up as she pointed the neck of her beer bottle towards it. 'Hey, I remember that tree.'

'You do?' Ethan's slow sexy smile let her know he knew exactly what she was referring to.

'Of course ... that's the one we engraved our initials into.'

'Is it?'

Now he was playing with her and she knew it. She jumped up and in five long strides she was standing beside the gum's massive trunk. Up on her tippy-toes she ran her hand over the initials carved into in the bark, her heart skidding to a stop when she noticed the love heart that now connected hers and Ethan's initials.

'Yes, I did that, many years ago, but please don't let the cat out of the bag because I got me a rough tough reputation to uphold round these here parts.' Ethan's voice soothed over her.

She turned to him, her heart now beating way faster than normal. Nothing had prepared her for the tenderness she was feeling for this fascinating man.

He walked towards her now, holding a bright yellow wildflower in his hand. Reaching her, he tucked it behind her ear, his fingers lingering on her cheek for a few seconds. 'I like the way I can make you smile like that.'

She gently tucked the flower in. 'How am I smiling?'

'Like you're on cloud nine.'

'That's probably because I am.'

'Good, you deserve to be.' He took her by the hand. 'Come lay with me.'

Although she ached to be skin on skin with him, doing things that would send her into a state of euphoria, she tensed, the ring that shone like a beacon on his wedding finger reminding her of his commitment to another.

As if sensing her hesitation, Ethan gave her a knowing look. 'Don't worry, I just want to hold you.'

Resting in the shade of the trees, Alexis snuggled into him, his bare chest feeling like heaven against her cheek. She sunk into him, her body relaxing with his gentle touch. Being in his arms felt so right, so much like home to her that she wished she could lay like this forever. She gazed up at the twisting branches, heavy with leaves, as the dappled sunlight flickered through and danced across her face. The song of the frogs near the water added to the serenity, as too did Ethan's slow steady breath. She felt herself drifting, more and more, until she was teetering on the edge of sleep, and then she fell, softly, peacefully ...

CHAPTER
18

Ethan woke with a start. Raising his arm, he squinted to see his watch. He swore out loud. Alexis stirred beside him; his other arm that had been wrapped around her the past couple of hours was now numb. With sleep-heavy eyes she looked up at him, and the smile that spread across her face when their eyes met made him want to stay there forever.

'Hey, you.' Her voice was merely a whisper.

He brushed a strand of hair from her cheek. 'Hey, you. Good sleep?'

'Sure was.' She stretched with the grace of a cat. 'Talk about sleeping like a log ... how long have we been out for the count for?'

'About two hours.'

She shot up to sitting. 'Holy crap, really?' Her hair was in complete disarray and it made her even sexier in his eyes. 'What time is it?'

'Almost five-thirty.'

'We must have needed it. Well, I know I did anyway.'

'Touché.' He sat up. 'As much as I'd love to stay here to watch the stars appear, we have to get a shift on. We're supposed to be at Mum's right about now.'

'Can you call her to let her know we'll be late?'

'Onto it.' He jumped up. Grabbing his jeans he dug his mobile out of the back pocket.

Alexis stood and walked over to her pile of clothes. 'Have you told her I'm coming along too?'

Ethan couldn't tear his eyes from her alluring curves, and didn't even try to when she turned to catch him perving. He closed the distance between them. 'No, I didn't. I thought it might be a nice surprise.' She went to say something but he held his finger to his lips as the phone was answered.

'King's residence.'

'Hey, Peter.'

'Ethan, are you almost here? I'm just about to put dinner on the table.'

Peter had been cooking? Ethan almost fell over backwards. 'You've cooked dinner?' Maybe, for once in his life, the chat they'd had the other night had actually sunk in.

'I sure have. Roast pork and all the trimmings, on the weber of course, the kitchen's no place for a bloke.'

Ethan loved being in the kitchen, but he bit his tongue. He had to give credit where credit was due. 'Right, well, we'll be there in about half an hour.'

'Bugger me, that long?'

'Sorry, we got a bit tied up here.' Glancing at Alexis he couldn't wipe the look of satisfaction from his face. A wispy smile tugged at her lips, making him crave taking her into his arms so he could kiss her, hard and passion-filled.

'Who's we, Ethan? You got a lady friend you haven't told us about?'

Damn. Ethan could have slapped himself. Talk about foot in mouth. 'Oh, yeah, I wasn't going to say anything, so I could surprise Mum. Alexis is here, visiting.'

'Alexis Brown?' Peter sounded as shocked as Ethan had felt the day she'd pulled up there.

'Yeah, the one and only.'

'Well, I'll be damned, hey?' There was a short pause. 'I thought that was her, driving past the house yesterday when I was taking the bin out, but then I thought I was being ridiculous.'

'What made you recognise her?'

'She looks exactly like her mother.'

Ethan bit back the words dying to leave his lips.

'So what's she doing back here?'

'Oh, you know … ' Ethan wasn't about to go into detail in front of Alexis.

'No, I don't know. Why she'd want to come back to the place her parents died is beyond my comprehension.'

Ethan turned his back to Alexis, who was now getting dressed, and dropped his voice. 'Yeah, well, each to their own. Can you not tell Mum she's here, please?'

'Too late. She's sitting here staring at me with wide eyes now that she's overheard the conversation.'

'Oh, bugger.'

'Sorry, buddie. Thems are the breaks.'

'Is there enough dinner for Alexis? Otherwise we'll just grab some takeaway on the way home.'

'Of course there's enough, I always cook for an army when I make a roast. You should know that?'

'Should I? I don't think I ever recall you cooking one.'

'Well then maybe you need to jog your memory, Ethan.' Peter sounded as if he were ready to start a battle.

'We'll be there as soon as we can. Thanks for cooking dinner.'

'Everything okay?' Alexis asked.

'Yup, all good.' He tugged on his jeans, and then rolling the rest of his clothes into a ball he shoved them into the saddlebag. 'Peter's cooked dinner, which is a nice change, so are you happy to eat there?'

'Oh, yes, if you like.'

She didn't sound too keen. He turned to face her. 'Are you sure?'

She waved her hand through the air. 'Of course. I forgot to mention I passed him yesterday, wheeling his bin out to the curb.'

'Yeah, he mentioned that.'

'You sure everything's okay?'

He gave her a brisk nod as he headed towards the horses. 'Yes, right as rain.'

Alexis walked beside him, her hands in her pockets. 'By the sounds of it, you and Peter still don't see eye to eye, huh?'

'Nope, and it's all getting a bit old, to tell you the truth.' He buckled the saddlebags on.

'It would be.' She ran her hand down his arm, her fingers leaving a hot trail. 'Wish I could make it better for you somehow.'

Oh, he knew exactly how she could make everything better, if only for a little while, but he bit back the words. 'Thanks, Lexi, but there's nothing anyone can do.' In one sweeping move he was in the saddle. 'Now come on, let's head off before we run out of daylight.'

*

A rain shower had freshened the earth, leaving a lingering scent of the ozone. The summer song of frogs and crickets sang out as Alexis and Ethan climbed the front steps of the suburban cottage. Before Ethan had time to knock, the door swung open and Joyce's face lit up like a Christmas tree.

'Alexis, look at how gorgeous you are.'

Ethan smiled as he watched his mum wrap her frail arms around Alexis and then release her, only to hold her at arm's length.

'You know you look just like your mother did at your age.'

'That's nice to know.' The sadness that possessed Alexis's eyes, if only fleeting, tore at Ethan's heart. And the way she swiftly bit it back and hid it from sight of his mother cut him even deeper. If only he could fight her inner battles for her, and take her heartache away.

'It's so lovely to see you, Missus King,' Alexis said as she hugged her again and gently rubbed Joyce's back, the subtle heartbroken look she gave Ethan was one he knew all too well. It was hard to watch someone fade away because of cancer.

'Please, call me Joyce, love.'

'Okay, sure.'

Joyce was about to invite them in as heavy footsteps sounded down the hallway and Peter stepped into their space, his body language stand-offish but his hand outstretched. 'Welcome back to Blue Ridge, Alexis, long time no see.'

There was a cynical tone in Peter's voice that made Ethan uncomfortable, as did the way he was looking at her like she was the enemy. He was all too aware Peter had never liked Lexi's dad, not that he was going to let her know that, but it was no excuse for Peter to take his dislike for him out on Lexi.

'Hi, Mister King.' Alexis shook his hand, seemingly oblivious to the undertone.

Peter remained blocking the doorway. 'So how long are you back for?'

'Just a couple of days.'

'Fleeting visit then ... not really worth coming all the way here for a couple of days, is it?'

'Yes, well, responsibilities back home have made it that way, I'm afraid, and I think a few days are better than none in the scheme of things. I've got to be grateful for that.'

'You're one of them positive-thinking ones, hey? Just like your mother was ... fair enough.'

Peter's gaze stayed locked on Alexis and an uncomfortable silence settled until Joyce said, 'Well, come on, you two, you can't stand at the doorway all night. In you come.' She gently nudged Peter out of the way and waved them both in.

Stepping inside Ethan gave his mother a hug and a kiss on the cheek. 'I have to say, you're looking good today, Mum.' She was a skeleton of her former self, but at least her eyes were lively.

'Yes, it's one of those rare days when I feel all right. The chemotherapy will fix that soon enough, though.'

'When have you got to go for it again?'

'Three days time, but to be honest I don't know why I'm bothering.'

Ethan swallowed down the lump in his throat and matched his mum's forced smile. 'Because you're not getting away from us all that easily, that's why.'

'Live to fight another day and all that,' Joyce said.

'Yeah, something like that.'

'Well, let's move before dinner is completely ruined. We've already had to reheat it once, and I don't want to have to do it again,' Peter grumbled before turning on his heel.

Ethan was ready with a retort, but his mum's hand clutching at his arm made him stop.

The four of them headed into the kitchen, where the table had been set with what Ethan recognised as his mother's only-for-special-occasions dinnerware.

'This looks lovely, Joyce,' Alexis said. 'Where would you like me to sit?'

'Beside me.' Ethan pulled up a chair for her, then noticed that his mum seemed to pale and grab hold of the back of her chair for support. He rushed to her aid, his arm going around her waist to hold her up. 'Are you okay?'

With a wobbly smile Joyce waved him off. 'Yes, I'm fine. Stop fussing. Just get a bit dizzy at times, that's all.'

Ethan pulled her chair out for her and helped her sit down. 'Are you sure you're up for this, Mum?'

'Yes, Ethan, I said I'm fine.' She placed her hand on his cheek. 'Love you.'

'Love you too.'

Straightening, he looked over to Alexis, who was wiping the corner of her eye with the paper napkin. She laughed uncomfortably when she caught his gaze. 'Got something in my eye.'

Joyce reached her hand – now only skin and bones – out across the table and placed it over Alexis's. 'Don't worry, love, it's okay to cry. Almost everyone does. Cancer's a very confronting disease. You would remember me from years ago, not how I am now. It must be a big shock for you.'

'Yes, it is,' Alexis said and a tear slid down her cheek. 'I'm so sorry you're going through this.'

Joyce smiled with a strength that outshone anything Ethan had ever seen, or even felt. 'It's okay, not your fault I've been dealt a bad hand.' She patted her bald head. 'Sorry I've gone bare up here. I usually wear a scarf when I go out, or a wig, depending on my mood, but at home I like to relax. They both make my head itch too much.'

'Please don't apologise.' Placing her crumpled napkin down, Alexis cupped Joyce's hand in both of hers. Her eyes were glistening with unshed tears, but she succeeded in blinking them back. 'You still look just as beautiful as you ever did.'

'Oh, love, do you know that's the first time anyone has said that to me since I got this damn disease.' Her eyes watered and tears fell. 'So thank you.'

Ethan felt like a bastard for not thinking to say this to his mother too. And Peter was an even bigger one for not reminding his wife just how beautiful she was at a time like this.

Alexis's resolve broke and now both women were crying while clutching each other's hands.

Ethan felt as though the wind had just been knocked out of him. Watching the two women, both so very close to his heart, connect on such a deep level was overwhelming. Busying himself so he didn't end up a blithering mess, he picked up the tray of vegetables from the sink and placed it in the centre of the table while clearing his throat one too many times.

Alexis flashed him a tender look and he returned it before going back to get the jug of gravy. Peter elbowed him out of the way, and Ethan barely saved dropping it. Even so, a few splatters slopped onto the kitchen bench. 'Bloody women, hey? Sopping all the time, can't live with them and can't live without them.'

Peter's sarcasm at such a poignant moment made Ethan want to punch him in the face. Not that he ever would, but the urge to do so was out of his hands, as it had been many times before. Luckily, he had strong restraint. 'Oh, come on now, Peter, have a heart,' he said through gritted teeth as he wiped up the gravy he'd spilt.

'You know I don't have one of those.'

'You damn well got that right,' Ethan mumbled beneath his breath as he returned to the table.

'What was that, Ethan?' Peter turned from the sink, his bushy brows meeting in the middle. His look showed Ethan that he'd heard every word.

'Oh, nothing, just talking to myself,' Ethan said.

The two men sat, Peter at the head and Ethan beside Alexis, and then they started to serve up for themselves.

Taking a swig from his beer, Peter then grabbed his knife and fork and began tucking in. 'So, Alexis, what brings you back to Blue Ridge after all these years away?' He shoved a mouthful of food in, eyeing her as if he were interrogating a suspect.

'Oh, I just thought it might help me understand some things, that's all.'

'Interesting ... what sort of things?'

Ethan flashed him a stern look, as did Joyce.

'Peter, let the poor girl eat her dinner in peace, will you.'

Peter shrugged. 'Sorry, I'm just making conversation. Would you rather me talk about the weather?'

Joyce huffed as she glared at him.

'That's okay, Joyce. I don't mind answering.' Alexis turned from Joyce to Peter. 'I'm sorry, Mister King, but I still don't believe my dad had anything to do with my mother's death, or his, so I thought coming back here might help to jog my memory.'

'You did, did you?'

'Yes, I did, and so did my psychologist.'

'You're still seeing a psychologist about your parents' deaths?' Peter looked dumbfounded.

Ethan gripped his cutlery tighter. 'Peter, lay off, would you ... '

Alexis placed her hand on Ethan's leg beneath the table, gently pressing it. 'Yes, I am, Mister King, and I'm not ashamed to admit it.' It was said with utmost confidence.

Looking back down at his plate, Peter forcefully jabbed a piece of roast pumpkin. 'Well, we were very methodical with the investigation and covered every angle and every lead, so I don't think you're going to uncover anything new.' He pointed his fork at her, the pumpkin lodged firmly. 'I'll bet my life on that.'

'I didn't mean to insult you, Mister King. I know you did the best you could at the time,' Alexis said. 'I just feel I have to do this.'

'Fair enough, whatever floats your boat. So you still haven't recalled anything from that night?'

'Absolutely nothing.'

'That's got to be frustrating,' Peter said.

'It is.'

Silence hung once again. Ethan slid his hand beneath the table, and gave Alexis's hand still resting on his leg a gentle squeeze. She graced him with a tender smile.

'So how is life in Townsville treating you, love?' Joyce's meal remained untouched, other than half a piece of potato.

'Yeah, good, I suppose.'

'Dare I ask how your grandparents are?'

'They've both passed away.'

'Oh, love, I'm so sorry.'

'Don't be. That's just the way it is.' She gave Joyce a smile.

'Sadly, yes it is.' Joyce turned her attention to Ethan. 'Have you gone and seen Grandpa lately, love?'

'I popped in to see him last week, and have been meaning to the past couple of days but time has just got away from me.'

'You should make more of an effort after what he's done for you, Ethan.' Peter's tone was lethal.

'Should I? When did you last call in to see him, Peter?'

'A few weeks ago, and he barely even spoke a word to me, so why bother, I say. Whereas you, well, we all know you're his favourite so he'll never ignore you, will he?' He shrugged. 'I don't even class the man as my father anymore, after what he did to me. I honestly couldn't be bothered with him.'

'Peter ... ' Joyce's voice was exasperated.

His jaw clenching, Ethan stared down at his now almost empty plate as he drew in a slow, steady breath, and when he brought his eyes back to Peter's he could do nothing to hide his fury. After what Peter had done, having the gall to say such a thing was beyond his comprehension. Standing, his chair tumbled out behind him, and crashed to the floor. He really didn't want to do this in front of his mother and Alexis, but enough was enough. 'You know what, Peter, it's not my fault that Grandpa left the place to me. Maybe it was the fact you haven't given two shits about him, or Diamond Acres, for years, as well as a few other things we don't need to mention.' The image of Peter's lips and hands glued to a woman other than his mother clung to Ethan's thoughts.

Peter stood now, and although he puffed his chest out he couldn't match Ethan's presence. 'How dare you?'

'How dare I what ... speak the truth?'

Joyce looked from one to the other. 'Please, Ethan, Peter, don't do this.'

'I'm sorry, Mum, but I'm tired of taking all of his bullshit on the chin.'

'My bullshit?'

'Yeah, your bullshit. For once in your life, Peter, man up and take some fucking responsibility for the wrongdoings in your life.'

Peter folded his arms defensively. 'What wrongdoings are you referring to?'

'There's too many to list.'

'Who in the hell do you think you are, coming into my house and speaking to me like this?' Peter's cheeks were glowing red and the veins in his forehead protruded.

'Who the hell do I think I am? I'm supposed to be your son, not that you've ever really treated me like one.'

'Why should I when I didn't father you?'

'You son of a bitch.' He felt Alexis place her hand on his arm, and her voice whisper his name, but he was too far gone to surrender now. 'You can go to hell.'

'That's really nice in front of your poor mum.' Peter smiled cynically, as if he'd just won the battle.

'Oh, don't you dare pull that card. You of all people don't have the right to talk about what is right and wrong when it comes to my mother.'

'What's that supposed to mean?'

'You know damn well what that's supposed to mean.'

The two men glared at each other.

Joyce stood, her hands gripping the edge of the table. 'Please, you two, stop this right now.'

Hearing her words, Ethan snapped out of it. He dropped his head, and shook it. 'I'm so sorry, Mum. I think it's best if Lexi and I leave.'

'Yes, so do I,' Peter grumbled.

'Oh, will you just keep your mouth shut, Peter.' The tone in Joyce's words was fierce and Ethan found himself reeling from it. He'd never heard his mother snap at Peter like that.

Glaring at his wife, Peter stormed out of the room, his heavy footsteps fading as he headed down the hallway. The slamming of a door let them know in no uncertain terms that he was now out of earshot.

Ethan looked to Alexis, who seemed to be at a loss for words, and then to his mum. 'I'm so sorry, to both of you. I just ... '

Joyce held up her hands. 'Save it, Ethan.' She sniffled, and tears fell. 'I know he's a handful, but he's my husband, and as much as you hate the fact, he's also your stepfather, so please, for my sake, just try and keep the peace. I haven't got long left on this earth and I really don't want to die being reminded just how much you two hate each other.'

Feeling like the biggest arsehole to have ever lived, Ethan strode around the table and took his mother into his arms. 'You have my word that from now on I will treat him with respect. I don't want your life to be any more stressful than it already is.'

'Thank you, Ethan.' She hugged him tighter.

'I'm so sorry.' Ethan made a silent pact that he would let nothing, no matter what, take away from his mum's final days on this earth.

CHAPTER

19

While watching the ceiling fan spinning at top speed Alexis ran the events of the previous night over in her mind. The hatred between Ethan and his stepdad was obvious and heartbreaking. Peter wasn't the easiest man to get on with, her father had always disliked him, but just why Ethan and Peter were so spiteful towards each other was beyond her. After asking Ethan on the way home if there was something he could pinpoint that would explain why and his answer of, *'Nope, nothing,'* she was at a loss. As if regretting his curt reply, he'd gone on to say they just clashed and then reminded her of the saying that you could pick your friends, but not your family. Something made her think he wasn't telling her the whole truth, but it wasn't her place to push it. Ethan was entitled to his privacy. She just wished there was something she could do to help mend the rift, if not for Ethan's sake then for his mother's. If she didn't have her own problems she might be able to lay here and think of a way, but she had more pressing issues at hand.

Sleep having evaded her for the past couple of hours, she crawled from her bed and opened her curtains. It was early, the sun hadn't risen yet, but the light was peeking out from behind the distant mountains. It was nice to have spent the day with Ethan, despite the events over dinner, but she really needed to turn her focus back to why she'd come here in the first place. With only two more nights before she headed home, time was of the essence.

Wrapped in her robe but barefoot, she wandered down the hallway, out the back door and then, descending the steps two at a time, she tiptoed across the lawn, the grass wet with dew. Reaching the shed, she tugged the door open and it screeched in protest. The dank smell hit her as she turned on the overhead light. It flickered to life, igniting everything in an iridescent glow and Alexis gasped. Unlike the cottage, it still looked the same in here as she remembered it from all those years ago. Cobwebs clung to the roof's beams and tools hung from hooks on the wall above the workbench, most rusted with age. She couldn't help but wonder if some of them were her father's. Walking over she reached out and trailed her fingers over them, trying to feel her father's essence within the cold metal, but to her dismay, there was nothing.

Noticing a rusty bike in the corner she recognised it as her own. Excitement quickened her pulse – if that was still here it was possible that more of her past was in here too. And then she spotted something shoved into a corner of the workbench that sent her reeling back to her childhood. Reaching out, she picked it up, the blue teddy bear looking its years. She hugged it to her, her fingers instinctively rubbing its worn ears. She would take this home and wash it, keep it for a child of her own, if she were lucky enough to ever have one. Looking around she spotted a few boxes in another corner, and she couldn't help but wonder what was in them. The largest was a toolbox she hadn't seen before.

Watching out for snakes and spiders, the cool shed an ideal place for them to escape from the blistering summer heat, she tugged the toolbox towards her and was surprised it felt so light. Wiping the dust from the top she spotted Charlie King's name written in black paint. Why was it stored away in here of all places? Wouldn't Charlie have wanted his toolbox kept down at the homestead? Curiosity claimed her. Keen to open it she groaned when she saw the heavy-duty padlock. Someone didn't want this thing to be opened easily. Looking back up at the wall, she found exactly what she needed, a hammer and a chisel. She would break the bastard of a thing off if it damn near killed her.

Grabbing what she needed and then kneeling back down on the floor, she got to work, smashing and banging until the lock finally broke free. Unlatching it and then lifting the lid, her eyes came to rest on a bundle of letters. As if they were made of the frailest glass she picked them up, pulled off the rubber band from around them, and then placed them in her lap. Picking up the one at the top she unfolded it. Her hands shook. Part of her already predicted what these were. Even so, it felt as if someone had just sucker-punched her in the chest when she started to read.

Dear Lexi-Loo,

Her breath caught in her throat, and tears filled here eyes as she read on.

This is the forty-ninth letter I've written to you, and still I haven't heard anything back from you. It makes me very worried. I hope you're okay. I wish I knew your phone number, because then I could just ring you, but Grandad and Grandma say they don't know it. I hope you're not mad at me for anything, and that you are reading my letters and not just throwing them in the bin. I really should stop writing them, I suppose, but I can't because it makes me feel not so far away from you. Stupid, I know, but that's me. I hope you're doing okay, and Katie is too. I couldn't even begin to imagine the heartache you'd both be going through. It's so lonely here without you around. I don't have anyone to boss me and tell me what to do anymore, and you'd think being a boy I'd like that, but I don't. Grandad bosses me around, and so does Grandma, but it's not the same as when you do. I think Wild Thing misses you as much as I do, too, which is a lot. Hopefully you can come back and visit sometime. I'd like that. Please don't forget me because I'll never ever forget you. Promise.

Ethan AKA Boof xo

Alexis covered her mouth and stared down at the letter in her lap, her tears blurring the writing. Why in the hell had Missus King decided not to post these? Such a cruel thing to do when she knew all too well how close Alexis and Ethan had been. There had to be a good reason, other than her not liking Alexis and her family. But what? What could have made her do this? Or was she just a heartless witch that cared about nobody but herself? If she were still alive, Alexis would have asked her to her face. The thought of talking to Missus King no longer scared her like it did when Alexis was a child. And then it occurred to her, maybe it was Mister King who'd chosen not to post them; the fact they were in his toolbox pointed in that direction. He'd always liked her and Katie. Well, at least she'd thought so, so why would he do such a thing? She needed to go and see him at the home, and hopefully catch him on a good day, so she could find out. Would Ethan agree to her joining him on the visit he had planned for tomorrow? She guessed they wouldn't let a stranger visit Charlie when he was suffering with dementia.

Flicking through the pile, an envelope slipped out and dropped to the floor. It was one she knew very well. How could she not recognise the swirling gold design embellishing the blue when it was she who had picked it all those years ago, the address on the front written in her very own handwriting. She dug through the pile, coming across the five letters she had sent to Ethan, all of them having been opened and then shoved back into their envelopes. Questions filled her mind. She needed to tell Ethan she'd found them, and see what he thought of it all.

*

Twenty minutes later, Alexis pulled up out the front of the homestead. Picking up her bag from the passenger seat, the only contents being the letters – she'd tipped everything else out all over the bed in her rush – she climbed out. Before she'd even walked up the steps, the front door had swung open and Ethan was striding out to greet her. Gloriously shirtless, his tanned, well-built chest was drawing her attention a little longer than she should have allowed.

'Hey there, Lexi, I was just going to have some breakfast and then come over to your place.' He stopped just short of her, smiling his dazzling, knee-buckling smile. His hair was wet, his feet were bare and the scent of soap lingered.

'Well, now you don't have to.' Reaching up on her tippy-toes she brushed a kiss over his cheek, liking the way his stubble grazed her lips. 'I've beat you to it.' She could feel her body language was tense, but could do nothing to relax it.

He eyed her inquisitively. 'Are you okay?'

Not about to lie, she threw her hands up in the air. 'Far out, I can't hide anything from you, can I?'

'Nope, we've already established that.' He placed his hand on her arm. 'If it's because of last night, I'm so sorry, I was out of line acting the way I did, no matter how much Peter pissed me off.'

'No, it's nothing like that.' She went to reach in her bag but then thought more of it. 'How about we have a chat over a coffee, huh?'

'That serious?'

'Sort of.'

'Shit, okay. Come on in.'

Alexis followed him inside, scooping Elvis up and into her arms when he came racing up to her. The dog wriggled excitedly, trying his best to give her a hello lick up the cheek, but she avoided it, just, as she placed him back down to dance at her feet. The tall entrance hall was exactly as she remembered it. Heavy exposed timber beams ran across the ceiling, making the place feel big and imposing. Though it was quite impressive, the grand scale intimidated her just as it had when she was young. It made the cosiness of the cottage seem all the more inviting. Ethan led the way, and while following him she drank in every detail of the place, hoping it might bring back memories, as painful as they might be. She paused at the foot of the staircase then gazed up, following the intricate design of wrought iron that wrapped around each bannister and then to the shadows beyond. She thought about the stained-glass window up there and couldn't understand why she could remember it when she had never stepped foot up there, other than to look for Katie that night. Then something else scratched at her consciousness, as though clawing its way to the surface. She silently begged it to come forwards, to reveal whatever it was, when Ethan's hands came down on her shoulders, making her jump.

'Lexi, you're acting really weird. What's up?'

Annoyed he'd broken the moment, but refusing to let him know, she turned, smiling. 'Oh, sorry, I was just admiring how beautiful the place is, that's all.'

'Right.' He shook his head as though he didn't believe a word, and then taking her hand in his, he said, 'Come on, don't leave me hanging. I want to know what's bothering you.'

Alexis allowed him to lead her to the kitchen, a room she didn't think she had been in before. Elvis trailed behind them and, scuttling to one corner, he plonked down in a lush looking doggybed. His eyes darted from one side of the room to the other as he watched them both.

'Coffee?'

'Yes, please.'

'How do you take it?'

'White, no sugar.'

'Sweet enough, hey?'

She couldn't help but smile. 'I sure am.'

'You got that right,' he said with a dashing grin before making the coffee.

Alexis pulled a chair up at the breakfast bench, the sweeping view out the bay windows distracting her from her thoughts for a few blissful moments. She could just make out Wild Thing in the paddock, his head hung low as he tugged at the grass.

Ethan passed her a steaming cuppa and she took a sip, starting from the heat of it. 'You're not having a coffee?' She placed her cup back down, deciding to let it cool.

'No, I've already had three this morning, I've been up since five.' He turned on the tap and filled a water glass. 'So, what's up?'

Alexis shifted in her seat 'I found our letters.'

'You what?'

'Our letters ... ' She took them out of her handbag and placed them on the bench. 'They were hidden in a toolbox in the shed.'

He thumbed over his shoulder, out the bay windows. 'The shed out there?'

'No, of course not. I wouldn't go snooping through your shed.' She pushed the bundle of letters towards him. 'I found them in the shed at the cottage.'

In three strides he was standing opposite her, his naked torso pressed against the kitchen bench. Close enough for her to reach out and press her palms against his chest and tell him just how much he meant to her, but she refrained and instead sat on her hands to stop herself.

He picked the letters up, and just as she had done, he stared at them for a moment as though he couldn't quite believe it.

'The ones I sent you are in there too. Opened, but shoved back in their envelopes, whereas all of yours are just the letters.' She shook her head. 'So weird.'

'I never put yours into envelopes. I just gave them to Grandma to post for me.'

'Oh, right, well that explains that then.'

Ethan's jaw clenched. 'What the fuck?' He was shaking his head now as he leafed through them all. 'Why would Grandma have done this? If it were Peter, I'd get it, but Grandma ... ' He shrugged. 'I suppose maybe that's where Peter got his mean streak from. I've just never seen it until now.'

'Well, about that, I found them in a toolbox with your grandfather's name on it, so maybe it wasn't her after all.'

'No, he wouldn't do that to me, to us.' Placing the letters down, Ethan leant against the bench, sighing heavily. 'Well, there's only one way to get to the bottom of it.'

Alexis pulled her hands from beneath her legs. 'You thinking what I'm thinking?'

'If you're thinking we should go and ask him, then yes.'

'Oh thank goodness.'

'Why so relieved?'

'I wasn't sure you'd agree to it.'

'Of course I want to know why in the hell they never got to you.'

Alexis sighed. 'It really means a lot to me that you wrote so many.'

'Of course I did. I missed you like crazy, Lexi. Have you read any of them yet?'

'Only one so far, and it made me cry, so I thought I might save the others for later.' Wrapping her hands round her cup, she stared into her coffee. 'And it made me start to think about how life could have panned out for me and you, if Mum and Dad hadn't passed away.'

'What do you mean?'

'In a relationship kind of way.'

'I've thought about that a lot too.' He sighed. 'And we'll never know because that's just how life has worked out for us, hey? Nothing to gain in regrets.'

'I suppose not.' She shook her head, her throat choking with emotion. 'I wish things could have been different.'

'Oh, Lexi.' Ethan strode around the bench and took her into his arms.

Alexis's head throbbed, a headache moving in for the kill. She rubbed her temples, groaning.

'What's up?'

Alexis sighed. 'Damn emotional stuff always gives me a headache.'

'I know how to fix that.' He moved behind her and his thumbs started to knead away the knots in her shoulders until she felt as though she was going to melt.

'That feels amazing,' she purred.

'Good.' His hands slid down her shoulders to her back, his fingers leaving trails of fire upon his skin.

She could feel his breath on her neck, his scent sending her to dizzying heights. She closed her eyes as she fell deeper into the moment. 'Where did you learn how to do this?'

'I didn't. I'm just a man of many talents.' His voice was husky.

Alexis laughed softly. She felt her desire flame even fiercer, her longing for him to tear her clothes off intensifying by the second. His lips brushed her neck, and when he placed a lingering kiss so soft yet so intense she gasped. She arched her head back so he could do it again. She knew it was wrong of her, with him still wearing his wedding ring, but it felt too good not to.

'You want more.' His voice trailed over her ear, soft, sexy, promising.

'Mmmmm, yes.' She quivered just thinking about it.

Brushing her hair to the side he did as she asked, his lips trailing like flames from behind her ear to where her neck met her shoulder, only stopping to kiss her along the way in all the right places.

Her mouth opened in a soft whimper. The tender way he touched her and cared for her made her ache for him to take her and make her his own.

But, although Jasmine was gone, he was still a married man.

She tried to put the brakes on, but couldn't.

Slowly, Ethan swung the barstool around so she was facing him. His eyes met hers and hovered and she revelled in his smouldering gaze. He brushed his hand down the side of her cheek, making her skin prickle with goosebumps. Then he leant in to meet her lips, and just when she was about to lose herself completely in their kiss, he dipped his head and kissed her neck, shoulders and collarbone, raining kisses across her tingling skin.

A sweet breath released from her parted lips, and she uttered his name in a whisper.

He raised his eyes to hers. 'I love you, Lexi.' He said it so softly, she scarcely heard him.

Oh how she loved him too, but should she say it out loud? Would it be wrong of her?

Her eyes went to his wedding ring. Panic rose within her. She couldn't do this, he couldn't do this … *they* couldn't do this.

Disentangling from his hands, she fought the lump in her throat and stood up quickly as if she'd sat on a thorn. Catching his gaze she could see the look of hurt in his eyes and it stabbed at her heart and soul. 'I'm sorry, Ethan. I really like you, a hell of a lot, but I just don't think we should do this.'

He looked down at his hand and then back at her. 'I think I'm ready to take this ring off, to let her go, Lexi.'

'You might well be, Ethan. But the fact of the matter is, you haven't yet, and that speaks volumes. It doesn't make it wrong for you to do this but only when the time is right. And besides, it hurt when I left the last time, when I was only thirteen. I can only imagine how much more it will hurt leaving you after we've made love.'

His gaze was hot now, matching the fire within her. 'Then don't leave. Stay here, come back home, to me.'

She shook her head slowly. 'That just isn't possible.'

'Why isn't it, Lexi?'

'Because my whole life is in Townsville, and I couldn't leave Katie there on her own … not when I'm the only family she has.'

'Well, bring her with you.'

'She's not going to move back here. She's in love, and her man lives there.'

'Don't you think that if she knew you were happy, and in love, she would want you to be here, with me?'

'Well, yes, but ... ' She couldn't think of anything else to say.

'Fair enough, I understand. It's just ... ' He stopped as though trying to contain his emotions.

Seeing him so upset shattered Alexis's heart. 'What is it?'

'I can't let you leave here without showing you how much I love you.'

Without waiting for a reply he stepped towards her and claimed her lips with his own, leaving her with an aching sweetness that was so exquisite her heart stumbled, as too did her resistance.

She gave into temptation and skimmed her fingers over his hair. A shiver of excitement skipped down her spine as she sunk against him, grasped his bare arms with trembling fingers and gave herself to him. His hands going to her waist, he tugged her in even tighter and she savoured his sizzling hunger for her.

Groaning, he lifted her singlet up and over her head and then with ease undid her bra and let it drop to the floor. His hands went to the button on her denim skirt, and in seconds it and her knickers were at her feet. Never letting her eyes go, he unzipped his jeans and kicked them off, along with his underpants. She raked her gaze over him, finding it almost impossible not to moan as she admired his assets. The sexy curve of his lips let her know he knew exactly what she was thinking. She felt her body burn as his eyes moved slowly and provocatively over her, making her feel alive with desire. Tiny fires danced over her tingling skin. Heat glowed inside of her as if she'd swallowed a flame.

Pulling her to him, he nibbled on her ear. 'I want to take this nice and slow, savour every moment.' His voice was husky and he breathed against her neck as she nuzzled into him.

'Me too.' She fought back tears, the moment so intense it was impossible not to well with emotion.

Ethan carried her down the hallway, kissing her the entire way. Then, climbing the stairs, he cradled her to him and she buried her face in his neck, her arms around his shoulders. Reaching his room he placed her down on the bed so her head rested on a feather pillow. He climbed over her as not to give her enough time to close her legs. She spread them wider apart, wanting, needing, craving for him to be inside her. He pressed his body into her, and then buried his mouth in the crook of her neck, his teeth pressing just hard enough to send pleasure-filled waves throughout her body. Brushing his lips over her erect nipples she gasped, tumbling deeper into him. He kissed around them, licking at the pink-pebbled flesh before pulling on them with his teeth. She arched her back, silently begging for him to bite down harder, and when he did, it sent her tumbling into a deep, warm place where nothing else mattered.

Only she and him.

Here.

Now.

Together.

If only it were forever.

Blinking open her sleep-heavy eyes Alexis took a few seconds to recall where she was. The bedroom was dark, the curtains pulled to block out the daylight, which crept around the edges as if sneaking a peek at what was in the room. The heavy drapes had been open as she and Ethan had made love, so he must have gotten up and closed them after she'd fallen asleep. With her head against his chest she could hear his slow, steady heartbeat as he slept. Skin on skin, her arm was draped over him, their legs entwined at the ankles. She ached with the idea of never experiencing this with Ethan again. The heights he'd taken her to and then fallen into with her had been higher and more intense than she'd ever experienced before. There was something that bound her and Ethan together that she couldn't explain with words, only with touch. It was as if their souls were one and the same.

Ethan stirred, and she held her breath as she waited for him to wake, or hopefully continue sleeping. What would she say, or do, if he woke? Thankfully he continued to breathe as if he were asleep. Alexis sighed with relief. She hesitated in the moment, wondering what to do. Part of her wanted to stay here, like this for the rest of the day and well into tomorrow, but she knew this wasn't a forever kind of thing. Maybe when they were teenagers it would have worked, but it was not so easy now.

The reality of their different lives came crashing down on her, like a tsunami, drowning her in guilt, shame and anguish. She wished she could give him the world, but life just wasn't going to allow that. She had responsibilities back home and he had them here. Ethan deserved better than this, better than half of her. She couldn't move back here on a whim and give him the life he wanted, and that crushed her to no end. Would it be wrong of her to slip back to the cottage, just for a while, so she could get her head around what had happened?

She felt she just had to.

Slowly untangling herself, Alexis slid from the cosiness of the bed and Ethan's arms. Finding a towel that had been tossed over the back of a chair, she wrapped it around herself. She needed to go downstairs to get dressed. Tiptoeing towards the door, the sheets rustled as Ethan stirred and then yawned.

Damn it.

Almost out the door, she froze.

'You sneaking out on me?' His voice was gravelly with sleep.

'No.' Turning, she leant against the doorframe, feeling guilty as hell now.

The bedside lamp fired to life, bathing the room in a warm glow. Ethan pushed up on his elbows, his hair wild and his chest marked where her nails had dug into his flesh in rapture. 'You okay?'

Alexis clutched the towel in tighter. 'Yup, all good.' She sounded just as torn as she felt.

'No, you're not.' He went to hop out of bed but she held up her hand.

'Please, don't ... I just need a bit of time to let all of this, all of us, sink in.'

'So there is an us?'

She stared at him, her mouth open but nothing coming out. What was she meant to say to that, to him? It wasn't as if she could deny the chemistry, the deep love, between them.

'Please, don't answer that, Lexi.' His eyes filling with sadness, he shook his head. 'Can you at least come back later and have dinner with me? I don't want things to be awkward between us when you go.' All the need and desperation within his eyes made her heart stall.

'I can definitely do that.'

'Good, great.' Pulling the sheet with him he stood, walked over to her and placed a lingering kiss on her cheek. 'Thank you for a beautiful few hours.'

'It was more than beautiful,' she choked out.

'Yes, it was.'

'I should go.'

'Okay.'

And then she just stood there, mesmerised by the love emanating from him and the essence that was all of him.

'You want to come back to bed?' His voice was oh so inviting.

'Yes, but no.' *Not until you take that ring off,* she thought, but she wasn't going to say it. He needed to do that of his own accord. She took a step back and now in the hallway she turned and spoke over her shoulder so she didn't need to look at him anymore – it hurt too much seeing the heartache in his eyes. 'I'll come back in a couple of hours, for dinner.'

'Sounds like a plan.'

She rushed away, afraid that she would go straight back into the bedroom and wouldn't be able to walk out again.

Standing at the top of the stairs she ran her hands over the cold balcony rail. Her senses suddenly heightened and a vague feeling of unease claimed her. Was it because this was where she'd fallen from that night? Looking to the left her hand flew to her chest when she saw the stained-glass window. With the sunlight piercing through, a spectrum of reflected light bounced back at her. Her past suddenly crashed into her present and then she remembered, standing here, calling out for Katie, when a set of headlights had shot through the stained glass. A car door had slammed. Then there were raised voices, two men, and one of them was Mister King. Her heart quickened. Minutes later Missus King appeared from behind, and when Alexis turned to look up at her, her eyes were wild. Her cotton nightie hung to her ankles. She could see her nipples through the sheer material, and Alexis recalled it made her uncomfortable. Looking down, she noticed Missus King's white nightgown was splattered with red, which was odd because she had always looked so clean and neat. She remembered wondering if it was tomato sauce or maybe even red wine. Now it occurred to her that it might well have been her parents' blood. The shock of this sent her mind reeling. Missus King, of all people? She might have been a grumpy old bat, but she certainly didn't seem like a murderer. And besides, why would she want to kill Alexis's parents?

None of this made any sense.

In a daze, her entire body trembling, Alexis found herself whispering what Missus King had said to her, 'What are you doing up here, Alexis? You should know better.'

'I'm looking for Katie, Missus King.'

'Don't lie to me, you're snooping, aren't you?'

'No, Missus King.'

'You little liar.' She grabbed her by the arm, so tightly that Alexis remembered crying out in pain. And then there was a sound behind them, like footsteps, and she tried to see who it was, but it was too dark.

Missus King turned and pointed to whoever it was. 'Go back to the room, now!'

Was she talking to Katie?

Kneeling down, Missus King took hold of both her arms, so tightly her nails dug into Alexis's flesh. Instinctively, Alexis rubbed her arms as though it were happening right now. Missus King was shaking her, telling her that she was a naughty girl and that her parents needed to learn the meaning of discipline. There was something about her eyes, a fierceness to them that terrified her. And then Mister King called out for Alexis, asking where she was. Alexis tried to answer, but Missus King clamped her hand over her mouth to quieten her. Alexis tried to wrestle free so she could run to Mister King and then before knew she it she was falling, tumbling, her head hitting the rungs of the railings on the way down. Then everything went black.

Slammed back into the present and with all the strength going out of her legs, Alexis crumbled to the floor. She wrapped her arms around herself in a bid to stop trembling. She bit her lips closed, not letting the sobs escape her for fear of luring Ethan out of the bedroom. She couldn't handle this *and* him right now. An urgent need to get out of here, out of this house, overcame her and she shot to standing. She ran down the steps two at a time. Still running, she hurried towards the front door, not realising she was holding her breath until she was racing towards her car, the towel still wrapped around her. It was then she remembered her clothes were still inside, as were her shoes, but she wasn't going back. She'd get them later, when she came back for dinner. If she came back. Getting into her car, she took a moment to glance up at Ethan's bedroom, and was shocked to see him standing there, watching her, a strange look on his face. How much had he just seen, and heard? She tried to smile, and gave him a wave. He returned her wave, but not her smile. She couldn't blame him for being confused, seeing her running towards her car still wrapped in the towel. She would have to think of a way to explain it all later. Revving the VW to life, she turned it around and headed back towards the cottage – her safe haven.

*

It was the magic of twilight; the sun setting at the same time as the moon was rising. The light surrounding her was almost surreal, dark blue mixed with purple. Alexis took a deep breath. Placing her hand over the tree-of-life pendant resting against her chest she tried to draw comfort from it. Standing on the verandah, she took in the vastness of this place and her soul resonated with the heartbeat of the earth. She'd spent the last couple of hours curled up in her bed, trying to make sense of the memories of everything that happened back at the homestead, but hadn't come up with any definitive answers. How could she say anything to Ethan about it, or the police for that matter, when nothing was making any sense to her? The fragments she did remember where disjointed and vague, and for the life of her she couldn't piece them all together. It was driving her nuts. She wasn't about to stir up a hornet's nest until she felt she had some hard evidence, or at least a clear memory of exactly what had happened. And she didn't have that ... yet. She still held out hope that within in the next forty-eight hours, she would find the way to put it all together.

She just had to.

The only thing she knew for absolute certainty was that she was madly in love with Ethan, with all of her heart and soul, and she didn't want to dismiss such an amazing feeling. Couldn't dismiss it. Not after what she felt while making love with him. She didn't want to spend the rest of her life wondering what could have been, and regretting her fear to ever find out. So tonight she was going to tell him she loved him and that when he was ready to take his wedding ring off, she would be waiting for him, how ever long that took. She wasn't sure how they would make a long-distance relationship work, but she was prepared to give it a shot. That was all she could offer right now. She just hoped that sat well with him.

Heading inside, she grabbed her car keys from the kitchen bench. Dressed in her favourite turquoise-coloured, boho-style dress she walked back out to her car, feeling the soft material floating around her ankles. She wondered whether Ethan would like how it looked on her, and also if he would like the scent of her perfume. She'd gone to the effort of dusting some blush on her cheeks and putting on a soft musk-coloured lipstick, as well as choosing her favourite pair of dream-catcher earrings. She drove down the dirt track, towards the homestead and towards the man who had brought so much love and light back into her life. She just hoped she wouldn't feel the way she did when she had run from the homestead a few hours ago. She knew it was going to be scary, stepping back in there, but she had to find the strength to do it. Justice for her parents depended on it. And her love for Ethan.

The front door was open when she arrived, so with a calming breath she pushed open the flyscreen door and let herself in. Her heart raced and her mind started to spin, but she did her very best to breathe slowly, deeply. Instead of freaking out about what was going on inside of her, she focussed on the present. It was a distraction tactic that worked wonders for anxiety. In a few moments her heart slowed and her mind behaved. Doctor Jacobs had taught her well. The delicious aroma of beef stroganoff made her mouth water. Wandering down the hallway, she was met by an overexcited Elvis as she called out Ethan's name. She took a moment to lean over and give the dog a pat, and once satisfied with her love for him, the fluffy bundle of joy totted back off to the kitchen, and Alexis guessed, his comfortable doggy-bed. He was a super spoilt pooch, and it warmed her heart that Ethan was the kind of man to do so much for his furry mate. It spoke volumes.

Reaching the door to the lounge room she spotted him on the couch. One of his arms was draped casually over it, his head resting back. He was shirtless, revealing his muscular chest dusted with dark hair. Her heart raced at the sight of him. She imagined his lips against her skin, velvety yet hard as he consumed her breaths, pleasuring her and loving her like only he could. Quietly, she crossed to the sofa and straddled him, her arms sliding around his neck.

His eyes still closed Ethan stirred, a smile on his lips before he'd even opened them. 'You smell so good I could eat you.' His blue eyes met hers. 'Did you get your head around everything?'

'I did.'

His hands slid around her waist. 'You did?'

She nodded. 'I enjoyed making love with you.'

'You could have fooled me with how you hightailed it out of here, without your clothes, or shoes, for that matter.'

'Oh, that, I can explain ... '

He shook his head. 'You don't have to. You were freaked out. I get it.'

'Yes, you're right. I was freaked out.' She wished she could tell him the real reason. 'But now I've had some time to think about it all, I feel good about what we did, and I want more of it, with you. Where you're ready, of course.'

'I'm ready, Lexi.'

She looked down at his hand resting on her thigh and her breath caught. Running a thumb over the white band that stood out on his tanned finger, she brought her eyes back to his. His warm, tender smile ignited her heart. No man had ever looked at her like that before, like he knew her more than she knew herself. 'You took it off?'

'I did.'

'Are you sure you're ready to do that?'

'Very sure ... you've unlocked my heart, Lexi-Loo. I can't imagine my life without you in it.'

She held his gaze as she placed one of her hands against his chest. 'I love you, Ethan, and I want to see if we can somehow make this work.'

A sensual gleam glistened in the depths of his eyes. With his hands now cradling the back of her head he brought her forwards, meeting her halfway, kissing her like he meant it, passionate, possessive, hungry. Her body melted under the scorching heat of his kiss that was much more intense than before. It was filled with more promise, more desire, more love – if that were possible. She pressed herself into him and he groaned, low and husky.

Just as they were reaching a crescendo, he pulled away, flashing her a wicked grin as he readjusted the crotch of his jeans. 'Hold that thought, because as much as I want to tear your clothes off and make love to you all night long, we're going to eat dinner first, otherwise the night will get away from us and all my efforts in the kitchen will go to waste.'

'If we must.' She eyed him sassily.

'Yes, we must. We need sustenance if we're going to make the most of tonight.' He raised his brows suggestively as he eased her off his lap and then stood. 'Come on, let's dish it up and then later I can have my wicked way with you.'

Floating way above cloud nine she followed him into the kitchen, her eyes locked on the way the muscles in his back tensed as he walked. He was the epitome of perfection.

He poured her a glass of red wine, the entire time watching her with desire-filled eyes. 'You sit and relax. There's not much more to do.'

'You sure, I don't mind helping.'

'Positive.' Grabbing a wooden spoon from the draining rack, he pulled the lid off the pot on the stove and gave it a stir.

The aroma was mouth-watering. Unable to help herself Alexis dived past him and succeeded in dunking her finger in. But with the sauce being so hot she quickly stuck her finger in her mouth and groaned in foodie heaven as she did. This man could not only run a property, keep a house clean and make love like he meant it, he could damn well cook too. What a catch.

Ethan gave her a playful shove. 'You're a sneaky bugger ... and bloody quick too.'

'Uh-huh. When it comes to snitching tastes of food.' Alexis flashed him a smile, her arm still tingling from his touch.

Setting out two bowls, Ethan put some fluffy white rice in each one and topped it with the stroganoff. Then he took out a knife and fork from the drawer. 'Would you like to sit outside on the couch to eat?'

'I'd love to.'

'Follow me then, sexy lady.'

Settled on the couch with their bowls in their laps they ate in silence, Alexis moaning every now and then with how delicious it was. Her bowl almost licked clean, Ethan took it from her and handed her the glass of red wine from the coffee table beside him. Then, grabbing his beer, they chinked them together.

'To us.'

'To us,' she repeated.

He motioned for her to snuggle into him and she gladly did so. Resting her head against his shoulder, he wrapped his arm around her. 'This is nice.'

'It is, isn't it?'

'So, where do we go from here, Lexi-Loo?'

'I'm not sure. I can't move here, though, if that's what your thinking? Not yet anyway. I'd only do that if Katie got hitched, and that's a long way off.'

'I kind of gathered you'd say that, and I understand you wanting to stay in Townsville, with Katie. So long distance it is.'

'Yes, for now, and then we can work it out further down the line.'

'Sounds like a plan.' He tightened his arm around her. 'As long as I get to love you, and you love me, we can make anything work. I just know it.'

She lifted her chin so she could look at him. 'You're an amazing man, Ethan King.' She paused, losing track of what she'd just said as she sunk into his eyes.

'And you, Lexi-Loo Brown, are the most beautiful woman to ever walk this earth.'

'That's so sweet. I love you, Ethan.' She reached out and touched his cheek and he pressed his face into her palm.

'Love you too, and will go on loving you forever.'

It was said with such conviction, such deep emotion, she paused and let it sink into her consciousness. 'Kiss me,' she said.

*

With the moonlight flicking over Alexis's soft skin, Ethan drank all of her in. He took the empty long-stem glass from her hand and placed it back on the table. Should he tell her what he knew, so he didn't have to tear himself apart over it anymore? Fear that if he did, she would run for the hills and never return, stopped him. It was not something that should ever have been kept in the dark, but it was a case of too little too late.

Not wanting to consume himself with the guilt of that decision, he ran a finger over her jaw and then upwards and over her lips, feeling where he was going to lay his kiss. He loved the way she moaned softly as her long dark eyelashes fluttered closed. He knew this was going to be hard, doing the long-distance thing, but he didn't care right now, he just wanted to be with her – the rest would come given time. Knowing she'd be driving away from here in less than forty-eight hours he didn't want to waste another precious second worrying about it, or anything else for that matter.

Groaning, low and hungry, he bent his head. Sliding his tongue over her parted mouth, he bit at her lip and then slid his tongue inside, so it twirled with hers in an erotic dance, filled with the promise of what it would feel like if they were to pleasure each other orally. She kissed him hard and hungry, making him the same, her hands sliding up his back and into his hair. With her pushing her hips against him, he deepened his kiss, wishing he could drink her in. She moaned and he caught it, pausing to sigh as her lips parted even more so. She raked her nails over his shoulders and down his back, her hands coming to grip him.

Slowly, he ran his hand from her ankle, up her calf, following the trail of her thigh beneath her silky dress, until his fingers met with the smoothness of her pants. Sliding his fingers beneath the soft material he found her centre, his self-control threatening to unfold as he felt her readiness for him. She was deliciously, achingly, desperate for him. Wet and warm, he longed to trail his lips and tongue where his fingers were. Massaging her, she arched harder into him, her head tipping back as she groaned in pleasure. He brought his lips to where her nipple was pressing through the sheer material of her dress. Grazing his teeth along it he bit down, just hard enough to teeter her on the brink of pleasure and pain.

'I need you. Now.' She was breathless, demanding ... and he liked it. One hell of a lot.

Clutching her to him he stood and carried her inside, her arms and legs wrapped tightly around him. He wasn't going to carry her upstairs this time, but instead make love to her everywhere he possibly could down here. He wanted to be able to walk around when she was gone and feel her presence everywhere, and remember making sweet, hungry love to her wherever he looked.

Halfway down the hallway he pressed her against the wall. With a look of ultimate satisfaction her legs dropped from around his waist as she allowed him to pin her wrists high above her with one hand. He rested his other hand around her neck, tight enough to make her feel at his mercy, but loose enough to let her feel she could escape if she wanted to. Raking her wanton gaze over him she then rested her head back against the wall, giving him an invitation that was hypnotic.

'Jesus, you're gorgeous,' he growled, leaning into her, his teeth grazing her neck before he licked and kissed his way up to her earlobe. Hovering there, he enjoyed the way she writhed against him before bringing his lips back to hers. This time the kiss was forceful and ravenous, hot and primal. While he kissed her, he pulled her pants down her thighs, letting them drop to the floor before undoing his jeans and yanking them down along with his boxers.

With his clothes around his ankles, he pulled her dress up around her waist, grabbed her hips and lifted her from the floor. She slung her arms around his neck. The groan that escaped her quivering lips as he slowly slid inside her was enough to send him to the edge. But holding back, he savoured the electric bolts of need coursing through him as he stroked the inside of her, soft and slow at first, his pace building as did hers. Her muscles clenched around him. He groaned in pleasure. His breath was raspy as he rocked harder into her, filling her completely. With a sob of relief she gripped him tighter, her entire body tensing for the inevitable tumble into ecstasy. Her hair was pressed against his face and his mouth was pressed into her throat. And then his chest heaved as he tumbled over the edge with her, freefalling together.

Alexis woke in a tangled mass of limbs, Ethan's rhythmic breathing music to her ears. She loved that it was still dark, for it meant she could stay right where she was. She snuggled in closer, her lashes brushing against his chest, not wanting an inch of space separating them. Ethan's arm tightened around her and her stomach fluttered as she recalled making love anywhere and everywhere. Ethan had made love so slowly and passionately that she'd cried. Never before had she experienced a love like this. He certainly knew how to send her to dizzying heights and then catch her as she fell, blissfully, breathlessly, into a pleasure-filled abyss. She sighed contentedly. This was definitely the start of something amazing, lasting, a forever kind of love ... one that she believed could take them into the next lifetime.

Gentle rain fell outside and on the far side of the room the curtains fluttered, allowing slivers of silvery moonlight to sneak in and dance upon the dark timber furniture. Still lying on the rug on the lounge-room floor with a cashmere blanket tossed over their legs, Alexis thought about the night they had shared. Who knew lovemaking could be so intense, so earth shattering, so mind-blowingly addictive. She brought her gaze from the window back to the man she was nestled into. Smooth, powerful shoulders narrowed to a tapered waist sprinkled with just the right amount of hair, and strong, thick thighs. Ethan King was eye candy if ever she'd seen it, and to top it all off he had the most enchanting heart and soul. She felt like the luckiest woman alive, crossing paths with him again. Fate was working in her favour.

Glancing at the clock on the wall, illuminated by the moonlight, Alexis saw that they had two more hours of bliss before they had to get up and get ready to go and see Charlie. Her heartbeat quickened. What was he going to say about the letters? She couldn't even begin to guess. And maybe, just maybe, there was a possibility he knew nothing, or he couldn't remember, and then they'd never know the truth behind why the letters were kept hidden. That would drive her insane, the not knowing. She was sick of the not knowing. Would she ever get a straight answer to what happened on that horrible night? She realised that she might have to come to grips with the fact that she might never know the truth.

Closing her eyes, she tried to drift back to sleep, but her mind wasn't having any of it. It twirled and twisted between good and bad; hopes and fears; the past, present and future. She was content in the decision to give things a go with Ethan, but then she worried about how they could do that while living so far apart. Was it hopeful thinking on their parts that they could make something work that most couldn't? Long-distance relationships were never easy. And then, before Alexis could worry about that any more, her thoughts shifted to her recollection of Missus King at the top of the stairs, the skin on the back of her neck prickling. Had she really fallen, or had Missus King pushed her? For some reason she believed it was the latter but how in the hell could she ever prove that? And if she did push her, was it to kill her? Who had walked up behind them and sent Missus King into a frenzy in the first place? Had it been Katie? Or someone else? From what she could remember, the footsteps sounded heavy. A man, maybe? So many unanswered questions and so many possibilities. Should she go out on a limb and ask Charlie what he remembered of that night, and see if it matched up with her recollections? Would Ethan be pissed off with her if she did? For some reason she had the sense it might be the one and only thing Ethan agreed on with his stepfather, that she should just let sleeping dogs lie when it came to her parents' death. If that were the case, how could she be mad at him because that's what everyone else in her life thought too? Groaning, she tried to shrug it all off. For now, she just wanted to linger in the moment and enjoy the feeling of being wrapped in the arms of her man. There would be plenty of time to hash over everything later, and drive herself nuts doing it. As for Charlie, she'd feel her way once they were there, and if she got a moment by herself with him she might just ask him about that night.

*

A big-busted brunette stopped dead in her tracks as she entered the office. She shot daggers in Alexis's direction when she saw her standing beside Ethan at the counter. 'Hey there, Ethan, what's been keeping you from visiting us the past few days? We've missed your handsome face around here.' She smiled in a very suggestive way as she waited for his response.

'Hey, Casey, how's Grandad been?' was all Ethan said in response.

Alexis bit back a smile at the brush-off Ethan had just given Casey, who was now eyeing her with jealous dislike.

'He's remembering less and less, but he's having a good day today so you've picked a great one to visit.' She drummed her long pink nails against the chart she was holding to her chest. 'So who's this?' Raising one perfectly plucked eyebrow she gestured to Alexis with a discourteous tip of her head and a fake smile.

Ethan turned to Alexis, his tender expression letting anyone know in no uncertain terms how in love he was with her. 'This is my girlfriend, Alexis Brown.'

'Your girlfriend?' Casey's voice wavered.

He turned back to Casey. 'Yeah. Come to think of it, I reckon you two would've been in the same year at school.'

Casey looked like she'd just been slapped in the face.

'Hi, Casey.' The atmosphere had turned so thick Alexis swore she could have easily cut it with a knife.

Casey gave her a tight-lipped smile. 'Oh, yes, Alexis, I do recall you. And your sister was Katie, is that right?'

'Yes, that's right.'

'I think I was the grade beneath you. And of course, how could anyone around here forget who you are after what happened?' It was said with an acid tongue.

'Hey …' Ethan shot a warning glance in Casey's direction. 'Ease up a bit.'

'Sorry, you know me, babes, foot in mouth. How's your mum doing?'

Signed in, Ethan pushed the visitor folder across the counter towards her. 'Yeah, not bad, but not good either.'

'I'm so sorry you're going through this. If there's anything I can do to help?' Her voice was so painfully sugar-laced.

'Thanks, Casey, but there's nothing really any of us can do.' He took Alexis by the hand. 'I'll catch ya later.'

'Yeah.' Casey tipped her chin up as she watched them walk away.

Walking hand in hand with Ethan, Alexis said, 'Who in the hell was that?'

'No one really, just a girl that's tried her best to go out with me since Jasmine passed away.'

'She doesn't really seem your type'

'She's not.'

'I think it's safe to say she hasn't given up the notion of you and her getting together.'

'Nope, never going to happen.' He gave her hand a gentle squeeze. 'I was waiting until I met the right woman to be able to move on in my life, and then you came back into it. I'm a very lucky man.'

Alexis grinned. 'And I'm a very lucky woman.'

Ethan released her hand and pushed in the code to open the security door. Then they walked into the large common room where Mister King was sitting near the windows.

'Grandad ... '

'Ethan.'

Half the man he used to be, Alexis watched Charlie King slowly rise to his feet, slightly stooped and bowlegged from his many years in the saddle. He placed one hand on the small of his back and shaded his eyes from the bright mid-morning sun with the other. He was dressed in his Sunday's finest, his trousers and shirt impeccably ironed, the lines on his face etched deep from his years outdoors.

They reached him and eyeing Alexis, Charlie's smile faltered but then swept wide. He reached out and cupped her cheeks. 'Oh my good Lord. Alexis Brown ... is that really you?'

His face was a little red and Alexis put it down to all the excitement. She placed her hands over his, more so to stop her own from trembling. After knowing Charlie King as a towering man, well built, with nerves of steel, it broke her heart to see him in such a feeble state. 'Yes, Mister King, it's me, but how did you know?'

'You look exactly like your mother did at your age, a spitting image in fact.'

Alexis bit back tears. 'That's just what Joyce said.'

'Well, she was right.' He chuckled lightly as he dropped his hands to his sides. 'Sorry if I looked shocked, but I thought I was seeing a ghost for a second there. It really is so lovely to see you.'

'That's okay.' Alexis gave him kiss on the cheek and embraced him, feeling a certain kind of bond with the man after he rushed her to the hospital all those years ago and in doing so saved her life. 'It's so nice to see you, too, Mister King.'

Returning her hug Charlie gave her a quick squeeze and then pulled away. 'Please, Alexis, call me Charlie.'

'Okay then, Charlie.'

Ethan gave Charlie's shoulder a pat. 'So, how are you feeling today?'

'Yeah, you know, Ethan, same old same old. I'm remembering stuff from years ago, but having trouble remembering what happened yesterday. Strange thing, this dementia … I'm lucky it's only early days. But the darn thing is only going to get worse as time goes on. ' He shook his head as he sat back down in his lounge chair. 'Come on, you two, pull up some chairs. You're making the place look untidy.'

Both Ethan and Alexis did as he asked.

'So what brings you back here after all these years, Alexis?'

'I suppose I just wanted to make peace with my past.'

'That makes me happy to hear, in more ways than one.' He jokingly waggled a finger in her direction. 'For a second there I thought maybe you were back here chasing my grandson, but then a woman as beautiful as you would be married, right?' He lifted her hand, frowning when he didn't see a ring. 'Boyfriend then?'

'Umm.' Alexis wasn't sure what to say.

'Don't worry, I understand. Your private life is exactly that.' He patted Alexis on the leg and then folded his hands in his lap. 'Sorry for prying.' The shake in his head became more pronounced and Alexis had to fight the urge not to reach out and cup his face so she could help still it for him.

'So everything's going well at home, Grandad.'

'That's good to hear.'

'I got a truckload of brumbies in a few days ago and one of them is definitely a keeper for Diamond Acres. The rest I'll train up to be sold off to good homes.'

'You've always had an eye for the exceptional ones, Ethan, which is why I left Diamond Acres in your care. Not that your stepfather will ever bring himself to understand that.' He scratched his head. 'I know Peter is flesh and blood, but after what he's done to me and this family …' Charlie stopped mid-sentence as though biting back his words. His shoulders slumped and his smile disappeared.

'Elvis is doing really good,' Ethan said quickly, as if trying to divert Charlie's train of thought.

'Who's Elvis?' Charlie looked genuinely confused.

'He's your dog, Grandad.' Ethan said it gently, carefully.

Charlie paused for a moment, his brows furrowing, and then he smiled. 'Oh, yes, I remember him.' But as quickly as his smile had appeared, it vanished. 'I'm so sorry, I feel like a silly old fool.'

'Oh, Grandad, please don't think like that, and don't apologise. It's not your fault, what you're going through.'

'Yeah,' Alexis piped up. 'I'm only thirty and I still can't remember a damn thing from the night my parents passed away.'

'You can't?'

'Nope.'

'Well, there you go.' Charlie heaved a sigh. 'Mind you, the fall you had that night. It was terrible. When I found you at the bottom of the stairs I thought you were ... ' He shuddered and then cleared his throat. 'Anyway, at least you were okay in the end, otherwise I'd have never forgiven ... ' He cleared his throat again as if fighting back emotion. 'Myself.'

Alexis placed a hand on his arm. 'Why would you need to forgive yourself?'

Charlie stared at her for a moment, his Adam's apple bobbing in his weathered neck. 'It was my stairs you fell down, so I would've felt to blame.'

'Oh don't be silly, Charlie. It was an accident.'

'Yes, yes it was.' But something in Charlie's eyes was telling Alexis otherwise. And then, as if sensing her reading his thoughts, he turned back to Ethan. 'Anything else interesting happening in the outside world I need to know about now, and then possibly forget all about tomorrow?' He chuckled uneasily.

'Well, now that you mention it.' Ethan eyed Alexis over his Grandfather's shoulder.

Charlie caught the look and graced them both with an anxious one. 'What is it?'

Opening the backpack he'd brought along, Ethan pulled out the wad of letters. He held them up and the expression on Charlie's face told them immediately that he knew exactly what they were.

He looked down at the ground as if humiliated. 'Where did you find them?'

'In a toolbox in the cottage shed.' Ethan saved Alexis answering.

'Right. I'd actually forgotten where I'd hidden them,' Charlie said, and then heaved another weary sigh. 'It was your grandmother's idea, to keep them from you both. She asked me to burn them, but I just couldn't bring myself to. Which was why I hid them. I thought, maybe one day, I'd be able to give them to you both.'

'Really?' Ethan said. 'Why did she want you to burn them? And more importantly, why would you agree to it when you knew how close Lexi and I were?'

Charlie took his time to answer. 'She didn't think it would be beneficial for you and Alexis to keep in touch, after everything that had happened, and being her husband I felt I had to support her decision.'

'Beneficial?' Ethan shook his head. 'Are you serious?'

'Yes, very serious. Your letters, Ethan, they were, well, a little heavy on the emotional side, and we didn't think that was appropriate for kids of your ages.'

'Well, I don't care what your reasons were, it was wrong of you both to do that. Lexi and I have lost years together, all because of yours and grandma's meddling. Years we will never get back. We were good mates, Grandad, and you knew that.'

'I'm so sorry, Ethan.' Charlie shot him a wounded glance. 'We all went through hell after that night, and we all just wanted to move on with our lives. I hope you can bring yourself to understand that and forgive me for keeping them from you.' He turned to Alexis. 'And also from you, sweetheart, it was wrong of me and I hope you can forgive me too.'

Not needing a moment to think about it, Alexis smiled softly. 'Of course we can forgive you, Charlie.' She placed her hand on his and then gave Ethan a look as if to say, *Yes, we have to.*

Ethan huffed and looked to the sky. 'I suppose it's not worth holding grudges, but I can't say I'll ever understand it.'

'I don't expect you to.' Charlie gave him a lacklustre smile. 'We all make stupid mistakes in our lives, and agreeing to keep the letters from you both was one of my many.' The sadness and remorse in Charlie's voice made Alexis's heart break in two.

And it must have done the same to Ethan's because he gave his Grandad a light tap on the back. 'Yes, we do all make mistakes, and that was a stupid one. But I still love you, you old bugger.'

'I love you too, Ethan,' Charlie said. 'Do you two want to join me for lunch in the food hall? We have roast lamb on the menu today.'

Ethan looked to Alexis for her approval, and she nodded. 'Yep, we'd love to join you.'

'Good. Great. Let's go and get ourselves a good seat before the place gets too packed. Roast lunches bring all of us old farts out of the woodwork.'

It was over their dessert of trifle that Charlie shot them both a worried glance when Ethan stole a quick kiss from Alexis. He pointed from one to the other with his spoon, his bushy brows furrowed. 'Please don't tell me you two are an item?'

'What do you mean?' Ethan said. 'Didn't you work that out until now?'

'No, I didn't.' Charlie voice was stern.

'What's wrong with that, Grandad? We thought you'd be over the moon.'

'Sorry to burst your bubble but I'm not over the moon.'

Ethan drummed the table with his fingers. 'But why? Don't you want to see me happy?'

Alexis looked to Charlie for an answer, her heart sinking. She knew how much Ethan valued his grandfather's opinion, and blessing, and wondered if this was going to pose a problem.

His trifle only half eaten, Charlie slowly placed his spoon down on the table. He drew in a deep breath. 'I just think the past is best left where it is, and on top of that you two live very separate lives, what with Alexis in Townsville and you up here. How do you think you'd ever make a go of things living miles apart?' He seized Alexis's gaze. 'Unless of course you're going to move here?'

Alexis fidgeted in her seat. 'No, not for now, I have responsibilities back home.'

Charlie nodded. 'Yes, I thought as much.'

'I'm not going to leave Diamond Acres, if that's what you're worried about Grandad.'

'That's good, Ethan, because Diamond Acres needs you, and so does your mother.' He pushed to standing. 'I'm tired now, I think I'd like to go back to my room.' Wobbly on his feet, he stumbled.

Ethan stood and took Charlie by the arm. 'Are you sure you're okay?'

Charlie patted Ethan's hand. 'Yes, I'm fine, just tired, that's all. It happens when you're my age.'

'Okay, well, let's get you back to your room then, hey?'

Alexis went to gather her bag from the floor.

'You take me please, Ethan, and Alexis can wait here.'

Ethan looked as confused as Alexis felt. 'Is that okay, Lexi?'

'Yes, of course.'

'Can you please go and get me a jug of water to take back to the room, Ethan?'

'Sure.' Ethan was hesitant to let go of Charlie's arm but Charlie tugged free of his hold. 'It's okay, I'm not going to fall over. I just get light-headed when I stand up too quickly, that's all.'

Watching as Ethan went over to the servery, Alexis stood and rested her hand on his arm to keep him steady. 'Bye, Charlie.'

'Bye, Alexis, it's been lovely seeing you. Sorry if I've upset you.' He pulled her closer and bent into her ear. 'Please come back and see me tomorrow. Alone. There's something we need to talk about.'

Her mind, already spinning with Charlie's reaction to her and Ethan being together, was quickly filling with questions, but Ethan was back before she could ask what it was all about. She looked Charlie in the eye and he subtly held a finger to his lips.

'One jug of water with lots of ice, just how you like it.' Ethan hooked his arm into Charlie's. 'Now let's get you to bed, Grandad, you're looking pale.'

Charlie gave Alexis a wave. 'Lovely seeing you, Alexis, take care now.'

'Yes, I will, you too, Charlie.' Forcing a smile, she watched the men walk off, trying to work out why Charlie wanted her to come back tomorrow, alone, and also why he felt the need for a moment alone with Ethan. What in the hell was going on?

The radio hummed softly in the background, the announcer's voice as he introduced the next song a nice distraction from the tension in the room. Alexis traced the rim of her empty coffee cup with her finger as she tried to weigh up Ethan's gloomy mood. He'd been distant, and quieter than usual since they'd returned to the cottage from visiting Charlie yesterday, and although he'd stayed the night, they hadn't made love. Saying he was tired he'd kissed her goodnight and then rolled onto his side, away from her. It had torn her heart in two. 'I'm sorry the visit with your grandad didn't really go as well as you expected.'

Looking up from the magazine he was flicking through he smiled but there was a deep sadness in his eyes. 'Don't apologise, Lexi, it's not your fault.' He reached across the table, taking her hand. 'I feel awful Grandad reacted the way he did. I'm so sorry you had to hear that. He's really not himself these days.'

'It's not your fault either, Ethan, so no need to apologise. But, I have to say, with the way you're acting around me, you're making me feel as though you've changed your mind about us making a go of things.'

'Oh, Lexi-Loo, I'm sorry.' He gave her hand a reassuring squeeze. 'Please don't think he's swayed the way I feel about you, and what I want for us. I'm just a little taken back by his reaction, that's all. Grandad's done a lot for me and I don't want to disappoint him. I wish he could find it in himself to be happy for me, for us.'

'Okay, fair enough.' She hesitated, but then spat the words out that were dying to be said. 'You promise what you told me on the way home was all you talked about when you walked him to his room?'

As if measuring his reply, Ethan was quiet for a few seconds, then said, 'I don't like making promises. And besides, it hurts that you don't believe me. I'm not that shady, am I?' He grinned but Alexis saw right through it. There was something he wasn't telling her and it was really getting beneath her skin.

'No, of course you're not shady, you're far from it, but I'm sorry, something's telling me you're not speaking the truth.' The mixture of hurt and anger in his eyes stole her breath.

'I'm sorry you feel like that, but you're just going to have to find it in yourself to believe me.' Tension sizzled as he held her gaze and then stood. 'As I've told you, all Charlie did was repeat what he said to both of us, and then pleaded with me to listen to him and not make a huge mistake.'

'Why does he think we're such a huge mistake?'

'He thinks it would be better for both of us to be with people who live in the same town. And I suppose, as much as we don't like it, we have to try and at least consider his opinion ... as bloody hard as that is.'

'Can't you see how his words are affecting us, Ethan? Look at how you're acting with me now.'

'I know, and I'm sorry. Like I said, I'm just trying to get my head around it. Like I understood you needing time out when you raced back to the cottage after we made love for the first time, can you please do the same for me?'

As much as she hated the fact, he had a damn good point. 'Yes, okay.'

'Thank you. I've got work to do now. I'll come back in a much better mood later.'

'That would be nice.'

'You have my word.'

'I thought you didn't make promises.' Alexis regretted the anger in her voice as soon as she spoke the words.

'My word is not a promise, it's my word,' he said before grabbing the cups and his plate from the table and heading to the sink.

Trying to remain calm even though her heart was racing and she felt like screaming her lungs out, Alexis sucked in a deep breath and decided to change the subject, before they both said things they'd regret. 'So what are you up to today anyway?' She pushed her cornflakes around her bowl. She was only eating so she could do something with her hands. With the plug in and the sink filling Ethan spoke with his back to her. 'I've got a few paddock fences to fix, a tractor to service and I want to do a bit of work with the brumbies that came in last week, as well as checking in on Shooter.' Flicking off the tap he began washing the dishes. 'Feel free to join me, if you like.'

'Oh, no, you're right. I might head into town for a bit of a wander around. Being my last day I thought it might be nice to check it out.'

'Oh, okay.' The disappointment in his voice was evident, and it gave her hope that this was just a silly tiff they'd get over once they'd had some space. They'd had their fair share of arguments as kids, so she had to look at this one in the same way. It was hard when everything was so much more dramatic as an adult.

'I won't be long, though, so I can come find you once I'm back, if you like.'

Ethan wiped his hands on a tea towel. 'Yup, cool, sounds like a plan.'

'You need me to pick up anything in town while I'm there?'

'Nah, thanks, I'm all good.' He sauntered over and kissed her, his lips trailing over her cheek before he placed a kiss on her neck, sending a cascade of goosebumps all over her. 'Don't be too long ... I'll miss you.'

'I'll try not to be.' She flashed him smile. 'I'll cook us diner tonight.'

'That would be great, thanks. Here?'

'Yeah, is that okay?'

'Of course.' He met her lips again, leaving what felt like flicking flames dancing upon them when he pulled back. 'Catch you a later.'

'Yup, groovy.'

Tugging his socks on, he eyed her suspiciously. 'I'm not the only one that seems a bit distracted this morning? Are you okay?'

'Yes, all good, just tired, that's all.'

'Okay, well, we'll have a nice night then, make the most of what time we have left together before you leave tomorrow.'

'Sounds good.' Alexis watched him walk out of the kitchen, and as soon as the front door was pulled shut, she jumped to her feet, tossed her bowl in the sink and picked up her car keys. The Landcruiser revved to life outside, and the gravel crunched as Ethan drove away. Alexis picked up her handbag and slipped her thongs on. She couldn't wait a moment longer to find out why Charlie had asked her to come back.

*

After a quick pit stop in town to buy Charlie his favourite butterscotch lollies in a bid to try to win him over, Alexis drove to the nursing home. She thanked her lucky stars Casey wasn't anywhere to be seen when she walked up to the reception counter to sign in. She wasn't sure what she'd do if she were there, but Alexis had more pressing issues to cope with right now.

A middle-aged lady who had welcomed them when they'd sat down for lunch yesterday recognised her straight away. 'Oh, hi, Alexis. Charlie said you might call in today. He asked me to keep it to myself and told me to remind him who you were if he forgot,' she said. 'I love how he can hold his humour at such a challenging time.'

'Yes, it's a good trait to keep.' Alexis's hands shook as she signed her name. 'I'll go in now.' Placing the pen down she turned towards the door.

'Okay, love, he's in his room. He's not feeling very well today so you'll have to keep your visit short.'

Keen to get to him Alexis nodded. 'Sure, that's fine.'

The lady pulled a printed map from under the counter and proceeded to draw the path to Charlie's room. 'You'll be right to get there yourself, won't you?'

'Sure, will be.'

'Goodo.'

'Thanks.' Head down, Alexis followed the map and was soon at Charlie's door. It was ajar and he was lying in his bed, reading the bible. She gave the door a few light raps.

Charlie turned to see her. 'Oh, hello, Alexis, come on in.' He placed the book down beside him and sat up, propping a couple of pillows behind him.

'Hi, Charlie.' Pulling over a chair, she sat down, her bag clutched nervously in her lap. Remembering the goodies she'd bought, she took them out and handed them to him.

His face lit up. 'Oh, I love these.'

'I know, you used to give them to Katie and me all the time.'

'Did I?'

'Yes, you did.'

'Thank you, Alexis, that was very kind of you to get them for me.' He heaved a sigh as he reached over and placed the packet on his bedside table. 'So, I suppose you're wondering why I asked you to come back?'

'Yes.' She almost grimaced as she waited for his response. She was terrified that what he was about to say would have the power to turn her world upside down.

'I will save you any more of a wait, then, and not beat around the bush.'

'Good, because I don't think I can wait much longer.' She could barely breathe.

Charlie nodded, his stern gaze never leaving hers. 'As Ethan would probably have already told you, Mavis passed away a few months ago, and now I no longer feel the need to protect her as a good husband should. Nothing can hurt her now. I asked God to show me the way to repent my sins, and although I thought I'd done enough, here you are, right in front of me. He clearly wants me to tell you everything, so as afraid as I am to do so, I must. I don't want to go to hell when I die.'

'Okay.' Alexis didn't remember Charlie being such a religious man but then would she have really noticed at thirteen?

As if reading her thoughts he continued. 'I only turned to the Lord a few years back, when I felt I couldn't go on any longer, and through him I found the strength to continue. I'm so sorry, Alexis, but …'

He uttered something, but, no, she mustn't have heard right. Wide eyed, she stared at him. 'I beg your pardon?'

'I said, you need to stay away from my grandson.'

Her defences fired to life and she sat up straighter. 'Why?'

'Because …' He choked on his words as if forcing back sobs.

'That's not an acceptable answer, Charlie. I want to know why.' She gave him a look to let him know she was not budging until he gave her a satisfactory reason.

'I know, please, just give me a minute. I'm going to explain everything.' Lifting his glass of water from the bedside table he tried to take a sip, but with his hands shaking badly he spilt most of it down his shirt.

Alexis jumped up and took the glass from him. Then holding it to his lips she helped him to drink. Placing the glass down she pulled some tissues from the box and mopped up the water, noticing how Charlie was having a hard time holding her gaze now.

'What is it Charlie? Please, tell me …'

He picked up the bible again and clutched it to his chest. 'I wrote you a letter.'

'You did. When? Because I didn't get it.' She was trying to make light of the situation. 'Maybe it got caught up in the ones in your toolbox.'

But Charlie didn't even break a smile. 'Yes, you did get it.'

'I did?'

'Well, I'm guessing you did because you've turned up, out of the blue, after all the years when you avoided the place like the plague. To be honest, I didn't think you'd ever come back, but here you are.'

Abruptly, it hit home. The room spun. She fought a wave of nausea and took a shaky breath to try to regain her composure. Now fearful of the frail man in his bed, she took a few steps back. 'You sent that note?'

Charlie nodded and then looked away from her. 'Yes, I'm afraid I did.'

'So you know who killed my parents?' Her back hit the wall. Her heart thudded like boxer's fists against her chest.

'I do.'

'Was it, oh my god, was it you?' She bit back a sob.

Charlie remained silent.

'Well?' This time her voice was a roar.

Heavy tears rolled down Charlie's cheeks. His lips trembled. 'No, of course it wasn't me. I couldn't harm a bloody fly.'

Alexis heaved a sigh of utter relief, but stayed where she was, up against the wall. 'So, who was it then?'

He pulled a handkerchief from his top pocket and wiped at his face. 'It was Peter.'

Sourness settled in her gut. 'Your son?' Her hand fluttered to cover her wide mouth. As she thought about sitting opposite the horrendous man at dinner in his home, the urge to vomit almost overcame her.

Shadows passed over Charlie's steely gaze. 'After what he's done, he will *never* be my son ... the only reason I didn't reveal the truth was for Mavis's sake, not his. But now she's gone and I'm not far off losing my mind, so the truth needs to be told.'

Adrenaline took over her need to crumble to the floor in shock. She stepped towards the bed, her hands fisted at her sides. 'I don't care why you protected him all these years. It made my dad out to be a murderer. How could you, Charlie?' Venom laced her every word.

He met her eyes with a vicious judgement of his own. 'Do you think this has been an easy thing for me, carrying this dirty, disgusting secret all these years? There were many times I wanted to take my own life, but then I turned to the Church.'

'I understand it wouldn't be easy, but it doesn't make it excusable.'

'No, of course it doesn't. And there's something else, Alexis, that you must know.'

Alexis was struggling not to crumble. 'How could there be anything else to know?'

'Your mother and Peter were having an affair.'

She pointed at him, her teeth bared and eyes fierce. 'Don't you speak about my mother like that. She loved my father. She never would have cheated on him, especially with a man like Peter.'

'I'm sorry, but she did, for many, *many* months. And it drove Peter insane that she wouldn't leave your father for him.'

'How do you know for sure?' He voice trembled with both hurt and anger.

'Because I just know, and I also know that's what caused the massive argument that night that led to your parents' deaths.'

She shook her head, everything finally falling into place. All the times Peter would visit when her father wasn't home, the way Peter loathed her dad so very much, the botched-up investigation because Peter was the head of it, the heavy footsteps at the top of the stairs when Missus King had pushed her down them to avoid her working out who it was – that had been Peter. She sucked in a sharp breath. The hatred Ethan held for his stepfather, was it because ...? Oh my god. Unable to stand any longer she slumped back into the chair. 'Does Ethan know about this?'

'He doesn't know Peter pulled the trigger, but he does know about the affair.'

Although relieved Ethan knew nothing of the murders, she was still hurt he'd kept such critical information from her. It tarnished everything she felt for him. 'The son of a bitch.'

'Oh, Alexis, please be merciful on him.'

'Why the hell should I?'

'Because that man loves you like no tomorrow.' Charlie sighed. 'Poor Ethan is the one who caught them out the first time, not that either your mother or Peter knew this. He ran all the way back to the homestead so upset, not knowing what to do. And I told him to do nothing, swore him to secrecy, said it would do nothing but hurt you and everyone else involved. And that's the last thing Ethan would ever want to do, was to hurt you, Alexis. That's what I spoke to him about yesterday when he walked me to the room. I reminded him to keep his mouth shut, seeing as he was getting so very close to you, because it would do no good telling you now, it would only break your heart.' Charlie dropped his gaze from hers. 'And that was wrong of me. I should never have made him stay silent. It's time I repent for my sins.'

'No, you shouldn't have, and yes, it's high time all of you repent.'

Charlie couldn't meet her eye, and instead looked everywhere but. 'Your father died trying to save your mother, Alexis. He dived in front of the bullet. He was a good man.'

Anger pounded her heart even harder. 'I never doubted my father's virtue for a second, so don't you dare think it's your place to tell me my father was a good man.'

Charlie hung his head. 'I'm so sorry, Alexis.'

Unable to hold it back any longer she broke down and sobbed, her head in her hands. When she finally found the strength to look up at Charlie, he was watching her, tears falling. 'Why did you decide to tell me now?' she said, her voice just audible. She felt as if all the life had just been knocked out of her.

'With Missus King now gone, I feel free to speak the truth. You see, she reminded me of my duties as a father and a husband and I made a promise to her that night that I would never tell another soul what Peter had done. And that was so very wrong of me.'

Alexis eyed him with contempt.

'She was on her knees, Alexis, begging me. What was I meant to do?'

'Tell the truth, Charlie, that's what you were meant to do.'

'I'm so sorry, Alexis. I should have, I know that now.'

With everything coming to light a dark image claimed her mind's eye, of Peter, standing half in the moonlight that was pouring through the stained-glass windows, his shirt covered in blood, her parents' blood, an evil sneer on his face as he eyed her with pure hatred. And she knew in her heart of hearts that he was about to kill her too. 'Missus King pushed me down the stairs to protect Peter, didn't she?'

Charlie heaved a weary breath. 'She wasn't thinking straight at the time, Alexis, but she had a good heart. She didn't mean to hurt you.'

'A good heart?' Alexis roared. 'She was evil, Charlie, just like her son.'

Charlie was sobbing now. 'Please, Alexis …'

But Alexis could feel no pity. She'd lived more than half her life in heartache, when Charlie could have eased some of it with the truth right back when it all happened. 'Where was Katie all this time?' Her voice was shaking.

'She was in the lounge room, hiding behind the couch. I found her there just before I heard you crashing down the stairs.'

There were two heavy knocks on the door and she turned to see Casey staring back at her. She shifted her gaze to Charlie. 'Sorry to interrupt but I heard raised voices. Is everything okay in here?'

Charlie tried to smile. 'Thanks for checking in, but yes, we're fine.'

'Are you sure, Charlie?' Casey took a step towards the bed. 'It didn't sound like it from the hallway. I don't mind asking her to leave.'

'Oh no, that won't be necessary.'

'As long as you're sure, Charlie.' Casey glared at Alexis, her arms folded tightly. 'He needs rest, not being upset by the likes of you.'

Not wanting to take her bait, even though every part of her was dying to tell Casey to mind her own business, Alexis bit her tongue.

'Have nothing to say?' Casey's foot began to tap.

Alexis remained silent.

'That's enough, Casey.' Charlie spat from the bed. 'Now please leave us alone.'

Her smile wiped off her face in an instant, Casey spun and stormed out the doorway.

Alexis stood. 'I'm going, Charlie.'

'Before you do, I have one thing to ask of you, if I can be so bold?'

'What's that?'

'Can you not go to the police with this until Joyce passes away? It will break her, knowing what Peter has done.'

Alexis didn't need time to think about it. She shook her head. 'I'm sorry, Charlie, but my family and I have suffered for years with this, and as much as I don't want to hurt Joyce, I cannot keep this a secret. It's been kept quiet for way too long already. I'll be going to the police as soon as I've told Katie and Ethan the news.'

Nodding his head sadly, Charlie wiped at his eyes with his handkerchief again. 'I can understand that. You have to do what you have to do. I just hope you'll find it in yourself to forgive me for this one day, Alexis.'

'Give me time, Charlie, and hopefully I will. And if I do, I'll forgive but I'll never, ever forget what you've done.' Picking her bag up from the floor she slung it over her shoulder, walked out the door, down the hall and out to her car.

She rested her head against the steering wheel and cried for everything she'd just learnt, for the fact her father had died trying to save her mother and for the fact this was going to ruin her and Ethan. She just knew it. But there was no turning back. She had to clear her father's name, no matter the cost.

CHAPTER

23

Ethan stood, staring at the rays of the setting sun, his mobile pressed hard up against his ear so he could hear over the rumble of the tractor's engine. 'Okay, yup, thanks for the heads up, Casey.' And before she could say anything more he hung up.

Briefly re-reading the text he'd received from Alexis just after lunch, saying she was going to have a lay down because she'd had a migraine, he shoved his mobile back into the pocket of his jeans. His jaw clenched as he kicked at the dirt floor with the toe of his boot. What was she doing visiting his grandfather this morning? Did she know she was going to see him when she left, or was it a last-minute decision? If it were the latter, he had no reason to be mad at her, although he was annoyed that she might have gone to see Charlie to confirm what had been said between the two of them yesterday. Shit!

Panic claimed him as he imagined Charlie slipping up and telling her something she didn't need to know. Something that would break her heart. Something he should have had the courage to tell her himself. Years ago. Would she believe Charlie even if he had told her? It had taken Ethan seeing it with his own eyes to believe it when he'd walked in on them – thank god neither Peter or Peggy had noticed him. The only person he'd ever told was his grandad, and now, after all these years, that's where he wanted the information to stay, because not only would it hurt Alexis, it would break his mother's heart too, and she didn't deserve any more sadness in the short time she had left.

With grease-stained fingers he pinched the ridge of his nose, a blinding headache threatening to overcome him. He honestly couldn't take much more. Deciding to throw down his tools for the day, he kicked his toolbox shut, climbed up and into the tractor and shut it down, and then wearily wandered over to his four-wheel drive. Revving it to life, he headed towards the cottage, the entire time panicking about what conversation they would have when he got there. Something was up. He just knew it. Alexis would've come and spent some time with him once she'd come back from town if everything were okay. He didn't believe for a second that she had a migraine. With his sunglasses on and his Akubra pulled down low to ward off the flaming red sunset he drove quickly, his heart in his throat. Was he about to lose the woman he loved with all his heart and soul for a second time?

Climbing the front steps and striding across the porch he reached the flyscreen door and tugged off his boots. He prayed this wasn't going to be a night to remember for all the wrong reasons. For now, he wasn't going to mention that he knew she'd been to see his grandad unless she brought it up, because he didn't want to risk a repeat of the tension this morning. It was their last night together, and he wanted it to be filled only with love, not angry words. His heart squeezed painfully with the thought of seeing her drive away tomorrow. While watching her sleep last night he'd memorised her every feature, burnt them into his mind for safekeeping, just in case she never came back to him.

Calling out, he entered the cottage to the smell of food cooking and country music playing softly in the background. He breathed a sigh of relief – good signs that everything was going to be all right. He noticed that the dining table was set and a candle was alight at the centre of it. But Alexis was nowhere to be seen. He called out to her again. There was no reply. Turning to go and look down the other end of the cottage he found himself face to face with her. Freshly showered, Alexis looked and smelt divine.

She smiled and wrapped her arms around his waist. 'Hey there, sexy.'

Her smile looked forced but he couldn't be sure. 'Hey there, yourself.' He placed a lingering kiss on her beautiful lips. 'Dinner smells amazing.'

'Why thankya.' She dropped her arms from around his waist and went over to the stove. 'I've had it cooking for a good part of the afternoon.'

He joined her and peered into a pot of the most delicious looking food. 'Lamb stew?'

'Sure is.'

'My favourite.'

'I know, I remember you always loved it when my mum made it.'

She switched off the gas, dished them up a bowlful each and handed one to Ethan. He took it, noticing how quiet she was now, as though she were trying to hold herself together. All his fears came back to plague him, in full force. But he sucked in a quiet breath and hoped for the best.

After she had poured them both a glass of red wine, they sat down opposite each other.

'Oh, this is amazing, and just like I remember it.'

'Told you I could cook.' Her voice sounded flat.

'I never doubted you for a second.' He watched as she pushed her food around in her bowl. Maybe she was just sad about leaving? He didn't want to say goodbye to her tomorrow, or ever in fact. If only they could have a few more days. 'What would it take to make you stay longer?'

'Oh, Ethan, don't, please. This is hard enough as it is.' She tried to smile but it faltered, and that's when he saw her eyes glistening with tears.

He reached across the table and took her hand. 'I'm sorry, I didn't mean to upset you.'

Pulling her hand away she tucked it beneath the table. 'Please, don't apologise. It's not what you just said that's upset me ... ' She paused, her lips open to say something but nothing was coming out.

'Then what is it?' he said it gently.

Her gaze dropped to the tablecloth. 'I went to see Charlie today.'

The blood flowed heavily in Ethan's ears. All the air felt as if it had left the room. 'You did?' Now was not the time to say that he already knew.

'I did, and Charlie told me something that might tear us apart.'

'He did?' His heart smashed wildly.

'Yes, he did.' She brought her eyes to his and he watched with baited breath as she drew in a slow breath of her own. 'He told me your father and my mother were having an affair.'

'Oh, for fuck's sake.' Ethan shook his head slowly.

'Why didn't you tell me, Ethan?'

'Because I didn't think it was something you needed to know and I didn't want to hurt you.' When he looked at her again the heartache in her eyes crushed him.

'Well, Ethan, it is something I should have been told. You should never have kept that from me or from the detectives who came here from the city to investigate my parents' murder, for that matter.'

'What do you mean, that I should have told the police?'

'It would have helped the investigation.'

'How in the hell would that have helped, Lexi?'

'Because Charlie told me something else too ... '

'And what was that?'

'Peter killed my parents.' She spat the words out as though they were poisonous.

His brows drew together and his eyes narrowed. Where in the hell did she get off, saying something so disgustingly unbelievable? 'What a load of fucking rubbish, Alexis, Peter is an arsehole but he isn't a murderer.' Standing, he slammed his hands down on the table, the cutlery clanging with the force. 'Charlie told you this, did he?'

Her eyes flashed with both hurt and anger. 'Yes, he did.'

'As you already know damn well, he's got dementia, Alexis. He doesn't know what he's fucking talking about.'

She challenged him with a ferocious glare. 'He knew exactly what he was saying.'

He matched her gaze. 'It's a load of bullshit.' His thoughts stumbled. He tried to catch hold of the emotions flying around in his head. The room spun. A blinding headache smashed behind his eyes as he sat back down and folded his arms defensively across his chest. 'I can't even believe you would speak such crap out loud. Peter's a police officer, for god's sake, and a very well respected one.'

'And I can't believe you kept something so important from me, Ethan.'

He shrugged and regretted it instantly, the look on Alexis's face one of sadness and hatred. 'I made a mistake ... ' he blundered out. 'I'm sorry.'

Alexis pulled the napkin from her lap and tossed it to the table. 'It's too late for apologies.'

'Are you serious?'

'Never been more serious in my life. This whole thing. Us. It's a joke.' Alexis flew to standing, her chair crashing to the floor behind her. 'I wanted to do the right thing and tell you first, before I went to the police. Do you know how damn hard it was, coming back here today and cooking dinner and pretending everything was okay? I wanted to do this calmly, like adults. I thought you'd stand by me, especially knowing how much you detest Peter, but what a fool I was to think such a thing.'

'You're going to the police with this?' He almost laughed out loud. It was the most absurd thing he'd ever heard.

'Of course I am,' she shrieked, her eyes wilder than he'd ever seen them.

Standing again, his voice low and steady, Ethan said, 'Do you have any idea what this load of bullshit will do to my mum?'

'Yes, I do, and I feel terrible, but I can't just let a murderer keep living in freedom when he took both my parents' lives.'

He flashed her a look filled with deep disappointment and suspicion.

'You really don't believe me, do you?' Alexis said.

'Oh, I believe you when you say Grandad told you this, but I can't believe you'd be stupid enough to believe him.'

'You're the stupid bloody idiot here, not me,' she snapped back.

Ethan's eyes flared with rage. 'If you're going ahead with your absurd accusations you can forget about me, and about there ever being an *us*.'

'Fine, if that's what it takes.' Alexis looked at him with loathing. 'To be honest, I don't want to be with a man who could lie to my face all these years about his dirty stepfather sleeping with my mother.'

'Are you saying your mother was in a saint in all of this?'

She pointed towards the front door. 'Just leave, get out of my house.'

He stood his ground. 'This is my house.'

'It may be your house now, but it was my home until your father stole that away from my family and me. And I'm paid up until tomorrow, so get out.'

Dismissed, crushed, heartbroken, reeling from shock and anger, Ethan stormed towards the front door. He needed some fresh air anyway, and to get away from a woman who had turned out to be nothing he expected her to be.

'I'm sorry, Ethan, I really am,' Alexis said softly, 'but I have to do this for my father.'

Before he walked out the door her turned to her. 'And I have to do this for my mother. Goodbye, Alexis.' He slammed the door behind him, heaving fresh air into his lungs as he stormed towards his Landcruiser.

*

It was just shy of daybreak, with the golden light barely peeking out from behind the mountaintops when Alexis took one last look around the cottage to make sure she'd left nothing behind – she wasn't coming back to get it if she had. Leaving the keys dangling from the front door she pulled her bag down the garden path and towards her VW. It had been a sleepless night, but nothing less than she'd expected given the horrible circumstances. After drowning her sorrows in an entire bottle of red wine, she'd fallen into a drunken slumber for a couple hours before waking with a sudden need to throw up. She'd barely made the toilet and had spent a good hour clinging to the bowl as she'd heaved up every last drop. At three this morning she'd thought about calling Henry to tell him what she'd discovered, but decided that a few more hours weren't going to make the world of difference; she'd wait until she was more coherent. She would call him on her long drive home, and Katie too. She'd rung her little sister after leaving Charlie, to fill her in on what had happened, but had asked her not to repeat anything to Henry. Alexis wanted to tell him herself.

Groaning as she lifted her suitcase into the boot, she slammed it shut and then stood still for a moment to take one last look at the magnificent landscape of a place she would never return to. Though she tried to fight off the memories, she remembered standing in this very spot, saying goodbye to a sixteen-year-old Ethan, tears streaming down her face. She was relieved to have finally found out what happened so she could clear her father's name, but also utterly heartbroken after connecting again with a soulmate she'd never again see. She looked over her shoulder at the cottage for the last time.

Sitting behind the steering wheel she turned the key, dismayed to hear nothing. She did it again, and again, her panic rising. But there was not one bit of life in the relic of a car. Smacking her hands against the wheel she swore out loud. What was the universe playing at? Hadn't she endured enough in the past twenty-four hours? Taking a few calming breaths, which did absolutely nothing to curb her growing anxiety, she climbed out and kicked the back wheel. What in the hell was she going to do now?

The thud of horse's hooves made her look up as she shielded her eyes from the glare. The rider seemed to float in the mirage of the rising sun as he appeared from the far paddock. Of course it was Ethan, who else could it be? As much as she needed someone to come to her rescue, she didn't want it to be him. He was the very last person Alexis wanted to see right now.

Pulling his horse to a sliding stop beside her, he peered down, his lips set in a thin line. 'You changed your mind about going to the police yet?'

'Good morning to you too, Ethan ... and no, I haven't.'

'I've just had a call from Peter. Mum's on her way to the hospital in an ambulance and apparently it's not looking good. I'm racing back to the homestead now to jump in the Cruiser and head in there.'

Alexis's heart sank. 'I'm so sorry, Ethan.' What else was she meant to say?

'Does that change your mind?'

She shook her head, unable to answer him for the lump in her throat.

'I hope you're out here to leave then?'

She nodded.

'Good.'

'I can't though because my car won't start,' she whispered, embarrassed.

'Are you fucking kidding me?'

'No.'

'Well, I don't have time to help you. I want to be with my mother. I'll give you a lift into town and drop you off at the mechanic's. You can decide if you want to ask him to come and fix it, or if you want to figure out another way home. '

'Okay, thank you.'

'I'll be back in five to get you.' He gave his horse a kick and galloped off.

She watched him ride away, her heart feeling as though it were going with him. As much as she was angry at Ethan for not telling her about the affair, and also with the way he was reacting to the news and refusing to believe it, she couldn't help but love him. With a heavy heart she supposed she always would. It was just something she was going to have to learn to live with.

Sitting down beneath the tree shading her VW, she cuddled her knees to her chest, tears rolling down her cheeks. This entire situation was fucked. She was hurting the man she loved with all her heart and soul to save another man she loved with all her heart and soul, but blood was thicker than water and her father's name had to be cleared. Resting her cheek against her knee, she stared out at the paddocks she and Ethan had galloped across only days ago, holding tight to the memories they'd shared over the past few days because that was all she was going to have of him.

The Landcruiser roared up the driveway, a spray of grit flying out behind it when Ethan pulled up. Leaving it running, he climbed out. 'We should take your suitcase, just in case the mechanic can't fix your car today and you need to stay at the pub.' He went to take it from her.

She tugged it away from him. 'Leave it. I'll put it in the back myself.'

'Fine, have it your way.' And off he stormed, back to the driver's side. Then the door slammed shut.

It took three attempts to heave it up and into the tray but Alexis wasn't giving up. She was determined not to ask for any more help from Ethan than he was offering her already. Climbing up and into the passenger seat, she yanked on her seatbelt, making sure to stay as far away from Ethan as possible. Once settled, she stared out the window. The ride to town was going to be a long one.

With a grunt Ethan jammed his boot onto the accelerator, lunging the Landcruiser forwards. He was driving dangerously fast, sliding around corners as he went hell for leather. Alexis wanted to tell him to woo up a bit, but she bit her lips closed. She could understand that he was in a hurry to get to his mum.

The drive was grimly silent for the next twenty minutes, until they reached the T-intersection that led into town.

'You know you're acting like a shark circling for blood.' He barely looked at her as he growled. 'Anything to prove that your father was blameless, no matter what the cost to people who are still alive, innocent people.'

She bit the insides of her cheeks. His comment didn't deserve an answer.

'How can you do this when you know my mother is close to death?'

That was it. She'd had enough. 'How can you question me when my parents died seventeen years ago, at the hands of your stepfather?'

With his nostrils flared and his knuckles white from his grip on the steering, Ethan remained deathly silent and turned his focus back to the road. She welcomed the silence and turned to look back out the window.

They remained like this for the rest of the trip, the relief that flooded her when they reached the mechanic's shop was overwhelming. 'Thank you,' she muttered as she climbed out. She was unable to meet Ethan's eyes for fear of crumbling into a million tiny pieces that could never be put back together.

Ethan remained heartbreakingly silent.

Shutting her door, she walked to the back, dragged her suitcase out and then watched as he drove away from her.

That was it.

He was gone.

And he hated her.

And in a way she couldn't blame him. As much as she wanted to hate him for not believing her, for not supporting her, she couldn't. She loved him, with everything she had, and once again she was going to have to deal with losing the love of her life.

CHAPTER

24

Townsville – five weeks later

Morning broke through the apartment window in a stream of golden light. The rays caught on dust motes in the air, making them look like tiny diamonds. Alexis stirred, enjoying the moment while still half asleep, before being thrust into full consciousness. She flicked open her eyes, recalling the passage she'd read in the newspaper five days ago. It was the same thing she'd thought of as she'd finally cried herself to sleep, as she had every night since coming across it. A notice announcing Joyce's death and the date of her funeral had broken her heart. If only she could have been at the service yesterday, but she knew she wouldn't have been welcome.

A brief wave of remorse gripped her, but she shook it off. She did what she had to for her family. Charlie King was the one who had a lot to answer for, denying what he had told her, as did Peter King, claiming his innocence to the police. And still to this very moment, she knew without a single doubt that Charlie had told her the truth. She just had to rely on the truth being eventually discovered, hoping that there would be enough evidence to lock Peter away where he deserved to be. Henry was doing his best to get the case re-opened, but trying to prove that a copper was guilty of murder was close to impossible. Even so, she was never going give up on her quest. And Katie was backing her the entire way. She was going to miss her sister now she'd moved in with Zane as of yesterday, but she was over the moon to see Katie so happy and in love. If only she could have the same. She missed Ethan every second of every day.

Groaning, she climbed from the bed and minutes later she had the bath running so hot the mirror misted over. The scent of the bath oil lingered in the rising steam and she couldn't wait to sink into it, hoping to gain comfort from the water if only for a little while. Stripping off her pyjamas, she was just about to step in when her mobile rang. Her toe hovering just above the water, she weighed up whether to answer it. Deciding not to, she climbed in, sighing as she sunk into the water. It felt so good to be weightless, the burdens she was carrying suddenly feeling lighter.

Her phone, sitting next to the basin, rang again. She heaved a sigh, but once again left it go to message bank. A chime let her know whoever it was had left a message. She'd get to it later. But then it rang again and this time she couldn't ignore it, worried now that it might be serious. Climbing out she gathered her towel to her, quickly wiping her hands before she picked her phone up to answer it. Her heart in her throat, she imagined the voice at the other end of the phone telling her that Katie had been involved in an accident, or worse.

'Hello.' She sounded breathless.

'Alexis, it's me.'

'Hey, Henry, what's up?'

'Peter has just handed himself in.'

'What?'

'I've just had word from the police station that Peter has just walked in and confessed to killing your parents.'

'Oh my god, are you serious?'

'Would I joke about something like this?"

'No. No, of course not. '

She recalled the death notice and put two and two together. Emotions almost overwhelmed her. 'He was waiting until Joyce passed, so she didn't find out.'

'Yes, that's what he's told the officer who took his statement. He said he couldn't bear the thought of a woman as good as his wife knowing she was married to a murderer, but now that she was gone, he could finally be the man he should be and own up to his crime. He said it was either dob himself in or take his own life, and he said he was too gutless to do the latter. It's over, Alexis, it's finally over.'

She should be happy, and deep down she was, but all she could think about right now was Ethan, and how he was coping with both his mother's passing and his stepfather's confession. 'Poor Ethan,' she said as she slid down to the floor and pulled her knees to her.

'Trust you to be worrying about him. You need to start thinking about yourself, Lexi.'

'I'm happy, Henry, I really am, but I love him, and I can't help but worry about how this is affecting him. What's going to happen to Peter now?'

'He'll go before a judge, but because he's confessed it will just be a case of the judge deciding his sentence.'

'Thank you for letting me know straight away.'

'Of course. Lexi, are you going to be okay? Do you want me to come around?'

'No, I'm fine, I just need a bit of time to let it all sink in, that's all.'

'You sure?'

'Yes, positive. It's a Friday and you're a married man now. Finish work early this afternoon and go home and make love to your wife, or something, and enjoy the weekend.'

'Okay, but only if I really have to,' he said playfully. 'But seriously, if you change your mind, I'm only a phone call away.'

'Thanks, Henry, I know you are.'

'Do you want me to call Katie, or will you?'

'No, I'll do it once I've caught my breath, but thanks for offering.'

'I better go, got a stack of paperwork to do. I'll give you another call tonight, okay, just to check in.'

'Yes, okay.' With Henry ending the call, Alexis remained on the floor, her towel clutched around her, for almost an hour, sobbing hard. Until a firm knock at the front door brought her to her feet. As if on autopilot, she wandered out of the bathroom and towards it, expecting to see Henry's smiling face when she opened it, telling her he'd come over anyway.

*

Ethan stared at the door. The drive usually took five hours, but he'd made it here in just over four. How he'd done it without getting a speeding ticket he hadn't a clue – clearly luck was on his side. He hoped it stayed with him a little longer, because by Christ he needed something to get him through this. His hands trembling, he pushed them into the pockets as he waited to see if someone would open the door. If Alexis did, was she going to tell him he was a bastard for not believing in her before she slammed the door in his face? He wouldn't blame her if she did. He felt like the biggest arsehole alive, refusing to trust her when she told him, and thinking how he treated her afterwards broke his heart. He heard the lock click. He held his breath. This would be his only chance to make amends.

Her beautiful face appeared, wet with tears.

'Oh my god, Ethan.'

'Lexi.' It was all he could choke out, emotions overwhelming him.

'What are you doing here?' Alexis pulled her towel in tighter and tucked it into the top, so it was secure and her hands were free.

'Have you heard Peter confessed?' His voice sounded strained, but he couldn't help it.

'I have. I'm so sorry Ethan.'

'Please, don't say sorry to me. I should be the one apologising.' He gazed at her, more in love than he'd ever been with her.

Her hands reached up to cup his face, her eyes filling with tears. 'Apology accepted.'

'Really, just like that?'

'Yes, just like that. I've missed you so much Ethan, you have no idea.'

'Oh, trust me, I do. You're all I've thought about. I feel like I can't draw a decent breath without you near me.'

'I'm so sorry about your mum.'

He bit back raw emotions. 'She's in no pain now.'

'Come on, come inside.' She took his hand and he closed the door behind them.

With a gentle smile, one that reached right into his soul, Alexis brought her lips to his, so softly, so full of love, that he felt the weight that had been bearing down on him now lift away.

Breaking the kiss for flicker of a moment, he breathed the words he'd been longing to say. 'I love you, Lexi-Loo.'

She pulled back to seize his eyes with hers, the depth within them immeasurable. 'I love you, too, my beautiful man.'

Her lids fluttered closed when he traced her lips with the tip of his finger, lips that were lush and swollen from their kiss. He ached to slowly pull the towel from her, to kiss her every sweet inch, and he would take his time so she could feel just how much he loved her, but for now he had something more important to do.

'Lexi.'

'Ethan,' she said and then her eyes dropped to his lips, lingering there as if she craved for them to be upon her once more.

The urge to kiss her again was overwhelming, but he gripped what was left of his self-control, eager to get out what he'd come here to say.

He dropped to his knee and took her hand in his.

Her eyes widened in recognition of what he was about to do.

'Alexis Brown, I love you and I can't imagine my life without you in it, every single day. I want to wake up to you and go to sleep beside you for the rest of our lives. I know we don't live in the same town, but I'm sure we can work that one out.' She nodded.

'Will you be my wife?'

Alexis laughed and cried at the same time. 'Yes, of course I will. I love you so much.'

Not able to hold it back, a lone tear rolled down his cheek. He pulled the diamond ring from his top pocket and slid it onto her finger. It was a perfect fit, just like Alexis and him. Then standing, he wrapped his arms around her waist and drew her into a passionate kiss, one that left him hungry for more.

*

'I'm so glad we've come here, to this point.' Alexis rested her head against his chest and hugged him tight. 'I know we've both travelled a really rough road to get where we are, and we've both suffered immense heartache.' She looked up at him beneath tear-heavy lashes. 'But from here on in I reckon we should grab hold of life and live it to the fullest, together, side-by-side. I want to move to Diamond Acres, Ethan.'

Ethan smiled down at her. 'Really? Are you sure?'

'Yes, really, I love you, always have and forever will. I don't want to live another day without seeing you the moment I wake up and just before I close my eyes at night, like you said.'

'You've just made me the happiest man alive.'

'Good, now kiss me.'

And so he did.

ACKNOWLEDGMENTS

First and foremost a huge heartfelt thank you goes to my fantastic team at Harlequin headquarters – my wonderful publisher Rachael Donovan, who is always there to barrack for me and encourage me to be the very best I can be, my two equally lovely editors, Annabel Blay and Bernadette Foley (I love how you both just get me as a writer), the design magicians who have created magic once more with an amazing cover graced by a handsome bloke, and the rest of the encouraging and supportive team who have helped make *Moment of Truth* the very best it can be. I feel extremely blessed to be part of the Harlequin family and look forward to many more stories to come.

To my precious daughter, Chloe Rose. I love you more than words can say, sweetheart. You brighten up even my darkest of days, just by being you. You always amaze me with the depth of your heart and the kindness you show to the world, both human and animal. You're an old soul with so much to give and I'm so proud of the beautiful person you're growing up to be. The unbreakable bond we share means the world to me, and the laughter we share is priceless. I love you, my beautiful girl, beyond the moon and stars and into infinity.

To my awesome mum, Gaye, you're not only my mum, but my best friend too. I treasure every moment we spend together, and I feel extremely blessed to have you in Chloe's and my lives. Living around the corner from each other is ace! You know me inside out and back to front. You've taught me how to be a strong, confident woman, and made me believe in myself time and time again. Thank you, for all you've done for me and for Chloe. Love you a million bazillion.

To my gentle, wise, loving dad, John. You never judge and always support my decisions – even if you don't agree with them. Thank you for allowing me to make my own mistakes and still being there to help me through them, for being there to applaud my achievements and for loving me unconditionally. You rock and I love you heaps!

To my awesome stepdad, Trevor. I have so many wonderful childhood memories with you by my side (little Peter Rabbit comes to mind ☺), and as an adult you have continued to always be there for me, no matter what. We share an unbreakable bond, and that means the world to me. You instilled a belief in me that everything always works out in the end, and I can't thank you enough for this – it has helped me through many hard times. Love you lots!

To my amazing sisters Mia, Karla, Talia, Rochelle and Hayley – you are all such strong, independent women, and I love that. I feel so blessed to have all of you in my life and to share all of life's ups and downs with. Love you all so very much.

To my awesome Aunty Kulsoom. I love your quick wit and your kind and thoughtful heart. Thank you for being the coolest aunty ever! Love you heaps!

To the four women in my life who are not only my dearest friends but my soul sisters too – Tia, Kirsty, Fi and Katie. As I get older, (and hopefully wiser – lol!) I've come to realise how important it is to have friends who will be there for you through the good times and the bad, ones I can laugh with and cry with, ones that will love me no matter what, and also ones that will throw caution to the wind and share weird, crazy moments that we can talk about when we're eighty. With all four of you, I'm blessed to say I have that. Thank you, for always being the bestest friends any gal could want. Can't wait to see what adventures we're yet to share. Love you all tonnes!

And finally, but most importantly, a huge jump-up-and-down-on-the-spot thank you to YOU, the reader. I wish I could hug each and every one of you! Thank you for diving into the pages of my book, hopefully I've evoked many emotions along the way. My wish is that *Moment of Truth* has given you an escape from the responsibilities of everyday life, and maybe even kept you up reading until the early hours of the morning.

Until my next book, keep smiling and dreaming … life is beautiful.

Mandy xoxo

If you loved *Moment of Truth*,
please turn over
for a taste of Mandy Magro's
most recent bestseller

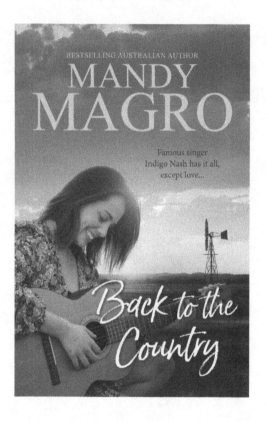

Out May 2022

PROLOGUE

Overwhelming exhaustion wrapped around Indigo Nash like a heavy cloak. What she'd give to be able to close her eyes and sleep for days, but just like every other day, she couldn't afford to be weary. No rest for the wicked, her actually wicked father would say, if they were on speaking terms. All work and no play is bad for the soul, her late mother would have said if Indigo's prayers were answered, and she got to hear her sweet voice once more.

Feeling way older than her twenty-seven years, she popped the last two NoDoz capsules from the blister pack and tossed the tablets into her mouth with a swig of coconut water. Her vivid green eyes glued to the glamorous woman in mirror, she stared at her reflection as if really seeing herself for the very first time since being discovered by the Capitol Records talent scout at a Nashville honky tonk five years ago. Although a spitting image of her mother – it was as if she were eyeing at a stranger. Just like the effervescent young woman she'd once been, her freckle dusted cheeks were nowhere to be seen. But thankfully, neither were the dark circles that that had become a permanent part of her gruelling reality.

Two hours before every one of her sellout shows was spent grooming herself into a picture of flawlessness – her fans and record label expected her to shine bright and she painstakingly strived to meet their expectations. And she liked to do this herself; the thought of other people plucking and preening her was very uninviting. Touching was for people she was close to, and they were few and far between. At first, it had been exciting to get all dolled up to maintain the Country Music's Sweetheart title she'd attained very early on in America, but now, it was downright exhausting.

With her make-up finally done, and her usually wild auburn locks styled to within an inch of their life, she placed her blusher down and stared in the mirror with a sigh. Her throat tightened – where had the wild-haired tomboy of her youth gone, the one who lived to ride a horse like she stole it, who ended each day covered in dirt with leaves and god only knew what tangled up in her knotty hair? Somewhere between her mother's untimely death, her older brother's disappearance, and this long, steep road to fame, she'd gone and lost herself. Completely. Something she always swore she'd never do.

She blinked past the unexpected surge of emotion – tears would ruin her mascara and she didn't have the time to fix it. She'd been so desperate to prove herself, to make a mark in this cutthroat world so she never had to return to the life, and man, she loathed. She could still hear her father's drunken voice loud and clear, on the morning she'd finally had enough of his cruelty: 'You are your father's daughter, Indigo Nash. You're never going to amount to nothing.'

Well, she'd gone and showed him, hadn't she? Not that he cared. But A Grammy would fix that.

Desperate for air, she shot to her feet, grabbed her coat and dashed out of her dressing room. Her bodyguard, and childhood friend, had lectured her again and again to never go anywhere alone, but she just needed a few minutes to gather her wits before going on stage. The back door of the tavern was almost as stubborn as she was, and she had to give it a firm shove before slipping out of the noisy bustle and into the snowflake-dusted night. Her breath escaping her in little white puffs, she tugged her sheepskin-lined R.M. Williams jacket in tighter as darkness engulfed her.

Closing her eyes, she drew in a slow, deep breath and, counting to six, blew it away. The sharp blow to her head came out of nowhere. With no time to react or call for help, she was pinned between a mammoth man and the wall of the alleyway. His hand, pressing painfully hard against her mouth, tasted like sweat and filth. His other hand gripped her wrists and twisted them painfully up behind her. He snarled into her ear, ordering her not to cry, and she bit back sobs. His chin dug into her shoulder, and his laboured breath was rife with the putrid stench of alcohol. Then, to her horror, she heard his zipper going down. Her blood froze solid in her veins. Even though this sick bastard was almost twice her size, she had to do something, anything. Now.

Gritting her teeth, she lifted her left leg, hard and fast. Her knee hit the mark and with a cry, he buckled. It gave her a moment to retaliate, to fight for her life.

'Harley! Help me!' Her scream echoed.

Her attacker swore viciously as she used every bit of strength to try to break free from his hold – kicking, punching, scratching – but he quickly overpowered her and wrapped his hands around her throat, terrifyingly tight. She gasped for breath, clawing at his fingers, but his grip constricted even more. Her boots lifting from the ground, her vision blurred … until, from the shadows, a fist connecting with the side of her attacker's jaw with a bone-shattering crunch.

Flying backwards, her assailant landed with an almighty thud, sending bins tumbling and rolling, his body limp, motionless.

Her knight in shining armour turned to her. 'Indy?'

Heaving a breath and shaking like a leaf, Indigo fell into the safe haven of Harley Knight's arms.

talk about it

Let's talk about books.

Join the conversation:

 facebook.com/romanceanz

 @romanceanz

romance.com.au

If you love reading and want to know about our
authors and titles, then let's talk about it.

BESTSELLING AUSTRALIAN AUTHOR

MANDY MAGRO

Novels to take you to the country...